IRISH *Fury*

IRISH WOLVES LEGACY

ANNE GREGOR

NEW YEARS EVE

MARGARET COLLEEN MORROW

AT SEVENTEEN, Mags felt like she was finally a woman. She and her best friends, Bébhinn O'Faolain, Gray MacGregor, and Blair Barr, who also happened to be her cousin, were attending their first "adult" New Year's Eve party.

It would be even cooler if most of the boys present weren't their childhood friends. On the bright side, the guy friends they hung out with were pretty hot.

The O'Faolains were an extremely wealthy family, but their wealth wasn't what impressed Mags. It was how much they loved one another. They shared the same kind of love she had for her parents and older sister, Mirren.

Bébhinn's dad, Hugh, Daniel's dad, Bran, and Jonathan's dad, Patrick, rented an exclusive club for the evening. Their children and friends had rooms to get ready in and sleep after the party, but seriously, no one planned on sleeping until they were hours into the new year.

She and her friends looked stunning—false modesty never

did a woman any favors. The four girls decided to wear all black. They didn't need to peacock to be noticed.

Bébhinn was drop-dead gorgeous, petite, fair, and with long, straight black hair, courtesy of her mother's Native American heritage. Gray was a stunning, leggy, bombshell with golden waves like her mother. Blair was an identical replica of her mother, Mags' aunt, Catriona. Blair was tiny and ridiculously stunning with miles of heavenly, brilliant, tight red curls that God Himself couldn't contain.

Mags was…well, she was kind of average, all things considered. She was almost five feet four inches with an athletic frame, a small but round behind, and moderately sized breasts that were thankfully round and perky. Her only two claims to fame were her father's green eyes and her mother's loopy brunette curls that fell in perfect waves down her back.

Her folks didn't have nearly as much money as her friends did, but she had never once been made to feel less. Could she afford a designer dress for the party? No. Was she capable of making a killer dress herself? Yes.

Her mom helped her buy a secondhand gown and transform it into the jaw-dropping showstopper that was currently skimming her body. The dress had started out as a boxy, black, floor-length number, high-necked, and stodgy. Now it hit mid-thigh, the front was still high, but the silk hugged her bare breasts perfectly, even with the added lining. The back was where the party started. After days of arguing, Mags had cut the back low enough to skim just above her behind.

It was simple and elegant and paired with her favorite pair of black high heels—yeah, she felt every inch a woman. Her mom cried when she'd modeled the final product, her dad gave her a stern warning about boys, but Mags could only fist pump while twirling in the mirror.

Bébhinn's cousins—technically her nephews, but Mags was

determined not to expend any brain energy on the O'Faolain's family tree that evening—Daniel and Jonathan, and their best friend, Ciar Murphy, weren't happy that Hugh said the girls could join the fun.

For those who weren't in the know, Hugh O'Faolain's word was law, and thank you, little, tiny, baby Jesus and all His Saints for that.

They walked into the fancy foyer, where, honest-to-God, attendants took their coats and purses. Blair, who was deaf, signed an "Oh my" on the downlow. Mags mouthed back. "I know, right?"

"Let's go get a drink, and then it's single ready to mingle time, bitches," Bébhinn said with a straight face before laughing her ass off.

"Christ, there are more people here than I thought there would be," Gray said while looking slowly around the room.

Gray was the most reserved of the four of them. Blair didn't count. If she looked standoffish, it was because she was daydreaming about her plants.

"Better scout out Jonathan, so Mags can get her crush-filled creeping over with," Blair signed.

"You bitch," Mags whisper-screeched. "I do not have a crush on that douche."

"Mags." Gray tilted her head and widened her eyes in disbelief. "You had at least a semi-crush on him since he and Daniel beat up that piece of shit Geoff last year."

Mags would never live down the shame. Her cheeks flamed red just thinking about the "incident."

Geoff had been her boyfriend for six months before she'd relented and sent him a picture of her in her bra and panties.

He'd shown his friends, of course. Her mom and dad found out—the whole damn family and friend group had. Jonathan had commandeered his family's private jet and flown to Scotland from Ireland to kick the ever-loving shit out of Geoff and the friends who had looked at the picture.

How did Jonathan know who'd seen the photo, one might wonder? Her best guess was that her Uncle Coll and Gray's dad, Thomas, who were best friends and owned a security company, and who weren't above using their tech skills to take down little, pedantic secondary school boys.

Mags admitted, only to herself, that she'd fallen a little in love with Jonathan O'Faolain that day, despite her mortification and all the adult speeches about online imprints lasting forever.

She'd never told her friends about her mini, very mini, crush on Jonathan, but they were too close to keep much of anything private. They all kept a few secrets tucked away or tried to, but the reality was that they knew most of each other's deepest thoughts. They were true friends because they never blabbed outside the group.

It was her fault that they had any fodder to tease her over. According to them, she stared at Jonathan during every get-together and hated any girl he dated. She wasn't good at subterfuge, clearly.

Gray took her hand to stop Mags from joining the party. "Seriously, you know he'll have a girl on him or more than one," she grimaced. "Don't let it ruin the night for you."

Mags deflated at the thought but knew Gray was right. "I won't, I promise."

Three and a half hours passed with gobs of laughter, dancing, and perhaps a smidge more champagne than they should have indulged. She'd spotted Jonathan, Daniel, and Ciar holding court with their fan club here and there, boys and girls, but she did her best to enjoy the rare night and forget Jonathan's existence because Mags knew she certainly wasn't remotely on his radar.

As midnight approached, Bébhinn dragged Gray onto the dance floor, though Gray quickly threw her hands up in a "no way" gesture. Bébhinn just laughed and danced in front of her. Blair excused herself. She wanted a closer inspection of the club's plants and flowers surrounding the grounds. That left Mags to slip out on one of the ballroom's balconies alone.

She could have gone with Blair, as she loved her cousin's passionate descriptions of anything green. She also could have joined her friends on the dance floor. Neither held much appeal.

Truth be told, she'd tried to enjoy the evening, and she had, just not perhaps as much as she had portrayed. Jonathan had different girls hanging off his arm all night, each prettier than the last. It was foolish and, at times, downright torture to watch. Jonathan was only into girls who looked perfect on his arm. She knew he'd never thought of her that way. He treated her like a pest on a good day—Bébhinn's little friend.

They weren't so far apart in age, but in school years...it just wasn't done. Mags settled her bare back against the cold stone of the balcony that overlooked the grounds and waited for midnight to come and go.

Thank God for the heated standing lamps, or she would have frozen to death. She heard the teenagers and young adults inside start counting down.

20. 19. 18. 17.

"Are you hiding, Mags?"

She almost swallowed her tongue in fright when Jonathan's husky voice sounded so close to her ear. "Christ, Jon," she panted, placing a ridiculously demure hand over her heaving breast.

14. 13. 12. 10.

"Have you ever kissed a boy?

"Yes." Barely.

His jaw clenched, but he asked, "Do you want to kiss me?"

8. 7. 6. 5. 4.

This was her chance. She wasn't about to play coy. "Yes."

2.

She had cold stone at her back and Jonathan's hot body pressed to her front. He dipped low and gently touched their lips together as firelights flashed in the sky.

For one heart-stopping minute, he deepened the kiss until she felt like her legs would give out, and even his hands at her waist wouldn't stop her toppling over.

He moaned as their tongues dueled, and she knew she'd found heaven. His hands left her waist and began to creep up her naked back, but that's where it ended.

Jonathan broke the kiss with a curse. "Christ, Mags. I—"

She had no idea what he'd been about to say because at that critical moment where euphoria met uncertainty, one of his drunk friends stuck his head out the door and yelled for him to get back inside.

Surely, he wouldn't leave her out here. Surely, he wouldn't leave her without a word.

He did.

When she'd pulled herself together enough to join the party, Jonathan was at the center of the dance floor completely sucking the face off a Barbie wannabe with his hands full of her ass.

While still deep in the kiss, he met her eyes over the girl's shoulder.

He never broke the kiss.

one

DUBIN, IRELAND

AILEEN BARR MORROW

"PLEASE, Charles. I don't want to ruin Bébhinn's wedding for Margaret. Let's wait to tell her until after," Aileen pleaded with her husband.

Her husband stroked her cheek and gave her a loving smile. Aileen had loved this man since her first year at university, and she still loved him fiercely, even though she wanted to take off her shoe and hit him upside the head with it.

"I would like nothing more than to give you anything and everything you want, Aileen, but we've told Mirren, and she agreed that Margaret should be told immediately, or we risk hurting her feelings. Hiding things from our youngest daughter is never a viable option," Charles argued in his sensible professor's voice.

"We're leaving the morning after the wedding for America, leaving no time to speak with her then. I've tried to get you to tell our daughters for three weeks." He nudged her side with his elbow, a wordless reminder that her procrastination was the reason that had put them on an untenable timeframe.

"I know," Aileen sighed, her breath shaky in dread.

"Mags is fearless like her mother, sassy, too, but I don't want you to think I'm complimenting all the backtalk you women have subjected me to over the years."

That made Aileen chuckle, which was Charles' intent. She pressed her hands together in her lap and attempted to regain a modicum of her normal self-assuredness.

"If we sit outside her house any longer, she'll accuse us of sexual deviancy in a car. Best get to it, then." Charles said with finality while squeezing her hands between his own.

He got out of their rental car and, like the gentleman he was, came to her side and opened the door and helped her out. He grabbed their overnight bags and wheeled them toward the beautiful townhouse that their daughter lived in with her best friends.

Only one friend now, she supposed, Aileen's niece, Blair. Bébhinn O'Faolain and Gray MacGregor lived with their partners. The O'Faolains assured the remaining girls that they would, under no circumstances, want or expect the remaining two girls to move out.

Before Hugh O'Faolain's passing, he'd purchased the two twin townhouses for his daughter, grandchildren, and their friends while they attended Trinity College. Aileen and Charles would have made it work, but it was such a blessing to have a safe home for their youngest daughter.

Charles knocked, and they smiled at each other when they heard slapping footsteps racing toward the door.

Margaret threw open the door and laughed in delight as she hugged her parents tight. "I missed you guys! Can you believe little Bébhinn is getting married? Though I suppose it's crazier to think that Gray is already married and has two children."

Charles managed to drag their bags over the threshold

while their daughter hugged them and danced and huffed her amusement.

"I'm so glad you're here," Mags said for probably the third time, warming Aileen's heart. "Blair is already with Uncle Coll and Aunt Cat and Josephine and Thomas at the O'Faolains. They're all waiting for us for drinks before we load up in several vans that Rowan rented to take everyone to the party at Three Wolves Distillery. You'll die when you see the fancy cocktail dress I'm wearing tonight and the one for the wedding tomorrow.

"Surprise! I made them. I know, I know," she bowed in faux modesty, "I made them, so of course they're amazing."

Despite the horrible news Aileen was there to deliver, she couldn't help but laugh at her daughter's exuberance. Her youngest daughter's over-the-topness was probably Aileen's favorite part of Margaret's character.

They moved into the living room while her daughter regaled them with her new passion for making clothes that she could then hand-embroider.

"Wearable art. Basically, a twofer," Mags laughed, excited about her newest artistic adventure.

"That's brilliant, sweetheart. You are so talented. You'll have people falling over themselves to wear your one of a kinds."

Charles joined the girls after he took their luggage to Gray's old room, where they would get dressed for the evening ahead. "Diversifying your brand already, Mags?" he teased. "Are you sure you shouldn't have majored in Business instead of The History of Art & Architecture?"

"No way, Dad. History is in my blood thanks to you. Besides, I get a lot of embroidery inspiration from the past. Now, if you guys are ready, why don't we change and head to the O'Faolains?"

Aileen surreptitiously wiped her sweating palms across her jean-covered thighs. Charles glanced her way once, then twice when Aileen hadn't made a move to interrupt their daughter.

He had to be furious with Aileen for leaving this until the last minute, and yet Charles loved her still, faults and all. He bit his tongue and bided his time. Because of that, because he was unfailingly her staunchest supporter, she managed to drum up a modicum of his courage.

"Mags," Aileen interrupted her daughter, "before we do that, would you sit with Dad and me for a moment? There's something I need to speak with you about."

two

THREE MONTHS AFTER – THE NEWS

MAGS

"CHRIST ALMIGHTY and all His Saints, Margaret Colleen Morrow. Get your bloody shit together." Mags cursed herself as she jogged down one of Dublin's busiest streets, dodging pedestrians while praying the large tote banging against her spine didn't bust a strap and knock some innocent passerby senseless.

"I'm so going to get fired," she repeated for the hundredth time, her whining getting on her own last nerve.

It had been three months since her parents had exploded some shit news all over her person. Not only had the news rocked Mags with fear, but it had also changed the trajectory she thought her life was headed in.

Mags remembered the night before Bébhinn and Gray's big day. She'd been so excited to celebrate two of her best friends. That was before her mom told her she had something she needed to say. Mags recalled every hair on her body had stood to quivering attention.

Mags recalled how her mom's face had flushed red before going startlingly white. Her mom was generally self-possessed, but she wasn't that night. Instead of getting out whatever she needed to say, she cleared her throat no less than four times and fiddled with a string at her cuff obsessively.

The most alarming—she wouldn't meet Mags' eyes.

At her mother's continued silence, her dad placed a hand over his wife's and said in his smooth, professor's voice, the one Mags and her mother teased him about, "Aileen."

Scrunching her eyes closed once, she finally sighed and met her daughter's worried gaze. "The cancer is back."

As Mags dodged another slowpoke walking three damn dogs in the middle of the footpath, she internally winced at how her mother's pain-filled image had seized Mags' chest as the awful words had kept coming.

Recurrence. Lymph nodes. Lumps. Swelling. Collarbone.

Those words sounding one on top of the other—terrifying.

Her mother had beaten cancer once before Mags was born, but Mirren had told her how scared she'd been, though she'd done her best to stay positive for their mother's sake.

It had been a blow to hear her mother was sick. More than a blow, it had felt like she'd been set on fire and was still burning. Mags made a conscious effort to be strong every day—every moment of every day, if she were honest. A world without her mother wasn't one she allowed mental space to contemplate. She couldn't.

Her mom and dad had always gotten by financially. They weren't wealthy by any stretch, but Mags had never wanted for anything, and though there were times she might have gotten a tad bit envious of her friends, she knew how loved and lucky she was.

She was still loved and lucky to have both her parents.

However, the secrecy of her mother's health took its toll on Mags. According to her folks, Mags' Uncle Coll, Josephine, and Thomas MacGregor had paid for her original cancer treatments. They financially supported her when she had to take months off from teaching.

She didn't want to burden them this time, even though Mags had furiously argued that they would never consider her a burden and would be hurt.

Her father might not have agreed with his wife, but her mom was the love of his life, and he would acquiesce to her wishes.

Her mom took another leave of absence, while her father took a sabbatical from the university to research and write a sequel to his one and only historical fiction, written during his first years of teaching in America.

He'd explained the situation with his wife to the university board members, and they were more than happy to grant his request for leave.

Her parents believed that the facility that offered her mom the best and healthiest outcome was John Hopkins. So, they left the morning after the wedding to live in the United States for an unknown number of months. Baltimore, Maryland, to be exact.

They'd told family and friends that her dad got a huge grant to write a novel, and they were going to treat it like an extended holiday.

The subterfuge was exhausting. Mags had complained to her dad, telling him that all the lying was bullshit, and she was sick of covering for them.

Her dad very kindly but firmly replied, "Your mother is scared, Margaret. She's scared to leave her daughters and grandchildren. She's scared about what she's missing now and what she might miss in the future.

"The treatments are brutal, and though I know her brother and friends would bring her comfort, she doesn't want her ravaged body to be the last thing they remember her by in case she doesn't make it.

"It's why she chose America for treatments over France, like last time. She didn't want to be close enough that you and Mirren would stop your whole lives to live at her bedside.

"So, I don't like lying either, but I'll do it for her, and so will you."

And that was, as they say, that. Mags begged forgiveness, which her dad had assured wasn't needed because they were all struggling with the entire situation.

"Your mom getting cancer again sucks, sweet girl. Hiding it sucks, watching you and your sister and your mum cry sucks. Don't ever believe that you're the only pissed off Morrow."

That was two months ago, but Mags heard her father's honesty and encouragement in her head every day. By then, she'd been wallowing for four weeks and feeling ridiculously lonely. After her dad's kick-in-the-pants speech, she'd attacked her life with the same fearlessness her mom used to attack cancer.

Mags wasn't one to wallow for long. Wallowing was for lazy people who lacked direction and motivation. She had both in spades and only had to make a few adjustments...or forty. Some had been harder than others.

Her parents were frugal people and had plenty of money in savings for an occasional splurge and emergencies. However, with neither of them working, their budget had to be tighter. Thankfully, they found a modest one-bedroom to rent close to the hospital that was affordable, and her dad made all of their meals and was a king of budget shopping.

Her mom said there were several stunning parks near them, including one with the most beautiful flowers. Mags adored the pictures her parents had sent and immediately set to work on a white dressing gown covered in the American flora as a get-well gift for her mom.

Once they'd settled in America, her dad called to discuss automatically depositing a bimonthly allowance directly into her bank account. Mags shut that down immediately, assuring him that she lived rent-free and ate most of her meals at school for cheap or at the O'Faolains. Mostly lies, but hey, Mags was embracing their new gray.

She'd work six jobs before she made her parents stress over their youngest child's finances when Mags was quite capable of making her own way.

"Watch yourself, brat," a grizzled old man barked at Mags as they nearly collided outside an ancient-looking tobacco shop.

"I'll show you, brat, ye smoked trout," Mags growled back under her breath, using one of Granny MacGregor's favorite slurs. She missed that woman, even though she hadn't been biologically Mags' grandma, she had been in every way that counted until the day she'd passed.

Mags' life had become nothing short of a dog performing a series of competitive, timed jumps and twirls, chaotic but choreographed to within an inch of its life.

Her days began at four in the morning at an elderly care facility, where she helped prepare the patients' breakfast, serve, clean what seemed like hundreds of pots and tableware, and finish with lunch prep.

From the care facility, she had to rush across town to one of Dublin's most popular chippers, where she immediately started cleaning and slicing hundreds of potatoes and filleting a quadruple number of cod. She'd convinced the owner that she was a brilliant filleter—seriously, how different was a knife than scissors and needles?

From ten thirty to two in the afternoon, she and two other grunts fried their little hearts out for a queue of customers. Too bad the stingy manager didn't allow employees a free meal once in a while. Her body wasn't meant to survive on ramen alone.

However, after the chippers, afternoons were all hers. That time became all about artistic pursuits—clothing design and embroidery—simple, classic pieces where she created art with stranded cotton. Some of the embroidery designs were bold and in your face, while others were hidden, just waiting to be discovered, peeking from a lapel, cuff, or collar.

Mags' final part-time gig was bartending Friday and Saturday evenings. She would have loved to ask Ciar Murphy or his father for a job at one of their pubs, but it would have raised too many questions, and since she was not only hiding her mother's cancer but her own dive into poverty, she couldn't risk it.

However, just a month ago, her dire situation improved, and her due diligence had paid off. The wife of Ireland's Prime Minister actually wore the embroidered vest she'd spent innumerable hours designing and hand stitching. She wore it to a charity event where she'd been asked who the designer was.

Wait for it—her name, Margaret Colleen Morrow, had been broadcast as the designer who dressed the Prime Minister's wife. It had been broadcast on television and written in the papers.

Mirren, her older sister had literally tackled Mags not four hours later, having flown from Edinburgh to Dublin immediately, and demanded that she take the opportunity and run.

Like, literally, run.

Mirren secured an attic above a gallery within hours and hired a cleaning crew to make the space presentable before contacting some of her acquaintances at the Daily Mail to run an article about the "highly sought after new designer" along with Mags' new website that their Uncle Coll had designed in less than ten minutes.

The art gallery whose attic her new sewing business had taken over was owned by her sister Mirren's employers. Kain and Lillias Smith owned a ton of shit, and thank the Lord, they loved her sister, which meant the rent was affordable—affordable with three jobs and an agreement to do light dusting in the gallery and clean the restroom at the back. Bonus, there was a stairwell to the attic inside the back entrance, and she could use the toilet without bothering anyone.

There was no central heat and air, but thankfully she hadn't had to deal with frigid winter temperatures yet...wait a few more months. She definitely needed to save for a space heater.

Her mom and dad had screamed at the news. Her father said later that her mother hadn't looked so happy in weeks.

What her parents and big sister didn't know was that Mags was actually living in the attic, which had no running water, heat, or air.

Because if she had mentioned that, she would have had to discuss all sorts of regrettable things, like dropping out of university. She'd blown off her financial aid deadline because she'd been too busy crying over her mother's cancer. The result—she couldn't afford Trinity.

The snowball effect hadn't stopped there. The late, great Hugh O'Faolain had purchased the townhouse she'd resided in for his daughter and her best friends, of which she was one, to use while they were in school.

Except Mags wasn't able to be in school anymore, at present anyway, and needed to move out. Bébhinn and her family would have never asked her to move out—they would have been pissed had she even suggested it—but Mags wasn't and had never been a charity case. She would never abuse their kindness.

Blair had gotten back from her extended internship in Wales the week before, and Mags made sure to tell her before she walked into the townhouse they'd previously shared and saw her room empty.

Blair had been bummed that they wouldn't see each other as often, but she understood and was excited about Mags' new flat—if only she knew—and her new business, which all of her friends were supporting, sharing her information.

She put off Blair wanting to come see her place, claiming that she hadn't even found a second to tell Bébhinn or Gray, but she would next time she saw them, and then maybe they could all do a tour together.

Mags prayed that she could put that off until she had maybe started bringing in enough income to perhaps afford a flat that her friends wouldn't freak out over.

The PM's wife had, unbeknownst to her, thrown a lifeline to Mags, and she'd grabbed it with both hands. She still had a long road with a lot of obstacles ahead, but almost all of her struggles could and would be fixed with money.

So, her afternoons were spent meeting clients in their own homes—her new abode wasn't an option, thank you very much—and sewing and embroidering until the wee hours thereafter. A few more weeks, and Mags would start to make a return on the long days.

Weekend days were spent on designing and sewing, while weekend nights were spent bartending at a cool jazz club. The tips were great and kept her head above the teeming water of financial ruin. Ninety percent of her earnings went toward rent, fabric, and stranded cotton. When her stomach complained, she chewed gum and wielded her embroidery needle with added fervor.

"Thank Christ," Mags whispered under her breath as she pushed through the chipper shop and realized her luck was turning. The obnoxious manager was late. Sending a pleading look toward Eze, a giant Nigerian math genius and her newest best friend, to keep his comments about her chaotic life to himself, she slipped her apron on over her care center scrubs and grabbed a potato.

three

JONATHAN

"GIVE me and Bran half an hour, and we can all go get something for lunch." Jonathan's dad, Patrick, said as he clapped his son on the shoulder.

"Your mothers want pizza," his uncle Bran informed Jonathan, Daniel, and Bébhinn before he followed his brother out of the boardroom.

They had just finished the quarterly financial review of O'Faolain's extensive holdings. Daniel would eventually take over as CFO, a title currently shared by their fathers. Dan loved nothing more than crunching numbers.

Jonathan, on the other hand, took more after the creative Byrne sisters. His mother, River, and his two aunts, Raven and Rowan, were successful interior designers. The three sisters and his aunt Bébhinn operated Triskelion Territory Designs.

Jonathan wasn't a designer in that sense, but he was damn good at architecture. He'd been drawing buildings since he was a young child. His parents bought him his first drafting tool set when he was five. One more year and he would have his Master of Architecture degree.

His dream was to open his own small firm, though he would still be very involved in O'Faolain business interests.

"I love how there was no asking us to go to lunch," Jonathan laughed. The O'Faolains were a tight-knit family. A consequence tended to be that they stepped on each other's toes inadvertently or purposefully on occasion.

"I would complain, but pizza does sound good," Daniel laughed.

"You should replace the word pizza with food if you're going for honesty," Bébhinn said before reaching over and tapping an empty sleeve of crackers.

"Hey, I had to come prepared," Daniel defended. "When Neil gets going on one of his slideshows, there's always a chance the meeting could drag through lunch."

Jonathan noticed he was tapping his fingers repeatedly on his thigh, an irritating tell of his when he was nervous, which was why he started keeping his hands under the table in stressful situations.

Now or never, Jon. "Everyone still meeting Sunday at Murphy's?"

It was excruciating to pretend like he didn't care either way, but any sign of strain and Daniel would pick up on it immediately. Dan was his cousin but ridiculously intuitive to Jonathan's moods. Telepathic twins had a better chance of hiding things than he and Daniel.

"Yes," Bébhinn clapped her hands once in excitement. "It seems like ages since everyone was in town at once. Blair is finally back, thank God, and Gray said that she and Ciar are in dire need of adult time. Dagr finished a huge case and is completely free, and you two twats aren't working out of country or jet-setting bimbos to the Caribbean islands for once."

Jonathan winced. He and Daniel really did have horrible taste in women. It wasn't completely their fault. When a person had wealth and influence, it tended to attract the worst of humanity.

"Just because Ciar let Gray tie him down and you tackled Dagr doesn't mean Jon and I can't still enjoy the perks of being single," Daniel smirked.

Bébhinn probably hadn't noticed that Daniel's grin didn't quite reach his eyes, but Jonathan had. He'd known for a while that Daniel wasn't as elated with their lifestyle as he used to be and still tried to portray.

Jonathan understood. Daniel wasn't satisfied with their single escapades like he used to be, either. He tapped a discordant rhythm on his thigh for another two minutes while Bébhinn and Daniel razzed each other, waiting for her to disclose any further revelations about their mutual friends.

Specifically, information about a tiny brunette with an attitude and mouth the size of an American semi-truck.

Margaret Morrow. Mags. The bane of his existence for years had vanished. She hadn't been to more than half of their friend group's get-togethers, and when she did make one of them, she would smile and laugh with everyone, even him, but she was different.

Her eyes never strayed to him like they used to. If their gazes clashed, hers would skate away. She was never home, not that he ever saw, and he would know. There was a camera facing her townhouse next to his, and he watched it religiously.

Further evidence of Mags pulling away from the group, or at least him, was that she never busted his balls over who he dated. She didn't stalk the women's social media accounts and report how horrible they were and send it to the group chat. She hadn't interrupted one of his dates in months.

Even when they were in one another's company, she didn't feel present.

Margaret Morrow was a ghost, or rather, she'd perfected ghosting him.

"Mags better not bail, or I swear I'll track that shady bitch down and drag her to Murphy's," Bébhinn interjected.

Finally.

"Why wouldn't she come?" Jonathan asked with what he hoped sounded like bored, barely there interest.

"Oh, I'm just kidding. Kind of," Bébhinn laughed. "After the Prime Minister's wife told all of Ireland who made her vest, Mags has been inundated with clients, which is amazing, but I am worried that with school and her sewing, she'll burn herself out. She's missed the last few girls' lunches."

"I'm sure we'd know if anything was wrong. Mags has never been a person to whine in silence," Daniel joked.

Before Jonathan could ask Bébhinn anything else, his dad and Bran poked their heads in to announce that their car was waiting, and their moms were leaving Triskelion now.

Sunday, he swore to himself, Sunday he would get some answers.

four

MAGS

NO MATTER how many times Mags counted the loose change in her purse, it didn't miraculously multiply. She'd scrimped all week to have enough to buy a meal and at least one drink at Murphy's with her friends, but alas, fabric was a lot more expensive than when she was only buying stranded embroidery cotton, and her last purchase had left her woefully short.

Work was going well, at least. By the end of the week, she should have her first-ever order complete, and once she got paid, she could breathe a little easier. The client was a bit snobby, but Mags could admit that the middle-aged woman had excellent taste.

She wanted a tailored blazer. Mags allowed clients to pick the fabric color within reason, preferring soft, muted earth tones over jewel tones. However, the embroidery design and placement were all Mags. No discussion. No give.

Embroidery was her art, and no one would tell her how to

express it. Plus, by meeting a client personally, she was able to determine what would work best for them.

She'd heeded Mirren's advice and took teaser progress pictures along with doodles and sketches for the website and shared them on TikTok. She was slowly growing a fanbase. People especially loved the videos in which she walked viewers through a particular stitch or explained how historical prints and architecture inspired her designs.

Mags just needed time and patience. Success would be hers eventually. Time and patience.

The only negative besides her growling tummy was the image of the tiny, brown tabby kitten she'd found dead on the top of the stairway outside her door that morning. The poor thing had been partially mangled, its wee neck bent cruelly.

Mags could only surmise that she'd foolishly left the back entrance open, and some predatory animal had, for whatever reason, dragged its prey up the stairs. Thank God the gallery's back entrance was solid metal with a security pad.

She shuddered imagining what would have happened had her carelessness opened up the Smith Gallery to criminals. As it was, she'd had to wrap the kitten in a scrap of leftover cloth and detour into one of the city's parks to bury the poor thing, albeit shallowly, before she made the one-mile trek to the gym she was a member of.

The gym wasn't a looker and far from the fashionable one she used to take classes occasionally with her friends, but it was cheap and had showers. So on the days when she craved a full shower and not the cloth baths she took in the gallery's bathroom, she went there.

They had a few spin and yoga classes. The best part was that the locker room had small lockers to rent for cheap, where she could keep a set of toiletries.

Her eyes lit up when Ciar's dad's pub came into view.

Murphy's had been kind of a rite of passage for her and her friends, and it still felt like coming home. The creak of the wooden floors, the clink of pints being drawn, and the smell of Ciaran Murphy's famous crab cakes always made her smile over the nostalgia.

Nowadays, Ciaran worked less in the kitchen. Ciar's Russian Aunt Alya had taken over since she and her daughters had moved permanently to Dublin. Word on the street, which was really just her friends' text group, was that Ciar and Ciaran were fighting over the chef.

Ciaran seemed to be winning, but the girls were of the opinion that Alya was secretly sweet on the older Murphy. Time would tell.

She pushed through the heavy wooden door, mentally reminding herself of all the lies she was currently working, and smiled as she spotted her group by the bar.

And there it was, the first blow of the evening. Jonathan had a leggy model wrapped around his waist, her curtain of straight, fake blonde hair hanging perfectly down her back like a curtain.

He was no longer her obsession.

Not her problem.

She instantly gave herself a little mental pep talk. *Be yourself, Mags. Enjoy this time with your friends. Do not let Jonathan O'Faolain dictate your happiness.*

Mags waved when she heard "Mags!" "About time," and "You made it!"

She gave hugs all around, with the exception of Jonathan and his...date. She did, however, force herself to smile and extend a hand in greeting.

"Nice to meet you. I'm Margaret." Petty, but she refused to give Jonathan's waste of space her nickname.

And...wait for it...Miss Model smirked as she rudely looked

Mags up and down while giving her fingertips in what must have been the world's limpest excuse for a handshake.

"Jasmine," she chuckled. "Right. The designer. I wouldn't have guessed."

As digs went, her jab dug in nice and deep. Mags knew she wasn't looking a hundred percent, but she was tired and hungry.

She could feel her friends stiffen. Gray took a step forward, ready to, most likely, snatch the woman from Jonathan and toss her out the door. Jonathan looked stunned. Whatever. Jonathan had a type.

Mags just smiled and said, "Right. My style's not for everyone, that's for sure. Nice to meet you, Jasmine." She quickly turned to Blair before her smile faltered into a grimace and signed, "Do we have a table, or are we just hanging at the bar? I don't mind either way."

Blair, Bébhinn, and Gray took the hint and turned to face Cormac, Ciar's uncle, to shout out their drink orders.

"Just water with lemon for me, Mr. Murphy," Mags grinned. "And where's the other Mr. Murphy hiding?"

"Yeah, well, be thankful the good brother will be serving you today, Miss Morrow. Ciaran can't go an hour without haranguing the new cook—too much salt on the chips, too much batter on the cod, mash on the pie isn't whipped enough. The man is embarrassing himself."

"Aunt Alya isn't a cook, Uncle, she's a trained chef for the love of God." Ciar leaned against the bar and rolled his eyes. "You and Dad are being selfish pricks keeping her here. I've told her she would make triple at Gray Eyes."

"Gray Eyes doesn't have your dad, babe. Let it go," Gray teased, elbowing her husband in the side.

"I bet if I walked into that kitchen right now, I'd find Ciaran and Aunt Alya in a compromising position," Jonathan joked.

Jonathan had come closer to the group, leaving Jasmine sitting on a stool by herself. While Daniel was busy telling Cormac that he swore his brother's lips looked like they'd been kiss swollen when he'd come in for a pint last week, and everyone hooted with laughter, Jonathan leaned close.

"Mags," he started. "I'm sorry about—"

She cut him off, no longer interested in hearing him apologize for his poor choices yet again. "It's fine. It meant nothing to me."

Cormac dragged a bar rag around her glass of water. "No rum and Coke today, Mags?"

"Eh, I've got a few hours of work left when I get home, and alcohol isn't the best incentive." Which was true, but she would have gladly thrown one back if she had the funds.

Jonathan tried to get her attention when Bébhinn announced that everyone should place their food orders before they found a table.

Thankfully, Mags' phone screen lit up with a call from her mom, saving her from the group's scrutiny over her lack of a food order as well.

Backing away from the group, she said, "No food for me, Cormac. I was a glutton and ate way too much breakfast." Before the inevitable questions of what she stuffed her face with, she quickly added, "Hey, Mom's ringing, I'm going to step around the corner to hear her."

Congratulating herself on the smooth exit, she rounded the corner to the restrooms. She answered, "Hey, Mom, you're up bright and early."

"I'm sorry to bother your friend time, sweetheart, but I have such exciting news, I couldn't wait to tell you," her mom said, clearly excited.

"Oh, my God. Tell me, tell me, tell me!" Mags was already chanting "be healthy" over and over in her head.

"One month, six weeks at the most, and your dad and I can come home."

Mags heard her mom squealing and clapping her hands, and her dad laughing in the background. "No way, Mom. Finally. Holy shit! Finally. So, what does this mean? Are you healed? Do you feel healed? Do you have to do anymore treatments?"

"I have to do one more round of treatment, but my doctor said my scans are already good. He just refuses to take any chances. And yes, I feel healed," she laughed, "and so happy. I've missed you and your sister horribly. I can't wait to hold you in my arms again."

"Me too, Mom. It's been hard having you so far away, but we're down to weeks now. We can make it a few more weeks. And Dad? Did he turn in his manuscript? Or the first half, I mean?"

"He did, and the university press' publicist loved it."

Mags felt her heart soar and the weight of bricks fall from her shoulders. Her financial struggles were nothing compared to what her parents had been going through, and it seemed like her family's toughest times were finally moving behind them.

"Are you getting Ciaran's famous crab cakes for lunch or a juicy burger and fries?"

"Can a girl not order the cakes and the burger? Geez, Mom, you know I'm always starving. I already ordered, and the food can't come soon enough. Oh, and Ciaran probably isn't cooking the food today, since Ciar's aunt Alya kind of kicked him out of the kitchen a few weeks ago." She smiled when her mom giggled.

Mags hung up after she and her parents said goodbye. She still had a grin on her face when she whirled around to find Jonathan leaning on the wall behind her. She gasped in outrage at his listening to her private conversation, but fear quickly followed.

"What the hell, creeper?" She stepped to the right, prepared to go around him, when his hand snaked out and grasped her forearm, stopping her retreat.

"What the fuck is going on, Mags?" Jonathan demanded.

He loomed over her shoulder. Not a bit of mirth showed on his face. Stray beams of sun highlighted his white hair like a damn halo, distracting her and sparking flames she'd been doing so well extinguishing.

She shrugged out of his grip and took three steps back. "Stay out of my life, Jon. We're friends, but you aren't my keeper, and you aren't going to ruin the one afternoon I get with everyone." She could feel her chest rise and fall in an ever-increasing rhythm and cursed the heat blooming over her fair skin, the telltale blush shouting her distress.

"Not this time, Margaret. I hardly see you anymore. Why?"

"Maybe I get tired of your girlfriends sneering at me from their great heights. Or maybe, you and I just aren't as close as we once were." All lies. *Damn. Damn. Damn.*

Jonathan's jaw clenched. "What treatment did your mom have to have? Is she sick?"

Mags clenched her own jaw, creating lie number...who knew. "She got really sick with bronchitis and had to do breathing treatments. Jesus, nosy much? My family is not your concern."

"The hell they aren't," he growled. "Why did you tell your mom you were starving and ordered two meals when you didn't order anything but fucking water? What's your answer to that, then?"

Save her from O'Faolain stubbornness. "Mom has missed me, and she enjoys hearing funny stories. Telling her that I was stuffed on scones and cream isn't nearly as amusing as eating enough for a grown man. That's it now, Jonathan. You're going too far."

"One more question. If you're so stuffed to the gills, why do you look like you've dropped a full stone? You look sickly," the prick added unnecessarily.

"My apologies for not having Jasmine's glow. Without sounding like a broken record, I'm aware of your taste in women. You don't need to list all the ways I don't measure up. You made your distaste for what I have to offer clear a long time ago."

Mags was furious now. Furious that he reduced her to defending herself. Doubly furious that she brought up that horror show of a New Year's Eve kiss. Way to let him know she remembered it.

Without listening to another word from his infuriating mouth, she stormed past him and practically ran back to their friends' table. He eventually joined, a menacing look on his face, and a storm cloud encamped about his person. Their friends kept eyeing him. Daniel, Jonathan's first cousin and closest friend besides Ciar, whispered something in his ear, but Jonathan just shook his head.

In the meantime, they collectively agreed to ignore Jasmine and her snarky comments. Mags' favorite, "I'm bored, baby." Jonathan didn't acknowledge her and, in fact, managed not to speak to anyone for the rest of the lunch, including his date.

Mags was nursing her third water, dreaming of the ramen cup she'd be slipping in the gallery's breakroom microwave the moment she returned home, when Blair caught her attention.

"Can I come see your new place today?"

Fuck my life.

"New place?" Bébhinn gasped. "What the hell?"

"Wait, what?" Gray asked.

"You were supposed to tell everyone, Mags," Blair signed

with a frown. "Mags has had her own place for almost three months now."

Blair raised her brows in an "I never said I would lie for you" look. "Yeah, geez, sorry guys. Mir helped me find a place where I could live and work out of. Forgive me, guys. I should have told you that my bedroom was free. I've been so damn busy, I barely remember to brush my teeth lately."

Bébhinn swept her apology away with the wave of a hand. "I don't care about that. Dad bought the townhouse for me to use however my friends and I chose to use it. I'm just pissed you didn't let me help you decorate your new place."

"Me too, asshole!" Gray added.

"Why don't we all go now," Bébhinn said excitedly.

Mags hated shooting the idea down, but having her friends see the pallet on the floor and her clothes shoved in grocery bags screamed mortifying.

Her sewing machine, fabrics, stranded cotton, sketches, embroidery hoops, and patterns were perfectly arrayed, organized, and tidy. She was proud of her workspace and had taken several pictures of it for her website, neatly cutting out the bare surroundings.

She had gone to buy a cot soon after she'd moved in, because that wooden floor was as hard as stone. Unfortunately, after seeing the price of even that small piece of furniture, she couldn't sign off on the expenditure until she was actually earning money.

She needed at least another month to make the space less tragic, though she knew she wouldn't be able to put her friends off that long.

She could feel Jonathan's angry glare drilling into her face, which she studiously ignored. Why he was angry was anyone's guess, though if she had to guess, he wasn't happy that she'd brought up the kiss. She never had before, and he probably would have been much happier had it stayed buried. He needn't worry, she sure as hell would never tell her friends about one of the worst, most embarrassing moments of her life.

"Sorry, guys. Today won't work. I've got a few more long days ahead of me until I finish my first piece." She gave a "woohoo" and high-fived Gray. "The client wants it for a luncheon next weekend. Plus, I haven't had time to really buy much of anything for the place. It really is mainly a work studio, which you've seen in those pictures on my website."

"It is a beautiful space," Blair signed and smiled. "It looked like there was a ton of natural light. I know just the plants you'll want."

"I would love that, Blair."

"Does everyone understand what the little girl is saying. I would be exhausted," Jasmine interjected, derogatorily speaking about Blair, completely unable or unwilling to read her audience.

Blair pretended not to see what Jasmine had said, choosing to finish off the last few chips on her plate. Daniel, Ciar, and Dagr looked stonily in Jonathan's direction, and Mags could tell he was about to tell his date off when she stood on her own.

"I've got to run. I'm meeting my bestie for massages. Call me later, Jonathan, and I'll come over. I haven't been to your place for weeks." Jasmine tee-heed and was gross enough to wink. "Oh, and Margaret, though I'm sure your clients are… rustic, designers are usually more put together than," she waved her hand up and down, indicating all of Mags, "whatever this is."

Jonathan stood abruptly, his face red and his fists clenched at his sides.

"Jasmine, would you open your phone and go to your contacts for me?"

She was all smiles as she handed him her phone, opened to contacts like he'd asked.

He must have clicked on his, because the idiot woman actually cooed and said, "Oh, babe, if you're going to change your name, make it something like Lover."

He tossed her phone back, forcing her to fumble it before it almost hit the floor. "I deleted my contact information. Don't ever come near my friends or me again." When she hesitated, her mouth opening and closing but thankfully mute, he added, "Leave now."

She finally stormed off with a huff. Jonathan remained standing to address the group. "Sorry about that, everyone. She asked me to do something today, and I told her no because I was meeting my friends. I stupidly told her where we were meeting, though. She was waiting for me when I got here. I'll be smarter in the future."

There were a few halfhearted "Whatever's" to his apology. It seemed the group was over Jonathan's bad taste, and Daniel's, to be fair. Since the focus was off her flat, Mags decided to get while the getting was good.

Stepping past Jonathan, who was still stiffly positioned at the end of the table, Mags cheerily announced that it was past time she headed out.

"It was great to see everyone. I'll let you know if my client adores my first commissioned piece."

"The bitch better," Gray said.

"If she doesn't, I want her name," Bébhinn added. "My mom and aunts taught me how to make a person suffer regrets."

Blair got up then and elbowed Jonathan out of the way. She shocked the hell out of Mags by hugging her close, leaving just enough room to sign privately. "You're hiding something. I'll give you time, not much, but I'll give you time to come clean. I'm your friend, or I'm not. You trust me, or you don't."

Mags could only nod once, too stiff with shock and denial. There it was, though. She should have known that nothing would get past Blair. When they separated, Dagr stopped her once again.

"I hope you can still make it to Gray Eyes Thursday night for Bébhinn's charity dinner to raise money for Dublin's orphanages," he said while hugging his wife close. "Everyone's invited, including plus ones. Feel free to bring a date, Mags. Bébhinn thinks you have a secret boyfriend. We'd like to meet him if that's the case."

"I am so excited," Gray cheered. I have a new evening dress that I've yet to wear outside my bedroom."

"Since I know you like the menu, Mags, I'll expect you to be there," Ciar smirked.

Mags had to smile despite the panic slowly stiffening her muscles. She'd made Ciar buy her dinner at his fancy pub months ago while he extracted information from her about Gray.

She had three distinct problems with the event. First, she didn't own a black-tie dress. Second, she couldn't afford even a potato at Gray Eyes, though it was her fervent hope that there would be plenty of free hors d'oeuvres. Third, and it was surely redundant, she had no money to give to such an amazing cause.

Mags had known about the dinner for weeks. The miracle she'd been praying for to get her out of it had yet to present itself.

If she worked every spare moment, meaning no sleep at all, she could finish the last of the embroidery on Mrs. Lark's blazer and hopefully deliver it late Wednesday night instead of Thursday like she'd originally planned. If she could manage that, then after her shift at the chippers on Thursday, she could wrangle a bit of free time to get all fancied up.

Perhaps she could take a small percentage of her earnings to go to one of the swanky secondhand stores to find an appropriate dress. Many well-to-do women dropped off gowns that had been worn only once or twice.

Fingers crossed.

Before she escaped Murphy's, some invisible devil on her shoulder had her saying, "I might bring my guy if he isn't busy. No promises though."

Oh shit. Mags, you idiot.

JONATHAN

"WHAT'S YOUR FUCKING PROBLEM?" Daneil huffed next to Jonathan's shoulder as they hoofed it back to their townhouse.

"What do you mean, what's wrong? What the fuck was right about any of that?" Jonathan would have loved nothing more than to follow Mags and demand answers. Truthful answers.

"You didn't intend for the idiot Jasmine to join us today, and you apologized. What's the big deal? I can assure you, we're all used to your poor taste by now, bro."

"You have the same tastes, asshole. I'm not pissed about that. What the hell is going on with Mags? And don't feed me a line that you didn't notice."

Daniel's eyebrows winged high in surprise. "This," he swept his hand up and down Jonathan's body, "is about Mags?"

"Just answer my question. You noticed, right?" Jonathan was not making shit up.

"I mean," Daniel hesitated, "I guess. Normally, she never misses a meal, but she did say she had a big breakfast."

"And no rum and Coke?"

"I heard her tell Cormac that she had work to do."

"She said a bunch of weird shit to her mom when Aileen called."

"Christ, Jon. Did you listen to her private conversation?"

Jonathan felt his cheeks flush, but he refused to make excuses. "Yes. She was asking her mom about her treatments. I asked about that, but Mags said she'd had bronchitis, which I don't believe. She told her mom she was starving and ordered two whole meals for herself. That's fucking weird. Right?"

"I suppose that's odd. Still, you couldn't hear Aileen's side of things. Why are you so bent out of shape?"

Jonathan ignored the last, still ticking off his points. "She was courteous to Jasmine even though she was purposely rude. Mags always lets my dates have it when they act badly. She just took it with a thank you and a smile."

"Let me get this straight. You're pissed because Mags didn't tear into one of your dates? Do you realize how dumb that sounds?"

Admittedly, that did sound ridiculous once he'd voiced it out loud, but Mags had made it her life's mission to screw up his dates, to stalk and make fun of the women. Basically, anything to piss him off.

Ever since he'd kissed Mags—no, he wouldn't think of that night—she'd become disdainful and uncaring when it came to his choices, but still, her antics said otherwise. She hadn't said a word against any of his choices in months. Hell, he'd barely seen her but a handful of times.

"Fine, but what about moving out of the townhouse without telling anyone? Even you can't deny that that's totally not like her."

"She told Blair."

"Well after the fact," Jonathan growled. "Don't you think it's odd that she didn't tell Bébhinn or Gray? Her best friends."

"Have you considered that it's nothing more than what she admitted? That she's busy. You know how she gets when she's focused on something."

"Not so busy that she doesn't have a boyfriend, apparently." Jonathan was seething over the last. Had her new boyfriend been to her new flat? A flat Jonathan hadn't even known about until thirty minutes ago.

Daniel stopped walking, forcing Jonathan to stop or leave him behind. "What the hell is really going on? Do you...do you like Mags, Jon? I mean as more than a friend."

Jonathan felt his chest tighten. "What the hell? I care about Mags as much as I do all of our friends. I just don't understand why no one else thinks she's off." The truth was, even though they'd been antagonistic with one another, he and Mags were friends, but it seemed like they weren't even that anymore, and it was freaking him out.

"Forget it, Dan. I'll keep an eye on her when I can and see what's what." He started walking toward home once more.

The ache in his chest felt hollow. Margaret Morrow used to take up space whether she knew it or not. He was an O'Faolain. He was successful, a good son, and a great friend. He offered help and counsel, needing nothing in return. Was he a bit of a playboy? Yes. Did he make his intentions clear to the women he dated? Again, yes.

There was only one person on this planet who could destroy him with a look. Three years ago, he'd made that person cry, and he'd never been the same.

That New Year's had been the one moment where he'd intentionally set out to hurt another person, and it was because he'd been scared. Scared of what his feelings meant. How his feelings would change his life.

Margaret Colleen Morrow wasn't a one-night anything. She was a man's forever, and he'd made her cry because of it.

She never questioned his actions, not that night, and not since. He knew, though.

Mags was going through something and lying about it. If he did nothing else, he would discover what she was hiding.

six

FOR THE FIRST time in almost fifteen years, it felt like she could stretch her legs and let her inner demons embrace their freedom.

There were years that she'd given up hope of walking amongst the plebeians of the world. Her soul bled art, and her fingers burned to express.

Her soul had always embraced death and blood and pain. Nothing gave her a bigger high than cutting herself and watching the bright red blood drip and splatter over a fresh, white canvas.

Her hand immediately went to her pocket to stroke her first purchase after she walked out of purgatory, a beautiful pocketknife with a carved wooden handle and a wickedly sharp blade. It had cost her a pretty penny, but she'd extorted quite a sum from her naughty therapist.

Once good old Dr. Portman watched a few videos of their "special" therapy sessions—her sucking him off, bent over his desk, him on his knees, and her personal favorite, him coming all over her face while he called her his dirty little psycho—it hadn't taken much convincing to fork over his life savings and write up a glowing reference stating that she was no longer a threat to society.

Healed.

Reformed.

She hoped he would spend the rest of his life looking over his shoulder. He really should. She might get bored once her long anticipated revenge was finalized.

As she walked the busy footpath, she avoided her reflection. She'd be lying if she said her profile didn't have bile gurgling in the back of her throat, while the voices threatened to cut the sagging skin from her body.

"It would be nice to have even a modicum of support," she growled under her breath to the voices who were constantly haranguing. "I'm the one who got us out of that place, and I won't have you underplaying my efforts."

She nodded to a mother pushing a pram, and a group of men laughing and smoking cigars. She felt all her sensitive bits tingle when one of the men tipped his hat in her direction. The idea of having sexual relations with a man who wasn't her disgusting pig of a therapist had her panties practically dripping.

"You do know what you look like, yes?" The most derogatory of her voices snarked.

She felt her body stiffen in offense. "Need I remind you that you and your cronies are the reason we even caught the attention of the authorities and ended up in that looney bin?

"You are the reason. Not me. You."

The voices used to make her harm herself over and over and over again, but she'd grown, matured.

Well over a decade locked away certainly helped with her insecurities. If she cut herself, it was because she wanted to, not because the cold voices said she had to "or else."

"I wouldn't take that tone. If we choose to exert ourselves, and we

will if you start to bore us, we could make you walk over to that stone wall and start bashing your head in." Another voice, the emotionless one, warned.

"Plastic surgery yourself, please."

"You're getting soft. You left your selfish whore of a mother alive and well."

"Yeah. Dear old Mum loved seeing you in a cage, and you left that bitch to enjoy her Wednesday night Bingo."

"I think your arms need more cuts. They're the only thing that makes you interesting."

She took a deep breath and appreciated the differences between Edinburgh and Dublin. Both cities had history, but Dublin had a stronger...vibe, intensity, playfulness.

As she zeroed in on her destination, she wondered if anyone from her past even thought of her. Did they miss her, despise her, wish her well, or hate her?

Her mother's puny allowance while she was locked away was an insult. That weak bitch loved insulting her only child. "Joke's on you, Mom. Might want to watch your back."

She snorted in amusement, but honestly, her dried-up, untalented mother wasn't even on her radar—she would be when funds demanded—but for now, her focus was on who locked her away.

Well, her focus was on the sister of who locked her away. And wasn't that sweeter?

She grinned at a young child shoveling greasy, fried chips into his mouth, all the while imagining how Little Miss Embroidery adored the kitten's broken neck draped over the steps of her stairwell.

It was the little things, she grinned at the memory. Kitties were so breakable, and so were little embroiderers.

Embroidery, not her choice of art, but who was she to

naysay the prime minister's wife? This was a scenario with so many options.

She'd been inside the girl's attic. Sparse at best, a hovel at worst. But she knew desperation, and Margaret Morrow was desperate as fuck.

She heard herself giggle and loved the carefree noise. She'd just watched the young girl shower at a dirty gym, and while Margaret cried under the hot spray, she'd come up with her next psychological trap.

Making this young girl afraid of her own shadow gave her no monetary value. It didn't give her back the years she'd lost behind the white walls of an insane asylum. It was about righting a wrong.

An eye for an eye.

seven

MAGS

Mags: I just got paid, bitches! And my client loved the blazer. I took a ton of pictures for my website, but she won't let me post them until after her fancy party. Ask me why? No, don't ask me. But…paid…

Ciar: Send proof of payment, and I'll buy you a steak at Gray Eyes to celebrate. I know how you like your meat. *wink face*

Gray: Ciar! That was only funny like the first three times! So many hugs and kisses to you, Mags!

Dagr: Consider me a client. I want blankets for Imogen and Colm. Gray for Imogen and black for Colm.

Blair: You would pick those colors for tiny babies, Griffiths. Congrats, Mags!

Mags: I make all the embroidery choices?

Dagr: Of course.

Bébhinn: Congratulations a million times over! I can only assume you will be coming to our charity event. It's special for me. Tell me yes, for sure.

Mags: Yes. For sure.

Daniel: Congratulations. Seriously. When do we get to see your new flat?

Mags: When it's not embarrassingly bare. Patience.

Blair: I can't wait until you can post the pictures. Also, send me a picture of what dress you're wearing to Bébhinn's thing. I'm considering a dress that requires no bra or panties.

Gray: Slut. I might be considering a similar dress. Send pictures.

Jonathan: I'm proud of you, Mags.

MAGS CHOSE to ignore the last text. *I'm proud of you, Mags.* "Good for you, Jonathan. Now kindly screw off. Condescending bastard," she grumbled.

She grabbed her satchel tighter against her body. She was still carrying a ton of cash even after she'd gone to the bank and deposited most of her earnings. She'd kept out just enough to swing by one of her favorite secondhand stores to pick out a dress for Dagr and Bébhinn's event the following night and another bulk case of ramen cups—chicken flavored with corn, her favorite.

The dress was stunning, sexy, and most importantly, cheap. It was black, which was the perfect shade to hide the cheaper polyester fabric. The bodice was two thick but flowy straps that created a plunging neckline and offered a peek of her breasts with an even lovelier glimpse of her side boobs. The straps thinned at the back and were secured with gold hardware.

The skirt was simple and flowed over her hips, but when she walked, a high side slit played peekaboo with her leg. She had plain black heels at home, and she knew they would work perfectly. Truly, the dress was a knockout.

It was getting dark, and she still had two more blocks to trudge before she reached the gallery. Only three days into the week, and she was smashed. She actually had other orders she needed to work on that evening, but she swore to herself that she'd go to bed at a sensible hour.

Sleeping soundly might be a stretch, though. Mags had done something at the chippers today that was so awkward and so unlike her that her muscles were still spasming from shock.

Poor Eze. Poor, poor, poor, poor, poor Eze. That man had gone to work without an inkling of how royally Mags was going to screw his world up.

He only worked at the chippers because he enjoyed the monotony of the work, which allowed him to work through complex theories in algebraic geometry—she asked what that was about. Mistake.

He was an assistant professor at Trinity, but he accepted a full professor's position at the University of Oxford and would be leaving after December. When she congratulated him, he only said the opportunity would afford him the time to enjoy other pursuits. Spoiler, they're all math-related.

"I'll miss you, Eze, but I'm so excited for you." She'd embarrassed him with the sentiment.

"You can visit," he'd said gruffly. "The flight is only an hour."

She laughed. "With my finances, I think the train and ferry option would be a better option."

"I'll send you flight fare whenever you wish."

Mags had felt her cheeks pinken. She wouldn't allow him to do that, but it had been a very kind offer.

Eze had to have been close to six and a half feet tall. He was Nigerian royalty, which he only copped to because one of his father's guards came by the shop once to deliver a "royal summons." He had the most beautiful, dark skin. She didn't know what his hair would look like because he kept it close to his scalp and he usually had a woolen cap on, but his beard was thick and curly and shimmered in the sun.

He told her once that he'd had a serious boyfriend before he went to university in America. He was tightlipped about his private life other than that. So, before their shift ended earlier, and she asked him to please pretend to be her slightly amorous date for a charity event, his eyes bulged in surprise.

He hadn't spoken for so long that Mags was afraid her request might have broken him. "Eze," Mags said desperately, "forget I asked. It was dumb. I know you aren't interested in me for heaven's sake. I'm not interested in you. I mean, you're a looker, don't get me wrong, but...but—"

"You want to make some bloke jealous. Am I right?"

She'd hung her head in shame, but she wasn't a liar. "Yes. I thought he liked me like I liked him. He kissed me on New Year's Eve almost three years ago. He kissed another girl right after. I'm embarrassed that I still feel some humiliation over it. The real problem is that he's also one of my best friends. All our friends hang out together. He usually has an obnoxious date on his arm."

"Fine."

"What? Fine?" Mags practically screamed, shaking off some of the fish guts from her apron. "Really? Oh, Christ, Eze, you're saving my life."

He laughed, well, an Eze type of laugh, which meant he was still sober-faced, but there was a slight crease next to his eyes.

"Do you have a dress?"

"I'm taking care of that after work. Remember, I'm getting paid from my first client tonight!"

"Margaret," he started with quiet intensity, "I don't understand why you are hiding your difficulties from your friends, but that's your prerogative. In the meantime, while you're working on becoming a famous designer, I need you to know that I can help you financially. It grieves me that you won't accept my help."

"Being my friend helps me, Eze. I don't need more than that from you. Besides, hard work builds character. I should have quite an overflow in my character bank already," she laughed.

He wasn't amused. "Does starving build character as well?"

"Don't," she held up the hand not holding the filet knife. "How's this, I'll let you buy my dinner at Gray Eyes tomorrow night?"

"That was a given as you're my date," he huffed. "I do have a favor to ask of you as well."

"You do? Anything."

He grabbed another cod from the basket between them and began cleaning it. Without looking at her, he said, "My mother's sixtieth birthday is in two months, which I know isn't much time, but she loves fans."

"Fans?" she encouraged further detail.

"Nigerian women enjoy using a fan at important events that matches their outfit. It must have feathers."

"Feathers. Okay." Pulling teeth with pliers would hurt less. "Did you want me to make a fan for your mom?"

He let out a relieved breath. "Yes. With feathers, and the inside done in your embroidery. English roses."

"Oh, Eze, that would be stunning. Any particular reason you want roses?"

"I'm my mother's youngest child, and she's been upset with me about taking the job in England."

"Ahh," she finally understood, "and you want to give her something traditional with something of her son's new life incorporated."

"Exactly. I'll provide the fan."

"Any particular color?"

He looked at her sharply then. "You don't take requests when it comes to your embroidery. You've told me that a million times."

"I will for your mom's special present."

"All the colors, then."

"A true English garden. Perfect.

"This man. The one who let you get away. We'll make sure he regrets throwing you over for that other woman. Tell me about the charity."

eight

MAGS

MAGS' cheeks were going to be sore if she didn't tone down her smile. But who could blame her? She'd just finished depositing her paycheck at the bank. She had a sack containing a baked potato with butter and cheese she'd picked up from a food stand. She dared not splurge on a protein topper, but the cup of ramen she planned on having with it surely contained some, and the new, gently used dress in her tote was a stunner. All positives.

Not to mention that she only had one more shift at the elderly care center and the chippers tomorrow standing between her and enjoying a fancy evening out.

Mags was grinning as she closed in on the gallery, which was thankfully closed for the day. She would dust the front desk and client meeting room and clean the toilet while her ramen cooked. She planned to put in a few hours working on the stunning button-up a client ordered with embroidered cuffs. Lovely, lovely, lovely.

As she went through her mental checklist, she added making a sketch for Eze's mother's birthday fan.

One moment, she was strolling along, and in the next, breath was knocked from her lungs. Something heavy hit her from behind, sending her arms windmilling and causing her feet to stumble over the uneven stone of the footpath. She teetered briefly before gravity held sway, and she was propelled down a set of stone stairs she'd been about to pass. Her body hit every stair and rusted bit of railing as she fell.

Finally, blessedly, her forward momentum ceased. She was splayed on her back at the bottom of an outdoor stairwell that led, she believed, to the basement of the neighborhood bookstore.

She blinked repeatedly, noticing that the stars in the sky shimmered, seeming to flit around her vision in sparks and flares.

She didn't move, knowing enough to assess her injuries first. Eventually, she wiggled her fingers. One hand was still gripping her hot potato, and damned if the thought of her fall ruining her dinner didn't piss her off.

Next, her toes, then rotating her ankles, bending her knees, flexing her arms, elbows, wrists—deep breath—neck, back. She tightened her abs and slowly sat up, allowing her eyes to focus on the stairs she'd just become intimately acquainted with.

Thank goodness it had only been about six or seven steps, though it felt like a hundred. It appeared like she'd gotten lucky. Her skull was free of bumps, but if the painful breaths were anything to go by, she'd bruised her ribs pretty good, her left hip throbbed, and various abrasions were beginning to smart.

Overall, she considered herself lucky. Work might be out of the question, but an extra-strength pain reliever certainly wasn't.

She heard a moan escape her lips as she got to her knees

and swallowed several times in the hopes that tears didn't follow. She still needed to make it back up the stairs, which she assumed would be a lot slower going than falling down them had been.

She needed to move. Period.

Her ribs screamed as she made it first to her knees and then to her feet, where she swayed, the destroyed potato finally pulled free of her numb fingers to smack the stone at her feet. She tasted copper and realized she must have bitten her tongue.

"Oh, God." She sniffled once, then twice, then a third time, until tears finally started to trickle down.

With shaking hands, she rummaged through her tote and found her cell. She should call one of her friends, but she still wasn't ready for any of them to see how and where she was living. Tears were dripping down her cheek, the salt mixing with the blood in her mouth.

The thing was, she should call the garda.

Because this wasn't an accident, not even a clumsy one.

She still felt the shape of big hands against her shoulder blades, pushing and shoving. Somebody did this to her.

No, surely not. Mags was being crazy because of shock. People didn't go around shoving people down stairs.

A big dog? Possible, except she'd swear she felt long, thick fingers. Impossible. Silly. She tripped, plain and simple. She'd been distracted.

She needed a hot bath, one she had no access to, pain relievers, and sleep. But first she had to make it up the stairs, walk to the gallery, and then...walk up a full flight of stairs to her space.

"Damn it. Damn it. Damn it!"

She needed help. There were times in a person's life when being stubborn was a virtue, and times when it was plain stupid.

She wasn't stupid.

With shaking hands, she opened her phone and dialed.

"Margaret?"

"Eze. I need your help."

nine

SHE STILL TASTED cum and stale piss with every swallow as she leaned against one of the towering brick edifices near the Morrow girls' gallery.

The voices told her not to overstep. They told her that they could make her do whatever they wanted, when they wanted.

Finally realize you don't rule us, little girl? The most persuasive of her voices asked.

We rule you. We've always ruled you. We said you were taking too long to make the girl suffer—

We had to intervene. You are forever and always inept.

"I am," she agreed. She had gotten carried away, but the voices had brought her back. She'd already moved some of the girl's embroidery and sewing items. Personally, she wouldn't have minded the chaos, but the girl was more like her mother. She would notice any discrepancy.

A place for everything, everything in its place, daughter.

God, how her mother's voice grated even in her thoughts.

Moving items hadn't been enough for the carrion living symbiotically within her. They had forced her feet in the direction of one of Dublin's derelict neighborhoods to seek out a drunk, drug addict for his services.

The filthy man's assistance would earn him five hundred pounds...and a blowjob. The voices were "teaching" her humility.

Surely you missed being some disgusting man's whore.

The best part was when the scumbag refused your offer of sex. A hard voice said, belonging to one of the cruelest of her "friends."

Christ and all His Saints. How ugly does a woman have to be to repel a homeless addict?

She knew they were trying to get under her skin. She knew! Except they were usually right. They were cruel, yes, but they were honest.

Hiding inside the stoop of a jewelry shop that gave her a view of where the girl had tumbled down, she retrieved her new knife.

Yes.

Finally.

Bleed for us.

She let the cold, metal tip scratch against her forearm as she waited patiently for the girl to either emerge or for an alarm to be sounded.

She grunted an almost euphoric, "Mmm," when the knife's sharp point pierced her skin, her focus momentarily diverted as she watched a thin, red line of her blood skitter and crawl in a haphazard line.

Go. Kill the girl and be done with this. Leave your signature on her youthful body so that her sister knows who is ultimately responsible.

That last voice was the one who encouraged her to slit the wrists of that drugged out artist. That voice adored watching death glaze a person's eyes.

"Perhaps, I should just kill myself," she mused.

Threaten us again, and you won't enjoy the consequences.

You can try, but without our consent, there won't be any follow-through.

Yeah, the only follow-through you've ever managed is putting the last stroke on one of your mother's paintings, and when you swallow a pig's release. Whoops, I meant your Prince Charming.

Enough. The leader of the voices barked. *We aren't quite done with playing with the girl. When we are, we move on to Mommy Dearest.*

Keep to the plan, you sloppy mess, but cut yourself deeper while we wait.

ten

MAGS

WHY COULDN'T she be obsessed with a man like Eze? Strong, handsome, wealthy, caring, and a genius. He did come with one drawback. Listening wasn't his strong suit. The ass took her to the hospital instead of her place. Even though she'd demanded it.

Traitor.

Eze left his evening math class at Trinity to rush to her aid, so she couldn't, wouldn't, be angry at him.

When he gently picked her up as though she were a fragile, cracked egg, she sobbed into his shoulder, embarrassing both of them. He refused to take her to the gallery. In fact, he refused to speak to her until an emergency room doctor had looked her over head to toe, given her drugs, and a nurse had helped clean her face and arms.

When he told her he would return shortly, she'd assumed it had been to make arrangements for rescheduling his class, but he'd taken her keys from her tote and let himself into her work/living space.

When he walked back into the emergency room, where she was still being monitored, it was close to eight. He held the strap of one of her old school backpacks, pinched between his huge fingers, and had an unreadable expression on his face.

"The nurse just went to get paperwork for me to sign, so I can go home soon. I just need to be woken up every hour to check for a concussion, but I can set my alarm." When he remained watching her without comment, she started to fidget.

She smoothed her hands over the hospital sheet, blanching when some of the residual grime from under her nails marred the crisp, white cotton.

"Where did you get that bag?" she asked, nodding toward the pack.

His jaw flexed, and his serious dark eyes did not look impressed with her question. She was about to ask what his problem was when the nurse returned.

Mags signed several discharge papers and listened to the nurse's instructions. "You'll need to have someone with you throughout the night. You were lucky that your ribs aren't broken, as it is, you'll be moving a bit more gingerly than normal, I imagine."

Mags was prepared to lie about having someone for the night, when lo and behold, Eze found his voice.

"She will be staying with me. I will follow your guidelines." As Mags opened her mouth to shoot down the lovely offer, he held up his hand, demanding silence. "A car is waiting at the entrance. I appreciate your help," he nodded politely to the nurse.

Eze wasn't happy, and she had a sinking suspicion she knew what it was about. He'd gone to the gallery. Bad luck, that. She would explain her long-term goals and that she had her life in hand. Her bare quarters were temporary.

Despite falling down stairwells. The further from the scene they'd traveled, Mags realized it was shock that must have made her believe she'd been pushed. It wasn't the type of neighborhood where people feared random acts of aggression.

A slick-looking Mercedes with a man holding open the back door was waiting for them when the nurse wheeled her through the lobby doors. When the man walked toward her wheelchair, Eze stepped between them.

"No, Abeo. I have her." Abeo gave a slight bow and went back to holding the door.

Eze gently placed her in the back seat and buckled her seatbelt. The evening became more surreal by the moment. Eze walked to the other side and slid into the backseat with her, his large frame taking up most of the space.

"Eze, I appreciate the offer of staying with me, but it isn't necessary, I promise."

He pinched the bridge of his nose, perhaps trying to stave off a headache. "We have several things to discuss, Margaret. Your living conditions are only one of them." Then, looking toward Abeo, who was weaving in and out of traffic like a pro, he asked, "Is everything ready for us?"

"Yes, Sir. Jol has seen to it."

Mags had so many questions, but Eze didn't appear to be in an accommodating mood, except that she did need one answered. "Where are we going?"

"Lansdowne Place. I have a flat there."

She knew his family was wealthy, but damn. She was beginning to believe that Abeo and whoever Jol was worked for Eze.

"Are you hurting?"

His voice startled her as she'd been blindly watching the streetlamps blink past her window. "I feel pretty good, really. The meds are helping. It's a wonder I didn't break out all my teeth on those steps," she chuckled. He didn't. "My ribs hurt, but that's to be expected."

Nothing else was said. They parked in an underground garage, and what was becoming a habit, Eze held her against his chest from the garage to the elevator, and even after walking into his spectacular flat.

"Wow, Eze. It's beautiful. You can let me down now." She began to squirm from his hold but gasped in pain when she twisted her ribs.

"Stop, Margaret," Eze demanded while a Nigerian woman, if her stunning clothes were anything to go by, appeared at his shoulder. Without a word, Eze followed her down a hallway.

They entered a bedroom done in stunning browns and muted reds. He didn't stop until they stood in an en-suite bathroom with a giant tub, steam curling above its rim.

He set her gently on her feet but kept hold of her arm. "Margaret, this is Jol, Abeo's wife. Jol, this is Margaret Morrow. Abeo is bringing your things. Jol will help you undress and soak before dinner."

Mags was beginning to wonder if she might still be lying at the bottom of those stairs because this definitely didn't feel real.

"Wait, Eze. Just wait a second." She rubbed both hands over her cheeks, trying to center her bearings. "I appreciate you coming to my rescue. I do, but this is too much. How about this, I'll gladly take a bath, which I don't need any help with, thank you, though, Jol, and then you take me home."

"No. Jol will assist you now."

So much for compromise. Without another word, he spun on his heel and left, shutting the door behind him. Mags looked at Jol and shook her head. "Is he always like that?"

Jol grinned as she began to unbutton Mags' blouse. When

Mags tried to take over, she got a stern look for the trouble. "No, he isn't usually like that. My husband said your call scared him, and then Abeo said you cried when Eze picked you up.

"Eze is a gentle man who feels deeply. I believe you are his first close friend. I've seen him lighter in spirit since you two met."

Mags let Jol do her thing, her cheeks only burning a bit warmer when she stood naked in front of the other woman. She helped her into the tub and adjusted a warm towel behind her neck.

"You will soak for thirty minutes. I will wait for you in your room." She turned at the door and added, "Comforting you comforts him, Miss Morrow."

Mags was curled up on one of Eze's living room sofas, a plush robe wrapped around her body, while she sipped on a delicious warm tea that Jol handed to her.

It was late, and her eyes were beginning to droop, but with everything Eze had done for her tonight, the least she could do was stay awake for what she assumed would be a lecture.

"I want you to hear me out without interruption. Can you do that?" he started.

"Of course." At Eze's disbelieving look, Mags tacked on, "I'll do my best."

Eze sat forward on his chair and steepled his fingers. "We haven't worked together long, but—"

"I knew you weren't destitute, but come on, Eze. All this," she said, and waved her hands around the room. At his pointed look, she realized she had interrupted. "Whoops."

"In that time, I've come to know how close you are to your

friends. How much you love them, and they love you. I know how much you love Art History at Trinity. I know your mother has cancer and is still out of the country, and that your parents asked you to keep it to yourself.

"I know you miss your parents. You miss the closeness with your friends because your deceit, whether well-intentioned or not, has been slowly building a chasm between all of you.

"I know you work three jobs, four if you include cleaning the gallery."

"Light cleaning," she couldn't help but interject, which he ignored.

"I know you dropped out of school because you couldn't afford it, and you didn't tell anyone. I know you live in an attic with no heat, air, or plumbing because you felt you didn't deserve to stay in your friend's townhouse if you weren't in school, and you were too embarrassed to tell them.

"If they are half the friends you say they are, you should have trusted them with the truth, despite what your parents asked of you.

"You called me tonight because you didn't want to bring them anywhere close to your truth, but what you didn't account for, Margaret, is that I am a good friend, too, and I won't let you continue on the way you have been."

Mags felt her heart pounding a frightened rhythm with every word Eze spoke. "Can I speak now?"

"Yes."

"I can appreciate that you know so much about me, that you're as invested in our friendship as I am. And I won't deny that you're fairly accurate in most areas of my life, though I can't imagine how you figured out I'm not in school and why I moved."

"I teach at Trinity, and I happened to speak to one of your professors weeks ago, and I asked after you. As far as your reasons for moving, when we first met, you told me that your friend's father bought the townhouses for his family and their friends to live in while they were in school."

She really needed to get a handle on oversharing. It was truly coming back to bite her in the ass.

"Fine, but what you haven't considered is that I have a roof over my head."

"Barely."

Ignoring him, she continued. "I do have access to a restroom, and my gym has a shower. I work more than one job because fabric and embroidery thread aren't cheap, and to make money, you have to spend money. I believe in myself and know I will succeed. My living arrangements are temporary. I have food to eat—"

"Debatable."

"If there were ever a true emergency, I do have friends to call. I proved that tonight, and thank you profusely. I would sacrifice just about anything to not burden my parents. You don't know them, but they are everything that is love and security to me.

"You let the attic situation freak you out, but I promise that this is only a season in my journey. I put money in my account tonight for the first time in forever. I bought a gorgeous dress for tomorrow night, which you aren't going to get out of taking me to, because I so want a night out, and that isn't solely because of Jonathan.

"I'll let you buy me the most expensive rum and Coke the bar can provide. I did find out that the guests are supposed to pay a thousand pounds per plate, but I already worked that out. I kept enough money out from my check to make us dinner before we go.

"I already let Bébhinn know that they could sit us at the bar or out of the way of the dinner tables. We'll still have so much fun, and I swear I'm not a bad cook."

Eze let silence fill the room for several moments. "I already called and purchased our spots. I called the elder facility and let them know you wouldn't be in tomorrow morning. I will cover your shift at the chippers.

"You will rest and recuperate and let Jol pamper you tomorrow. You will move into the extra room here until you've saved enough to find a place of your own. With running water and a bed," he stressed.

"No. No way. You are my friend, Eze, but I'm not your responsibility. I refuse." She felt destined to surround herself with men whose overflowing testosterone was deadly.

"We are friends. I knew your finances were strained, but not to the extent they are now. That is easily remedied. You can keep the gallery space for your work. Living here will afford you a level of comfort and safety. And food.

"Either do what I ask of you and keep your life private, or I will tell your parents and friends."

Mags watched in horror as he crossed his behemoth arms over his chest, reminding her so much of Gray's father in that moment it felt like déjà vu. Stubborn men. Soft-spoken Eze was railroading her, giving her nothing but granite eyes and stonewall expressions.

She sat up and tugged the lapels of her robe tight, regretting the tug against her ribs immediately, but damned if she would let even the smallest whimper pass her lips. "You're being unreasonable."

"You'll still be running yourself ragged. You'll still be working an unseemly amount of hours. Your goal of becoming famous for your embroidery is still in place. The only difference is that you'll have a place to lay your head at night."

If she argued further, which she wanted to, it would seem

petty and childish. Worse, it would be foolish. "Fine. I accept... gratefully." Eze's lips tilted into almost a smile at that.

"But I'm going to the gallery to work tomorrow. I have a few adjustments to make to my dress as well. Also, if I'm staying here for a short while, I will help cook and clean."

Jol, who happened to be quietly moving through the living room at the time, said "No," before retiring to the back.

eleven

JONATHAN

JONATHAN'S PHONE started pinging with notifications the moment he exited a meeting at Three Wolves Distillery and switched his phone off silent.

He glanced at Daniel, who was getting the same notifications. He pulled up his texts and saw that there were already about ten messages in their mutual friend group, with more coming. The first was from Mags. Why the hell did his chest squeeze uncomfortably?

He'd felt her distance before, but ever since their get-together at Murphy's, he was positive her emotional distance was personally directed at him.

Mags: Don't panic, friends. I'll still make it to the charity tonight. I will be sporting a few bruises, unfortunately. 🫤

Jonathan felt ghost fingers gripping and squeezing his throat. It hurt to swallow, and his ears and cheeks felt hot.

Images of how she might have gotten hurt flashed behind

his eyes—a car wreck, she tripped over a loose cobblestone and face planted, she cut off a finger with sewing scissors, hit by a revolving door, or a dog attack. The possibilities were endless.

Bébhinn: What happened?!

Blair: Start talking.

Gray: The hell?

Mags: I accidentally tripped on my way home last night and fell down a set of outdoor basement stairs. My ribs – Ouch! At least my money makers (my hands) escaped a tragic end.

Gray: Oh my God, Mags! No way!

Daniel: Tell me you went to the hospital.

Bébhinn: I can't believe that happened. I'm sick. Were you alone? Where are you? I'm coming now.

Blair: Not taking no for an answer. Where are you?

Ciar: Answer now, or I'm calling your parents and your Uncle Colly.

Mags: Fuck off, Ciar. I've had your back more than once, and you bloody well better have mine! I was alone, yes, but I called a friend, and he came and carried me up the stairs and made me go to the hospital. Drugs for pain and bruising. I took a long, hot bath last night at his house, took all the meds, and feel much better today. I'm going to work soon. I promise to see everyone tonight. Stop worrying. My friend threatened to out me if I didn't fess up to my clumsiness.

Blair: Nice story. Where are you?

Gray: Were you in the bath alone, or did your friend, that we haven't met yet, garner a spot?

Bébhinn: Dagr likes to get me in the bath too. Did the bath soothe some bits but make other bits tender?

Ciar: Dagr. Control your wife. No one wants to hear your half-assed version of romance.

Jonathan was so tense by that point that he was still sitting stiffly in the passenger seat of Daniel's car. They were both reading texts and answering emails before they got on the road. Thank God, he wasn't required to navigate a vehicle after reading that shit.

Blair: All joking aside. Where are you?

Mags: I'm staying with my friend until my workspace above the gallery is finished and livable.

Bébhinn: Address.

Gray: Address.

Blair: Address. Now.

Mags: Fine, but you three are being ridiculous.
I'll send you a pin.

Jonathan watched the chat like a jungle cat stalking prey. Nothing. Nothing. Nothing. And then...

Bébhinn: Damn, girl. Better put my Sunday best on before I enter that zip code.

Gray: 😶

Blair: My, my, my. See you in thirty. Don't even think of not being there.

Dagr: Hey, just seeing this. Don't even think of coming tonight if being pampered in bed by your friend helps your recovery. 😌

Jonathan would strangle his new cousin the next time he saw the insinuating asshole. Did they all know who the mystery friend was? Daniel didn't, or he would have said.

Mags didn't send her address to the group. Why? "Message Blair and see where Mags is staying," Jonathan demanded of Daniel.

Daniel gave him a sharp look before putting the car in reverse and backing out of the parking spot. "Mags sounds fine. If you're so concerned, call her and find out whatever it is you want to know. Don't involve me."

Jonathan practically bit his tongue in two he was so pissed. Mags called a "friend" to help her when she'd been hurt. Mags' "friend" took her to the hospital. Mags stayed at a "friend's" house last night. Mags was staying at a "friend's" house for an indeterminate amount of time.

He wondered if the "friend" would be at the charity event that night. It was ridiculous to be angry with Margaret for having friends outside of their group or even a boyfriend, especially when he'd never given her any reason not to.

It was childish. He knew it was. He sighed and leaned his head against the headrest.

"Listen, Jon, far be it from me to give out relationship advice, but I think you need to admit that you have feelings for Mags, and you do feel something. Lie to yourself, but don't try to bullshit me. I don't think you've liked any of the women you've taken out since secondary school. It's like you're waiting for something or someone else."

Daniel emphasized "someone," and maybe he was right. And maybe he was just a prick who'd been satisfied knowing Mags had crushed on him for years. Knowing she felt something more than friendship for him had been enough.

But she'd taken away the "something more," and he wasn't handling it well. He'd never felt so undeserving of Mags' affection. When had he become such a prick?

She thought their New Year's Eve kiss had meant nothing to him, when the frightening reality was that it had meant everything. If he were honest, he hadn't had a moment like that with a woman since that night. Mags had shaken him that night, turned him inside out.

He hurt her that night. The horror of it was that he'd done it purposefully and had kept doing it with every woman he'd forced her to endure.

Had she given up on him? Did he want her to finally let him go?

No.

He unclenched his fingers from around his phone and pulled up his contacts. She answered on the first ring.

"Hey, babe," the woman purred.

"Sheri. Tonight's off. Sorry about the late notice." He hung up before she asked any questions, foolish or otherwise.

Daniel opened his mouth, but Jonathan quickly cut him off. "Don't."

twelve

MAGS

MAGS SIGHED the minute the gallery came into view, and her ribs screamed in protest. Oh well. All's well that ends well. Eze clearing her work schedule was a huge overstepping blessing. She was giddy to spend the rest of the day working on her second paid piece and sketching the fan design for Eze's mother.

Speaking of her rescuer, she hadn't seen him since the night before, when he "laid down the law," so to speak. He was busy at Trinity and picking up the slack at the chippers.

He laughed when she asked him if their boss would get someone to help clean all the fish. "Margaret," he chuckled, "I've worked at half speed since you took an interest in filleting. The faster my hands work, the more I can immerse myself in equations, but I've learned to do my thinking at the slower pace."

He'd still been chuckling when he excused himself at her bedroom door. *Ass.* Just because he was kind of like her hero now, didn't mean she wasn't plotting payback for the razzing.

Mags paused at the top of the stairs and felt her breakfast begin to make a second appearance. A small, headless bird lay still with its blood congealing around the gray feathers.

"Christ!" She screeched and slammed a hand over her beating heart, quickly moaning at the pain she'd inadvertently caused her bruised body.

The bird's head was leaning against her door, its small black eyes frozen and watching. "My God," she mumbled. Eze or Abeo must have let in a cat that, unfortunately, liked to eat its snacks outside her door.

She looked around the stairwell, the door, and finally to the window high above, the only source of natural light. It had to be a cat getting in. They were clever and resourceful. It probably sneaked out the moment it heard a human.

Stepping over the head, she let herself in and grabbed several paper towels, making quick work of scooping up the cat's interrupted meal and placing it in a garbage bag to toss in a bin on her way to Eze's. She'd be damned if she buried every damn thing the cat dragged in.

As she washed up, she decided she really needed to tell the gallery manager that they might have a gap somewhere in their exterior. They wouldn't want to take any chances that a cat or any other animal could gain access to the gallery proper.

Finally seated at her desk, her hands froze above the desk's whitewashed planks. A few things were out of order. The hair on the back of her neck rose.

Her scissors were on the windowsill. She could maybe believe she'd been in a hurry and placed them wrong, but several of her embroidery threads were out of their color codes.

Now that, she would never have done in a hurry or not. Her eyes slowly traveled around the small room, landing on the partially opened door of the space's only closet, and then it hit her. Eze had been there, and he'd been in a hurry. He might have looked at her sewing things out of curiosity.

It seemed out of character for him not to put her things back the exact way he'd found them, but then, he was emotional at the time.

Forcing her shoulders to relax, Mags settled in to enjoy a few hours of uninterrupted work. As her hands worked through an intricate bee pattern, her mind drifted to her friends. Their visit and care had been a balm to her spirit that she hadn't realized she'd been craving.

Jol prepared a whole brunch spread for her friends, and at everyone's urging, the housekeeper sat and enjoyed the feast, even laughing at the crazy exchanges.

The moment they walked into Eze's flat and introductions with Jol and Abeo were made, they dragged her to the back bedroom and forced her to strip to her bra and panties to see for themselves how badly she was hurt.

"God, Mags," Gray gasped. "You're so lucky you didn't break any bones. I'm still pissed you didn't call one of us."

Blair lightly ran her fingers over Mags' ribs and winced before signing, "Did your mom freak?"

At her hesitation, Bébhinn clasped her shoulders and forced Mags to look her in the eye. "Tell me you told Charles and Aileen." At Mags' grimace, she added, "You better have a damn good reason for all your recent cloak and dagger bullshit."

She had about ten reasons, but she refused to tell them everything. However, she could give them something. "This book deal is super amazing for Dad, but family finances will be tight for a few more months. I've taken a couple of part-time jobs to pick up the slack. My parents don't know, and I don't want them to."

Blair, ever the most intuitive, asked, "Why did you move out of the townhouse, then? You didn't have to pay rent."

Mags felt heat sweep over her body, exhausted by the subterfuge. She put her clothes back on while her three best friends looked at her with concern.

She decided on one more truth. She sat on the bed and faced the firing squad before her so her shaky knees wouldn't fail her.

"I didn't make the financial aid deadline and couldn't afford Trinity this semester. Your father," she looked at Bébhinn, "provided a roof over our heads while you and all of us were in school because he was the most amazing, thoughtful, honorable man to have ever walked the Earth. But...well, I'm not in school, and I have honor too.

"I had to take a few jobs to make ends meet while my parents are in America, but I'm excited for my business. I believe in myself, guys. This year has been shit for me, and there are some personal family things I'd like to share, but I can't. Not yet. Just know that I have a plan, and I feel optimistic."

Bébhinn cried and sat on the bed next to Mags. "Dad would have kicked your ass for moving out. I want to kick your ass, but you're scrappy, and I don't want a black eye for tonight. You should have trusted me. Us." Her voice hiccupped the last.

"Mags," Gray started before swallowing roughly several times, "you saw me at my lowest, and you refused to leave me there. You were the catalyst that brought Ciar and me back together. I would have been honored to help you. It hurts me that you didn't give me the chance."

That gutted Mags. Her own panic had blinded her to her true resources. It wasn't money she'd needed all these months. It'd been her friends' support.

"What jobs are you working?" Gray asked.

Groaning at what was to come, she told the truth anyway. "I work in the kitchen at an elderly care center Monday through Friday. I get there at five. Once the dishes are done from morning service and the lunch prepped, I hoof it to the chipper shop we all like on Crown Alley. I fillet fish and fry until the afternoon.

"Then I work on my projects above the Smith Gallery the rest of the day. I dust and clean the shop for money off the attic space, but" she attempted brightly, "I get to use their toilet and breakroom fridge and microwave."

"Where have you been showering?" Bébhinn asked tightly. "You've only been staying here since last night."

Mags blushed furiously, but she was done lying. "There is a gym not a half mile from the gallery that rents lockers and has showers."

"What else?" Gray asked.

"I bartend Friday and Saturday nights. The tips are great. You guys know that fabric isn't cheap. It'll all be worth it in the end, I swear."

"You didn't eat or drink at Murphy's last Sunday," Blair stated. She was tight-lipped, her face pale and pinched. She was beyond hurt.

"Well, I was running a bit short of funds, but I loved seeing everyone. Honestly, I didn't mind." Even Mags was getting slightly depressed at her "woe is me" bullshit. "Listen. It sounds bleaker than it is, and now that Eze, the guy who lives here, has decided I'm to live with him until I get on my feet, my life is truly turning around.

"I don't want your sympathy, guys. I'll take your love and support, but not your pity."

Blair was busy typing away on her phone, which was odd since she needed to watch everyone to stay involved in the conversation. Mags watched as Blair's face paled. Whatever she'd been reading wasn't good.

Blair looked up and stared daggers at Mags, while tears slipped from her expressive green eyes clouded with tears. "Your parents are living a few blocks from America's number one cancer hospital. Johns Hopkins. Her cancer is back, isn't it? That's what all of this is about. Don't lie, Margaret, or I swear I'll call Dad right this minute."

This was it then. No more running. She was tired of hiding, and Mags trusted her friends with her life and certainly with her mother's secret.

"It is. I found out the night before your wedding, Bébhinn."

In that moment, the painful band that had been constricting her loosened. She was able to explain the reason why her mom had insisted on secrecy, on wanting to fight the cancer on her own two feet and with her own money.

She agreed with her friends that their family and friends would be pissed when they found out. When Mags explained that her parents would be back in Scotland in a few weeks, and that she was showing all signs of having beaten cancer a second time, and that they wanted to break the news to everyone themselves, they had agreed to not tell their parents.

With liberal cold water splashed over everyone's eyes, they'd finally found their way to the kitchen and dug into the glorious spread Jol prepared.

She explained her relationship with Eze and that he was truly a knight in shining armour. They agreed and couldn't wait to give him hugs. Eze would not be happy.

As Mags' needle thrust and wove through the fabric stretched in her hoop, she couldn't help grinning. Who knew that honesty could feel this freeing?

Had her friends been hurt at first? Yes, just as Mags would have been had the situation been reversed, but now she had people in her corner who knew her struggles and would be nothing but uplifting.

Her friends promised to keep Mags' family drama a secret from their parents. Still, Gray and Bébhinn were absolutely firm on telling their husbands. She understood and agreed. If Mags had a relationship like they did, there would never be room for secrets.

Mags' hands flew over the cream linen in nothing short of joy. Jol had given her a strict curfew to be home. Eze's flat was home now, which made her smile widen.

If she shied away from wondering what woman would be hanging off Jonathan's arm tonight, she just as quickly remembered she'd actually be on the arm of a gorgeous Nigerian prince.

Suck it, Jonathan O'Faolain.

thirteen

"I GUESS *you got what you deserved, and in your case, you got what your body was worth. Nothing.*"

"*The girl is practically skipping and shitting flowers down the footpath.*"

"*We're going to take over, you dumb bitch. At this rate, the budding artist will bloom all over fucking Europe while you eat your weight in chocolate.*"

She gritted her teeth and took the criticism. She had miscalculated the drunken lout's effectiveness. A mistake she wasn't prepared to let happen again.

"I said, I've got it under control," she growled under her breath as she watched the seriously undertalented girl waltz into one of Dublin's most exclusive Eircodes.

How had she climbed from the bottom of those stairs only to walk into a better life minutes later? She needed to escalate her plans before the voices did.

"*Forgive us for underestimating you. Your track record of disappointment is legendary at this point.*"

"*We know you're waiting for the gallery's exhibition to make your so-called move. Surely, you know we don't trust you anymore.*"

"Headless birds? Christ, but you are an idiot."

"I have a plan for the exhibition. Give me more time," she begged.

"Tick tock. Tick tock. Tick tock."

"Give you more time? Your finances are finite, cow. We have just enough to exact revenge on Mirren Morrow-MacGregor Campbell before we need to turn our attention on your waste-of-breath mother."

"Consider your free will revoked."

fourteen

MAGS

MAGS MET Eze in the flat's foyer. His formal attire left her all but speechless. He was wearing a black bespoke suit that fit his large frame to perfection and custom-made leather loafers. That wasn't the head-turning moment of his look, though.

He chose to wear a large, and by large, she meant the size of his broad chest, coral and gold beaded necklace, and a black silk traditional cap with black beads sewn in a stunningly beautiful pattern.

"Oh, Eze, wow," she announced as she entered the foyer. "Your necklace and cap are works of art. Let me study the beadwork on your cap later. Christ, that had to have taken hours upon hours. Does the necklace represent anything special?"

Eze began to shake his head 'no' when Jol joined them. "It denotes his royal status." Eze frowned at his house servant and obvious longtime friend.

"I feel woefully ordinary," Mags laughed.

"Hardly, Margaret," Eze said with his usual solemnity. "There won't be a more beautiful woman at the event tonight."

Mags linked their arms. "We'll make a good showing of it unless the guests look too closely at my ribs. Too bad I had to bruise them up the day before showing so much skin," she clicked her tongue in irritation.

Eze cleared his throat. "I doubt the gentlemen will be looking at your ribs, Margaret."

The slight censor in his voice made her throw her head back and giggle. "Pretend your royal beads are pearls and clutch them whenever a man ogles the girls," she teased.

Abeo drove them to Gray Eyes, but Mags noticed another car following them closely. "Why is that car following us?"

"Eze's security detail, Miss Margaret," Abeo answered from the front seat.

"Security?"

Eze huffed out an irritated sigh. "My father insists."

Eze was always the quiet, stoic type, but under his usual unexcitable demeanor, Mags sensed he was stressed.

"Eze," she started, placing a hand on his arm. "If you regret being my date, I'd understand. It was childish of me to want to make Jonathan jealous, and your friendship sure as hell means more to me than being petty. We can turn around now, and I'll tell my friends that I didn't feel up to it after all."

He placed his hand over hers and patted. "I'm sorry, Margaret. I would never disappoint you by changing my mind. It's only—" he cut himself off and shook his head.

"I won't step a foot out of this car until you tell me what's got you so upset." Mags should have noticed the strain bracketing his eyes before now.

"You won't accuse me of dramatics?" he asked, and a small smile even peeked over his full beard.

"I would never. Spill it, Your Highness," she teased.

"Part of my security is a man I was in a relationship with for three years before leaving for university. I don't know if my father is testing me or if my mother believes she is giving me a gift. I do not understand why Nasir would subject himself to my security detail. He could have gotten out of the assignment."

"Who broke it off between you two?"

"I did, but we weren't exclusive. Well, he wasn't, but my life was going in a different direction anyway. He was a distraction to my true life's pursuit."

"Oh God, Eze, you're speaking about math, aren't you?"

"Of course."

God save her, but men were unquestionably obtuse. "Are you sure he wasn't as committed to you? I mean, did you talk to him about a future before you tossed him over?"

He looked confused. *Patience, Mags.* "Do you miss him?

"Yes."

And there it was. "Perhaps while I'm proving to Jon that I've moved on from my crush, we might also gauge a certain guard's reaction to me being by your side. If he didn't have regrets, he may have them after he sees how glorious we look together," she cackled.

His eyes widened. "I like this plan." When he grinned, Mags couldn't help but match his smile.

"Stage one. Be extra attentive while you help me out of the car. Stare into my eyes periodically as if no one else exists. I will smile at you, and you'll be mesmerized. You'll mesmerize me, too, of course."

The first part of the plan went off perfectly. Eze didn't have to point out which of the three guards was his ex. When Eze pulled her from the car, he held her tight and pressed his lips to her neck. Hiding her surprise, she held one of his hands to her lips and kissed his knuckles.

Nasir's glare scorched.

As they followed the host to their reserved seats, Mags

asked Eze how he was doing and if he thought they'd made an impression on his ex.

"To be honest, Margaret, I could never have faced him without you by my side." He grinned devilishly, then adding, "But perhaps you were right, and he carries some regret after all."

"He's watching us now from the left side of the room. Perhaps another peck on the cheek will encourage future dialogue." She waggled her eyebrows and grinned.

Eze stopped the flow of traffic to bend down and kiss her softly on the lips. She may have swooned. Following the host once more, Mags whispered, "Christ, Eze, but you handle a woman well for a gay man."

"Oh, I like women too." And then he winked. Well, okay.

fifteen

JONATHAN

"FOR THE LOVE of all that's holy, Jon, stop staring at her. Your face is screaming stalker," Daniel hissed in his ear, like the annoying mosquito he was.

The elbow to the gut proved how much his cousin needed swatting. Jonathan tossed back another swallow of his family's whiskey, which had him remembering his conversation with his dad earlier, though conversation wasn't a completely accurate description.

His father let Jonathan know that he expected an attitude adjustment before they met again, and that if he ever snapped at his mother again, he'd tan his hide no matter his supposed adult status.

He cringed in shame. He had been short with his mom. She'd been telling her sisters, Raven and Rowan, that she couldn't wait to hear all about Mags' date. Jonathan had childishly replied, "You need to get a hobby, Mom. No one else gives a shit."

And that was when his father grasped him by the back of

the neck and led him from the room. He'd gone back to his mother and apologized, because he was out of line and because he had hurt her feelings. Taking his anger out on her had been a new low.

The evening, unfortunately, didn't improve. He and Daniel were the only friends in the group who didn't know who Mags was bringing or whether it was the same "friend" who had taken her to the hospital and who she was now living with.

Even Ciar and Dagr were tight-lipped, and Jonathan knew that they knew since they were married to two of Mags' best friends.

Even Blair let him down. Daniel relented after hours of Jonathan needling him to ask Blair. Daniel said she rolled her eyes and shut the front door in his face.

Jonathan had been at Gray Eyes for two hours, and unfortunately, he was no longer in the dark about Mags and her friend. He wished he were.

He'd had to endure an introduction to the bastard, who couldn't seem to keep his giant paws off Mags. Jonathan saw red as he watched the man's hand curve around her ribs, her bare ribs.

The dress she wore was created to bring men to their knees, or perhaps it was the woman who wore it. He forced his eyes from her breasts, the creamy smoothness of their curves peeking from the deep cut of her bodice making it almost impossible to blink

It had been hell to watch that man's thumb sliding gently over the bruises marring Mag's ribs, visible when the soft light surrounding the room hit her just right. Jonathan wanted to get her alone and ask her if she was truly okay. If there was anything she needed.

He wanted to be the man who provided her comfort, but he'd left it too late.

Jonathan startled when Gray tapped him on the shoulder, not realizing that she, Blair, and Bébhinn had joined him at the bar.

"It sucks, doesn't it?" Bébhinn asked.

"Am I supposed to guess what you're speaking of?" Rude, but his personality had departed weeks ago. Also, he knew exactly what she was referring to, or who, rather.

Bébhinn sighed in what must have been disappointment. "Our group is meeting in the card room for a brief announcement. Don't be late, turd."

"It's not a good look, Jon, to only be interested in Mags now that she's gotten over you," Gray said solemnly. "She has enough heavy things dragging her down right now. She doesn't need you piling on."

He wanted to shout that he'd always been interested in her. He wanted to beg to know what things were worrying Mags. He said nothing, which he was pretty good at.

Gray and Bébhinn went to stand by their husbands, leaving Blair looking at him fiercely, her head of fiery curls and waves reminding him of Medusa. She looked like she wanted to turn him into stone at any rate.

"I saw you kiss Mags that night," she signed.

Jonathan would swear he'd been electrocuted. He didn't think anyone knew about that night. "You mean Mags told you?" There was no reason to deny the kiss, nor was he upset that Mags would tell one of her best friends.

"No. I saw you. I was in the gardens below. I watched you take advantage of her feelings for you. Then, I watched you leave her alone without a word."

"I shouldn't have—"

"Shouldn't have what. Kissed her? Left her? Kissed another girl a minute later? I ran back inside to get to her on the balcony, but she'd already gone back inside before I could get to her. She was watching you kiss that girl, and you were watching Mags while you did it.

"I understand we were all younger then, alcohol was involved, mistakes were made. But you hurt her that night, and you've continued to hurt her for almost three years. None of us would have wanted you to date Mags if you weren't into her that way, but you could have at least explained that to her after the fact.

"And now, now," she signed with more emphasis, her breathy voice forming the word as well, "she has finally found happiness, and you're moping about like a kicked puppy. I love you, Jonathan, but get over yourself."

Blair walked away without a backward glance to join their friends. His head throbbed with the mental beating the girls gave him, but he was far from giving up and walking away because of his mistakes.

The O'Faolains had plenty of stories about the many apology tours the men in the family had to take before they got the women they wanted.

Jonathan tracked Mags and her date across the room. They were clearly making their way to the back room to meet every-one. He saw his chance a moment later, when the two separated to speak to others.

Mags was telling an attractive middle-aged woman covered in jewels, "I will call your secretary tomorrow to set up a time to take your measurements and see the dress. Thank you for thinking of me. I've never embroidered a belt. I'm completely excited. Once I see your home and a bit of your space, I know I can come up with a personal design all for you."

"I look forward to it, Margaret."

The moment they separated and before she could reattach herself to her date's side, Jonathan swooped in. He quickly entwined their arms to lead her further away. She gave a solid tug, but he wasn't letting go.

"Let me go," she growled under her breath, thankfully not willing to make a scene.

He led her through the crowd until they were close to the high-stakes room where their friends were probably already gathered.

Tucking them behind a tall wooden column of intricate Celtic fretwork, he turned her to face him, studiously ignoring how damn beautiful she looked. He placed his hands on her shoulders gently, knowing that despite her showing up tonight, she had to still be in quite a bit of pain.

He looked into her eyes and prayed she would hear him out. "Listen, Mags, I know I have no right to it, but would you please say that you'll give me a moment of your time tomorrow, or the next day," he pleaded. "I don't deserve it, but for the sake of our history, please."

In this lighting, her green eyes looked more hazel, with hints of brown swirling through them, as she gazed at him with a sadness he had never seen in her before.

Not since the night he'd kissed her.

"I'm not sure what you need to talk to me about, Jon. I've assured you more than once after your latest date took potshots at me that, at this point, being belittled by your ladies is as easy to brush off as a fly's nuisance." She waved her hands between them like the state of their friendship wasn't a big deal.

"Apologies for my past mistakes, and the position they've put you in won't make them any less. I know that. I only want to talk to you. Just the two of us."

"Margaret," her date's deep voice sounded firm and just on the left side of aggression.

She immediately tried to step away from his touch, but he couldn't leave it at that. "Please, Mags. Only a moment."

"I'll text you when I have time, though I can't imagine we have anything that needs sorting."

Jonathan had to let her go when she wrapped her hand in her date's. The man stared intensely at Jonathan a beat longer before pivoting sharply on his heel. Jonathan was forced to watch as the stranger stopped before walking into the card room. He lifted Mags' chin and kissed her on the mouth.

The man, he refused to remember his name, took a beat to glare at Jonathan over her head.

Jonathan felt his body swell with rage. That bastard was staking a claim on his...on Mags. That man might be royalty in Nigeria, but he wasn't anything in Dublin, and he sure as hell wasn't an O'Faolain.

sixteen

PATRICK O'FAOLAIN

"SOMETHING IS GOING on with our son," Patrick growled over his shoulder while he flipped pancakes for the impromptu family breakfast.

Breakfast tended to be at his and River's flat on the second floor of the O'Faolain building since he enjoyed cooking.

His brother, Bran and sister-in-law Raven, arrived a moment ago. His half-brother, Ulf, had stayed in their extra bedroom last night, so his dour presence was counted. He was ferrying back to Wales today after he met his son, Dagr, and Dagr's wife, Bébhinn, who was Patrick's niece and sister, and Rowan's daughter, for lunch.

River had cajoled Ulf long enough last night that he'd finally relented to sleep over instead of going to a hotel, and clearly had regrets about his interrupted routine.

Dagr and Bébhinn had stopped by last evening on their way to a charity dinner that Bébhinn had helped plan to tell the family the big news.

Bébhinn was pregnant, only a few months. She admitted

that she couldn't keep it a secret from her mom another minute. She was not due until early next summer.

All of them had been overjoyed with the news. Still, there had been a moment during the hugs, kisses, and congratulations that Bébhinn and Rowan had burst into tears—not the joyful kind.

His father's passing still weighed heavily on all of them. Hugh would have loved a new wee one to cuddle and spoil. He would have loved to see his wife become a grandmother and to see his daughter hold her first child.

It had taken considerable effort on everyone's part to dispel the dark mood, but eventually the tears dried, and they sent the happy parents-to-be off.

Patrick, however, was still frustrated over his son's recent attitude. His boy was unhappy, upset about something. Whatever it was, Jonathan wasn't opening up to him like he normally would.

"Is he concerned about taking the Architects Register Admission Exam?" Bran asked.

"Surely not," Raven chimed in. "I've never seen anyone with more talent. He's been working with the firm we use for new builds or reconstructions since he got his bachelor's."

"Yeah," Rowan, who had just arrived, added. "He had no trouble with his masters, and he speaks positively about the projects the firm allows him to collaborate on."

"I don't believe it has anything to do with his job or the ARAE exam. Daniel hasn't said anything to you?" Patrick asked his brother.

"No, only that neither of them took dates to the Gray Eyes event last night, which was new for the two of them, but Daniel seemed fine with it."

Patrick looked at his wife, River. "You're awfully quiet." Very quiet. Very un-River-like. The moment he called on his wife, he watched her eyes flick to first Raven and then Rowan.

"You know something." That wasn't a question. The question was why she was keeping secrets. They never kept secrets from each other.

He flicked his own glance to first Daniel and then Ulf. They shrugged but nodded toward the women. As if they'd choreographed the move, River's sisters moved to sit on either side of her at the kitchen bar.

Patrick flicked the heat off on the range before turning his attention to the three smiling women. They still looked so alike, it made his heart pound to see them side by side, remembering when he, Bran, and their dad met the sisters for the first time.

Not letting happy memories fog his train of thought, he asked, "Well, wife?"

"I, no, we," she corrected, glancing again at her sisters who nodded agreement, "think Jonathan's in love."

"But there is a problem," Raven added.

"A big problem," Rowan agreed and winced.

MAGS

TWO WEEKS HAD PASSED since Dagr and Bébhinn's charity event and their big announcement. With all their closest friends—and Eze, whom everyone instantly approved of except for Jonathan—gathered around them in Gray Eyes' high-stakes poker room, the happily married couple announced that they were expecting a baby.

Everyone went wild with congratulations. No wonder Bébhinn chose a charity that provided shelter and love for children. Mags was still tingling with excitement for her friends. Another child to love on, as if Gray and Ciar's little ones, Colm and Imogen, weren't amazing enough.

Mags looked at herself in the mirror as the hot air from her blow dryer filtered through her dark brown waves. She pinched herself every morning to prove that she was truly living in such an amazing flat with an amazing friend instead of sleeping on an attic floor and being lonely. Her clientele was ticking up every week as well.

She and Eze had become closer, and Mags would be forever

thankful that she'd taken that job at the chippers because she'd made a lifelong friend from it. He surprised her by turning in both of their notices. He claimed that he used to need the monotony of the job to concentrate on the theories running through his mind, but since she'd moved in, he felt more clarity and had enough peace now to sit on his living room couch and let his mind wander where it would.

With the money she saved by living with Eze, she was able to devote her energy to her business. She quit her job at the elderly care facility to free up even more time, but kept the bartending gig because it was only two nights a week and the tips were crazy good.

They'd compared notes a few nights ago about the men they were trying to make have regrets. In her case, she wanted to get over the man and for Jonathan to have regrets. Nasir watched her with an unforgiving glare. Eze pretended not to see Nasir's pain-filled eyes following him, but he'd admitted that it went a long way to soothing his wounded pride.

Jonathan—he was more complicated.

It was hurtful and infuriating in equal parts that he was attempting to, what, pursue her? He had done everything to show her that he didn't think of her as girlfriend material, or even worthy of a date. Was this about making amends for the kiss and how he behaved afterward?

She shook her head at her reflection. "Let it go, already, Jon."

Whatever his reasoning, she knew it was in her best interest to ignore his newest nonsense and protect her heart.

Jonathan was the one man who could really hurt her. He'd proven the ability over and over and over again. She was mature enough now to understand that he wasn't doing it on purpose. Not since after the one kiss they'd shared, anyway.

She was the one who'd allowed her heart to be pummeled

and broken. She was fixing her past mistakes now and moving on. She might still long to feel his hands on her skin and his mouth devouring hers, but she'd become an expert at pretending where he was concerned.

She had two errands to run before she could go to the gallery for the day. With that in mind, she dabbed clear gloss on her lips and grabbed her coat and purse before hurrying out of her room.

Eze had just opened the front door, about to leave for Trinity, when he saw her walking toward him.

Eze's lips barely lifted, but Mags could see mischief brewing in his dark eyes. Her eyes flicked briefly to the hallway behind the open door and saw Abeo and Nasir standing at attention.

Let the games begin.

"How many classes do you have today?" she asked, coming to stand before him. His body was angled just enough that the men in the hall would see their profiles.

"Two and a study group. And where are you off to?" While he spoke, he took one of her hands in his and brought it to rest against his solid chest. "Busy day?" he asked her.

"Fabric shop. I need a few more colors for your mother's fan." She hadn't let him see any of the progress yet. Too bad he didn't know she had the piece in an embroidery hoop in her tote. She'd worked the last few nights on it once she went to bed. "I also have to drop a pair of scissors off at the sharpeners, then the gallery for the rest of the day."

"Are we still going to the gallery to see the artist your sister signed to Smith next week? I was going to make sure my schedule was clear at work."

"Yes," she grinned. "Mirren is so excited. She'll be here this evening. She has to meet the artist one more time before the show to finalize placement. Thank you so much for letting her stay here."

Mags finally had to come clean about some of the changes in her life to her sister. The most crucial update that affected Mirren's visit was her change of address. Mags promised to explain everything that night.

"I was hoping you might be home in time to have dinner with us. We have a lot to catch up on, so I figured I'd just make dinner, and we could stay in."

Eze attempted to hide his grimace, but he was no actor. "Eze, you ass! I burned one meal. One! Get over it."

He chuckled. "I'll be home, but only if Jol does the cooking."

"Amen," Jol shouted from the kitchen.

"Traitor," Mags shouted back. "Fine. Have a good day, Eze." When she went to pull her hand away from his chest, he tugged her closer with it. He looked at her and raised his brows in question. *Oh my.* He really wanted to put on a show this morning.

At her subtle nod, he bent slowly and kissed her. It was gentle and soft, tender and surprisingly romantic as their lips melded and their tongues tentatively touched. When it ended, they both looked surprised.

Eze cleared his throat and stepped back, running a hand down his button-up. Turning his head sharply to the men waiting beyond, he said, "Abeo, you will drive me today. Nasir, you will help Margaret with her errands and ensure that she gets to the gallery safely."

Mags choked on her own saliva. "That isn't necessary." She pinched his arm to let him know he was going a touch too far with the make Nasir jealous plan.

"Just making sure you don't fall down any more stairs."

Without another word, Eze walked briskly out the door, Abeo in his wake, leaving her awkwardly alone with Nasir. Pasting on a smile she didn't feel, she said, "Looks like it's the two of us today, then.

Mags: You could give a girl ideas after a kiss like that. I think my safety is the last thing on Nasir's mind after that stunt.

Eze: It wasn't all for show.

Mags: Your Grim Reaper persona is false advertising. You are a good kisser.

Eze: My lips are still tingling. Never fear that Nasir's feelings will get in the way of his job. He's nothing if not professional.

Mags: See you tonight.

As Nasir hailed a cab to take them to the fabric store, she called her mother to check on how she was feeling. She told her about some of her new paying customers and about Mirren's gallery party tomorrow night. Mags promised that she and Mirren would video call her that evening.

Mags tried several times to strike up a conversation with Nasir, but he chose to be blunt and snide every chance allowed. Sighing, she shifted her attention to the list of fabric and embroidery floss she needed to purchase.

Once the cab driver dropped them off at the fabric store, Mags turned to Nasir. "Here," she handed him her best fabric shears, "the sharpeners are only around the corner. Please drop them off while I shop."

She could tell he was about to argue, so she quickly shut down any argument. "I won't leave this store until you've returned."

He clenched his jaw in anger but turned to do her bidding. When he was only a few steps away, she couldn't help but add, "I wonder if you cared half so much for Eze's safety back in the day." He paused and his shoulders stiffened, but he continued on.

Her phone pinged a notification right as she reached the store's front entrance.

Jonathan: Will you meet me today?

Christ Almighty, he'd been asking that same question since the day after the charity event.

Mags: I'm working all day, and Mirren is coming into town tonight. I don't know if you're in some type of therapy that encourages apologies all around, but let me assure you, yet again. We have been friends since we were children, and we're friends now. Nothing has changed.

Jonathan: Everything has changed.

Mags: Whatever epiphany you've had, keep it to yourself. We'll meet up when all of our friends get together again.

Jonathan: Please, Mags.

She gritted her teeth and breathed deeply, trying for calm. Whatever his angle was, she wanted no part.

Jonathan: Tomorrow?

Mags: I'm working all day.

Jonathan: Tomorrow night?

Mags: I bartend Friday and Saturday until the wee hours of the morning.

Shit. Shit. Shit. Why did she tell him that? Too much information for a nosy O'Faolain.

Mags: Leave me alone, Jon. Honestly, this is getting old. I'm sure you have a Rolodex full of willing women to live in your self-important bubble with you. Don't text me again about this, or I will block you. We are friends. We have only ever been friends. Perhaps you should review the lessons you've been dishing out to me for years. The rules have been crystal clear since that New Years.

Mags turned her phone off and shoved it into her tote, vowing to herself to put Jonathan O'Faolain's bullshit behind her.

An hour later, she and Nasir were entering the gallery's back entrance, silently, of course, since Nasir refused to engage in so much as a comment about the weather.

Before she'd taken four steps, Nasir's strong arm had wrapped around her waist and swung her behind him. And then she saw what he had. "Damn it." It was a dead cat broken on the top step and partially lying over the top landing outside her door.

The hair on her body stood like frozen soldiers, and her breathing became choppy the longer her eyes raked over the poor, black-haired creature.

Mags laid her hand on Nasir's forearm. "It's okay. This type of thing has happened a few times since I've worked here. I let the gallery manager know that there must be a structural issue allowing all the animals in.

"This poor girl must have fallen or something," she added, while looking up at the high wooden beams. Even though a cat falling to its death did seem highly unlikely. Still...

"Let's get you and your packages inside, Miss Morrow, then I will dispose of the carcass."

"Oh, you don't have to, Nasir. Let me drop my bags off upstairs, and then I'll do it. I'm sure you've had enough of babysitting me."

He only watched her, expressionlessly. She sighed at his continued silence. He was taller than Mags, but not as tall as Eze or Jonathan. Still, he appeared lean and strong, with a strong face and lovely high cheekbones. His complexion was paler than most Nigerians she'd encountered, and his eyes were a lovely greenish brown.

He waited until she entered the attic before he bent to pick up the poor cat. Christ, Mags shuddered, the amount of death on her stairs was becoming creepy as hell.

eighteen

JONATHAN

JONATHAN OPENED the heavy wooden door to Triskelion Territory Design that sat next door to the O'Faolain's four-story family home. He was out of breath from jogging the three blocks from the restaurant where he'd been eating lunch with one of his colleagues from the architecture firm where he worked.

His mom had texted him that his dad was in an important meeting and she hated to interrupt him, and that she had an emergency with the office's kitchen plumbing. However, Jonathan would have sworn that his dad and uncle Bran met Ciaran and Cormac Murphy for lunch at their pub. He decided not to mention that she had interrupted his lunch meeting.

The moment his body crossed the threshold, his forward momentum came to a grinding halt. His mother and her two lookalike sisters were at their desks, watching the door with wide eyes.

Triskelion was the Byrne sisters' interior design business, with the office's stunning interior paying homage to their Irish and Native American heritage. His eyes darted around the space, seeing nothing out of place. No river of water flowing over the office's hardwood floors. He glanced at his phone's screen, where he'd pulled up how to shut off the water supply, and shook his head. Obviously, the YouTube tutorial wasn't needed.

The three women held pens in their hands like they'd been interrupted making lists, pretending a casualness that they were far from pulling off. Clearly, they'd been waiting for him to arrive.

"Oh, Jonathan," his mom started, "I'm so glad you had time to stop by."

"You said it was a plumbing emergency," Jonathan replied dryly, a dawning realization that his mother had lied.

"Sorry about that, she replied, shrugging her shoulders and grimacing, "I overstated things."

Right.

"Have a seat," his aunt Rowan said sweetly, indicating the lone chair set in the middle of their three desks.

Whatever this was, he, Daniel, and Bébhinn had learned as kids that it was easier to let the three women have their way.

He loosened his tie and unbuttoned his suit coat and the top button of his shirt before sighing and sitting before the tribunal as it were.

He didn't speak a word, only found his mother's eyes and held them. The slight flush to her cheeks was concerning. She was nervous.

"Jonathan, I know I asked you here under false pretenses, so I won't beat about the bush on why I called you. You're in love."

"You've been in love, you're just now accepting it," Aunt Raven corrected.

"And from what we've gathered, your courting skills might

need some tweaking. A lot of tweaking," Aunt Rowan said gently.

"I wouldn't normally dream of interfering, son, but you've been so unhappy lately that it's killing me."

Jonathan forced himself not to touch his scorching cheeks. His body temperature felt high enough to boil him from the inside out. He could feel sweat prickling his skin, creating an uncomfortable friction beneath his clothes.

He was stunned speechless.

And completely and utterly horrified.

He sent a silent prayer to the Heavens, promising every higher power listening that he would attend Mass regularly if only his cousin, Daniel, did not find out about...whatever this was.

He cleared his throat and, with joints stiff with embarrassment, stood. "I appreciate the concern, Mom, but I have everything handled. I have to get back to the office."

He nodded to his aunts and was about ready to turn and flee when his mother said, "Sit." He could have left regardless of her wishes, but he wasn't prepared for the fallout with his father if he hurt his mother's feelings, inadvertently or not.

He sat as gingerly as a man would with a raging case of hemorrhoids, chanting in his head that this humiliation had an expiration date.

"Your father hurt me once. Gravely. Deeply," his mother began.

That, he hadn't expected. Date ideas, maybe, flowers, dinner, jewelry, declarations of love. He should have known his mother wasn't some airheaded woman to make such suggestions. He frowned, thinking about his father ever hurting his mother.

"What are you talking about?" He felt his hands clench on the chair's armrests.

"We were new. Patrick was scared of loving me." She sighed and looked at her sisters, who both nodded encouragement. "He kissed another woman on the night we made it official."

Jonathan shot straight out of his chair. "The fuck he did that to you!"

"Sit, sweetheart, please," she encouraged. "The pictures were leaked to all the social media pages and newspapers in Tulsa, in all of Oklahoma, really. I was crushed. I left for Ireland. I left him."

His mother got up from her desk and came around the front to lean against the edge in front of him. "He fucked up. But do you know what he didn't do?"

"What?"

"He didn't give up. He made amends one hundred times over. He worked on himself. He faced his fears, but most importantly, he didn't take no for an answer. I don't know what happened between you and Mags, but I suggest you figure your shit out, and then you make sure she knows what she means to you."

nineteen

HANNAH

THE GREAT HANNAH TODD, *former mediocre artist, psychiatric patient, prostitute for candy, and your newest accomplishment, animal scourge of Dublin.*

Hannah clenched her jaw, refusing to acknowledge the digs. She knew killing that last cat would catch her flak. The bastard voices hadn't stopped reminding her, all day, all night, every waking minute.

It had been a last-ditch effort to control the situation and prevent them from taking over. Hannah found living outside the hospital surprisingly challenging and admitted that she was rusty in ruining people's lives.

The dead animals would have frightened most people or at least given them pause that something more nefarious was at foot.

Not Margaret Morrow.

That childish bitch practically skipped and jumped rope over the corpses. Now that she'd moved in with a man, getting to her had quadrupled in difficulty. His flat was in an area with several cameras and security measures.

She'd managed to follow his car once. He'd gotten out at Trinity. He looked too old to be a student, probably a professor, plus he was rarely, if ever, alone.

The voices told her to lie low. They had a plan. They always had plans, but they usually involved them crowing about how brilliant they were and how stupid she was.

She lost time two days ago. Five hours of time. They were up to something, and even when she did the breathing therapy to settle her mind that she'd learned at the hospital, the lost time remained void.

Damn her for the last animal stunt. They'd warned her not to go against them. Not to think for herself...

Oh, look, the dumb bitch finally remembered who she answers to.

It isn't her fault for going after cats. They kind of complement her cat-lady look: fat, hairy, and friendless.

Christ, Hannah. Truly, do something with yourself.

I think we should find another body. One more willing to follow us.

"I thought it would scare her," she hissed under her breath.

She sat at the end of her hotel bed, the white, untidy sheets bunching beneath her fat thighs. Take-out containers littered the room's long, white, shiny counter. The scrapbook she'd spent years of her life creating lay open beside her. Mirren MacGregor's smile beamed at Hannah from each and every page, making her eyes tighten and her teeth clench.

Shame and regret pierced her chest right above her heart. There were days when she barely remembered why she hated her so much. Days she forgot that she was an artist. That she had a mother, a brother.

Doesn't that feel good, friend.

Punishments always feel good, don't they?

Ignoring the voices, she moaned as the pain increased, finally looking at her chest. Ahh, that made sense. The tip of her steak knife was digging ever deeper into the flabby meat of her left breast.

She coated her free hand in the blood and gently pressed the print over one of Mirren's faces, obliterating one of the woman's hideous smiles.

There were days when she wondered how different her life would be had the voices never come to her.

Lonely. Cold and lonely.

twenty

JONATHAN

JONATHAN'S EARS burned every time he remembered the...intervention. "Christ have mercy," he muttered, staring at his reflection in his bathroom mirror. At least his mother had planned their "talk" while his dad and uncle were away.

Apparently, his mom and aunts figured out years ago that he had a thing for Mags. He hadn't been nearly as ambiguous about his feelings toward her as he'd thought.

He smoothed his hands over his suit jacket. Tonight, he paired his dark navy suit with a pale blue button-up. The gold and sapphire cufflinks that his father had given him for graduation glinted at his wrists.

He turned his head first one way and then the other. Women seemed fascinated by the white color. For him, it wasn't that unusual, given that he, Daniel, his dad, his uncle Bran, Dagr, and his father, Ulf, all had the same. The grandmother he'd never met sure had strong genes.

He'd gotten a haircut that morning, shaving the sides tighter than normal and leaving the top long enough to slick back or leave slightly tousled to cover his forehead. He chose the latter for his night out.

Daniel stuck his head in just as he spritzed a sparse spray of Tom Ford at his neck. "Do you really think this is a good idea?"

Jonathan had told his cousin what he was planning. Daniel was his cousin and best friend. They didn't keep much from one another. "Yes." He took his mom's words to heart, no matter how uncomfortable they'd been to hear.

His dad hadn't given up on making amends with his mom, and he wouldn't give up on him and Mags.

"The car's here, then. Ciar and Gray are meeting us, but they said they can only stay for an hour or two. And Gray told me to tell you that she is only doing this because Bébhinn gave up and told you Mags' secrets and then had the audacity to suffer from morning sickness and not come herself."

Jonathan tried to smile, but just recalling the things that Mags had been going through made his whole body clench in pain. She'd been suffering while he continued to flaunt his women in front of her.

He felt his eyes burn when he thought of the last time the group had met at Murphy's for lunch. She hadn't eaten or ordered a cocktail because she hadn't had any extra money for it.

And that wasn't the worst of it. Bébhinn was in tears when she related that Mags had been forced to drop out of school because she couldn't afford the tuition. She'd slept on the attic floor of the gallery because she didn't want to take advantage of his family's generosity of the townhouse since she wasn't in school. She'd worked three, practically four jobs, with the gallery cleaning.

Her mother had cancer, *for the love of God*. She'd been hungry, uncomfortable, and working herself to exhaustion, and she'd done it all without complaint. She'd met her friends with smiles and love like she always had.

And what had he done? Brought a woman into her world who belittled and insulted her during one of her only moments to enjoy her friends.

Daniel touched his arm as they left the townhouse, probably noticing that he was pathetically near tears. "You didn't know, Jon."

"I should have."

Mags had been ignoring him for over two hours, which was quite a feat considering he and their friends sat at the bar, and she was the bartender.

Gray and Ciar left half an hour ago, but before they left, Gray had had a private moment with Mags at the edge of the bar's main floor. He watched as her mouth fell open in shock—Gray must have told her that he knew about some, hopefully all, of her recent troubles. Her head bowed as her fingers pressed into her eyes. It killed him not to go to her.

Gray hugged Mags tight before pulling back and exchanging more serious words. He watched as Gray wiped what must be tears from below Mags' eyes. They silently looked at one another a minute longer before Mags nodded her head. Agreeing to something before parting ways.

Gray went to Ciar's side, her husband frowned, and wiped tears from his wife's cheeks. He frowned at Jonathan, clearly blaming the whole shitshow on him, which was fair, before hustling Gray from the bar.

As the couple passed Daniel and Jonathan, Gray leaned close and said only, "Be careful, Jon. Please."

He swallowed the lump in his throat and nodded before

turning back to Mags. She was smiling and laughing with customers, but the joy didn't reach her eyes. Her gaze cut to him. She frowned and mouthed, "Leave." Not a chance.

Daniel was in charge of turning any and all interested women away from them. He didn't want even a hint of a woman near him for those moments that Mags glanced his way.

He picked up his phone and texted her.

Jonathan: I'll drive you home when you get off.

He watched her glance at her phone on the counter where she was cutting oranges.

Mags: No thanks. I walk.

Jonathan: I will call your family if you don't. Would your uncle Coll think it's safe for you to be walking home alone? At night.

She slammed her phone down and refused to acknowledge his raised hand, signaling that he'd like to order another drink. A club soda with lime. He wasn't drinking alcohol before he spoke with Mags. He knew he'd need to have all his wits about him for that.

The pub was one he and his group of friends never went to, which was probably why she chose to work there. It would have made it easier to keep her financial issues secret.

Beside him, Daniel had been working away on his tablet, ignoring Jonathan's lame attempts to catch Mags' eye, when Daniel groaned.

"Incoming," Daniel muttered. "Why the hell are those two here, of all places?"

Jonathan turned in time to see Denny and Josh Hertz,

brothers from a well-to-do London family. He and Daniel had met them a few times over the years. Their parents sent them to live with their aunt in Dublin when they did something bad. Ireland was their timeout.

Those two were never apart, and rumor had it that they shared everything, especially women. Jonathan enjoyed sex, perhaps too much over the years, but the thought of him and Daniel ogling each other's dicks in action was going just that much too far.

To each their own, he supposed, except Denny and Josh had an odd sexual chemistry...between just the two of them. He and Daniel avoided them. Always.

"Daniel. Jonathan," Josh hailed.

As Jonathan was turning to greet them, he noted Mags' grimace when she watched the brothers waltz up to the bar.

"Back in Dublin again, I see," Daniel commented. He kept his voice neutral, neither caring nor uncaring of their presence.

"Yeah," Denny grinned as he sidled up to the bar, "we got into a spot of trouble. It'll blow over in a few more weeks."

"Dad won't let us come home for another month, though, the cranky bastard," Josh said with a shrug and smile.

Jonathan hadn't a clue how he and Daniel had ever tolerated them. The creepy vibe they gave off was beyond off-putting.

"I see you two are here for the same reason we are," Denny snickered and glanced over his shoulder—at Mags.

Jonathan felt Daniel go stiff beside him. Jonathan set his water down but didn't say a word. Yet.

Josh turned toward Mags then as well, making a show of checking her out. She wore one of the pub's t-shirts tucked into a pair of well-worn jeans. Her ratty tennis shoes were some he'd seen her wear over the last couple of years. The outfit should have appeared comfortable and nothing more, except that the simple clothes hugged her body to perfection. Her perfectly rounded breasts, tiny waist, and firm, round ass were all mouthwateringly highlighted. And these two pieces of shit were ogling her as if they had the right.

"We saw her first," Josh announced as he turned back to them, smiling. "So far, she hasn't been swayed by our charm and big tips, so Den and I decided that tonight we wouldn't take no for an answer."

"That's right," Denny agreed. "We don't take well to a 'no.'"

Jonathan didn't think, his body lunged without thought of consequences. He slammed his fist into Josh's face since he stood closer to him. The filthy prick dropped to the ground, screaming about a broken nose.

Denny landed beside his brother a second later after Daniel's fist connected. Mags had run up to them by that time, her eyes wild with worry.

"What happened? Oh my God, you guys, my boss is already calling the gardaí." And then she briefly touched Jonathan's arm and then Daniel's.

A determined look came over her face, and she placed her hands on her hips. "Call your fathers. Both of you. Right now."

Jonathan knew it was the smartest thing to do, though they'd both be catching hell for this.

Their dads answered almost simultaneously. He and Daniel explained the situation and suggested calling Dagr in for legal counsel, giving them Denny and Josh's family name so they could work on a plan while they drove to the bar.

While they waited, a few patrons helped Denny and Josh to a couple of chairs, and a waitress gave them a rag with ice for the swelling. He noticed the waitress didn't look pleased to be helping them. The brothers didn't appear to leave good impressions anywhere, it seemed.

Jonathan watched as Mags nervously shuffled her feet and wrung her hands. He wanted to comfort her. At the same time, he said, "Mags," Daniel said, "They deserved it, Mags. They were saying disgusting things about you, basically admitting they planned on following you tonight. I don't believe they planned on giving you a choice."

Her face turned pale at the news. "They've been coming in off and on for a few weeks. I admit, they're horrible. Oh God, I hope you don't get into any trouble."

She gave Daniel a quick hug and then turned to Jonathan, but hesitated. He didn't give her a chance to back out on the gesture. He pulled her to him and held her head gently against his chest. It took her a moment before she returned the hug.

Their dads, Dagr, and Ulf walked in while she was still in his arms. His father raised his brows in surprise. The entire bar was entranced by the spectacle. Seeing five big men with white hair gathered together didn't happen every day, at least for them. It happened most days for Jonathan.

Mags started to pull away from him. He panicked at the thought of her walking away. It was fully sinking in what Josh and Denny planned on doing to Mags, and Jonathan needed her to stay safely at his side. He couldn't prove that they wouldn't have walked away if she told them no, but everything pointed to them not listening to her.

He leaned close to her ear. "Stay by me." At her startled look, he added, "Please, Mags." She settled at his side. He liked that. A lot.

Daniel finished giving their family the rundown, including rumors they'd heard about the brothers. The gardaí arrived and took statements from those involved and witnesses. Josh and Denny had already been moaning that they wanted to press charges for assault and battery.

Dagr had been on the phone but joined them once more. At hearing that Josh and Denny wanted to press charges, he only smirked, saying, "Wait for it."

They watched as Denny, the oldest brother, answered the phone. He winced at whatever was being said on the other end. His face went white and then red and then white again. He gripped his brother's arm and shook his head no.

Denny put his phone away and approached the officers. "I'm sorry for the trouble. My brother and I had too much to drink before we got here and said some pretty stupid things to the O'Faolains. We absolutely do not want to press any charges, and in fact would like to pay the owner of this establishment enough to cover the inconvenience and lost sales."

Mags poked his side and grinned at him. *God.* It had been almost three years since she'd directed one of her smiles at him.

As one of the officers got off the phone, they approached Josh and Denny. "I guess we'll clear out, and you two will get a taxi home." It wasn't a suggestion.

"Yes," and "Of course," they said in unison.

The officer held up a hand to stop the brothers before they could slither out of the pub. "The O'Faolains weren't the only patrons here tonight to hear some of your drunken comments." The officer said drunken with just the right amount of disbelief and disgust to make Josh and Denny stiffen.

"No matter that you aren't pressing charges, I will be making a report of the incident. If, say, a person came into the station to report a sex crime, *any* type of sex crime, your names would be flagged. Okay then," the officer said with a smile that looked vicious, "off you go."

Everyone shook hands with the gardaí and thanked them for coming so quickly. One of the officers let them know that he was friends with Thomas MacGregor and Coll Barr and that they called while they were still en route to let them know that they were already looking into the brothers.

"I won't say much," the officer said, "but we have had some unsolved assault crimes come across our desks."

He didn't add anything else before he and his partner left, but it appeared as though Josh and Denny may have finally outed themselves.

Daniel asked, "Why did Josh and Denny change their minds about pressing charges?"

"Oh, that was me," Dagr smiled. "Their father is in politics, and I happen to know his attorney. I told him to expect hell to rain down on the family if they so much as sneezed toward one of my clients."

Jonathan's phone began to vibrate. He rolled it over in his palm to see the screen. Coll Barr. Mags was still standing next to him, probably because each time she tried to put distance between them, he gently touched her back or waist and brought her back.

She inhaled sharply when she saw it was her uncle calling. "Don't answer."

"I'm not interested in dying anytime soon, Mags." He accepted the call and brought it to his ear. "Barr."

There was no greeting from the taciturn Scotsman. "Your father called me. You will walk Margaret home and convince her to quit that job. And I'm not fucking asking. Tell her that her evasiveness with me hasn't gone unnoticed. If she would like me to visit, I will."

Mags was looking at him with wide, worried eyes. He took one of her hands and held it against his chest, and of course, every man around him was instantly glued to the link.

"Understood," Jonathan answered.

"Keep me informed," Barr growled.

"I won't do that, but I will explain to Mags that if she isn't more transparent with her family, to expect a visit." Mags winced, probably imagining quite well what her uncle was saying.

"Fine." He hung up.

twenty-one

MAGS

MAGS' head was spinning. In fact, it'd been spinning since she watched Jonathan walk into the pub looking like he'd just finished a photoshoot for Forbes Billionaires List, and People's Sexiest Man Alive—it should be a crime to look that damn good.

Jonathan's stunning face, which she regularly imagined hitting or kissing, wasn't the only thing that had put her off kilter.

Gray let her know that Bébhinn had argued with Jonathan and let Mags' secrets come flying out of her giant mouth. Bébhinn sent her apologies and begged Mags to blame it on her hormones.

Then came Jonathan openly eye stalking her for hours, and if that hadn't put her over the edge, he and Daniel punched people. She was sick when she found out that the brothers had decided to not take no for an answer with her that night. Denny and Josh deserved to have their asses handed to them. She'd just been so worried that Jonathan and Daniel would be in trouble.

The sleazy brothers' comments shook her up. She recognized that she had been taking a chance with her safety walking alone all those nights, which was why she allowed Jonathan to possessively keep her by his side. He made her feel safe. *Damn him.*

Everyone was heading home, so she gave Bran, Patrick, Dagr, and even Ulf a hug. They'd come for their boys, but calls to her family were the first ones they'd made, which meant they'd come to her rescue as well.

Her mom and dad had already texted and told her to call them the moment she was home. They hadn't known about the bartending gig until that evening. Sighing, she rubbed the back of her neck. She wasn't built for deception. She would have to tell her mother that her friends knew about the cancer, and that she needed to come clean to everyone too.

The pub was closing, and the patrons who had stayed to watch the drama were trickling out. She swallowed a moan as her boss made his way over to where she, Jonathan, and Daniel were still standing by the bar.

Mags quickly said, "I'll start cleaning the bar now, Ben. Sorry, I should have already gotten started."

Ben waved her words away. "Go home, Margaret. You and your friends have had a hell of a night." He shook the cousins' hands. "You got the scum out of my pub, mates. You're welcome back anytime."

After a few more backslaps and handshakes, Jonathan glanced her way nervously before clearing his throat and facing her boss once more. Mags was instantly on guard.

"About Mags' job, Ben. I'm afraid her family would like her to put in her notice."

Her jaw practically unhinged. "What the hell do you think

you're doing, Jon? My parents have asked me to do no such thing." She wanted to say more, but she was so amazed, shocked, and pissed off that she couldn't articulate further.

Jonathan seemed to be silently pleading with her to understand. "I'm sorry, but your uncle Coll told me to take care of it tonight. Or he would come to town and do it for you. I thought you would prefer this." He shrugged and had enough grace to look guilty.

She wanted to rage, but she wouldn't act like that in front of Ben, who didn't deserve to be in the middle of the family. She also wanted to be mad at Jonathan, but she believed that her uncle Coll would have done exactly what he threatened. She wouldn't kill the messenger.

"I apologize, Ben. You've been a great boss to work for. Regardless of what my family wants, I would gladly give a two-week notice so you can fill my shift."

"No worries," Ben put his hands up to stop her from insisting. "I've plenty of help. Listen, Margaret, I heard the boys' testimony of what those brothers had planned for you tonight. That had to have shaken you, and I know, as a father myself, that your family will want to keep you extra safe for now. Let them and be happy for it."

Ten minutes later, Mags had clocked out and grabbed her tote and coat. She already said goodbye to Jonathan and Daniel. It was one-thirty, and the air was cool, damp, and swirling with fog. Shivering, she pulled her collar tighter about her neck, looking for Nasir's disapproving countenance.

Eze had become just as overbearing as her family. Trip down some stairs once, and they thought she needed constant babysitting.

When she saw two men come out of the swirling mist, an involuntary scream ripped from her throat. In that moment of fight or flight, Jonathan and Nasir's faces came into focus.

"Oh, God," she wheezed. She'd been sure that Josh and Denny had stayed behind to harass her after all.

Jonathan grabbed the backs of her arms, keeping her upright when her watery legs wanted nothing more than to collapse on the cold, hard footpath.

"Mags, damn it, I'm sorry I scared you. I didn't think." The words poured fast and apologetic from his lips.

He brought her to his chest and wrapped his arms around her back. She stood like that for a few more minutes, catching her breath and her bearings. The pins and needles left her limbs, finally, and she was able to get her feet firmly under her once more.

She patted Jonathan's chest as she backed up, a kind of "Thank you, I'm fine now" gesture.

"Sorry about that. I thought—"

"I know what you thought," Jonathan cut her off. "Christ, but I keep fucking things up with you. I've got a car waiting across the street for us. Let me get you...home."

He didn't like that home was with another man. "I appreciate everything tonight, Jon, really, but Eze always sends Nasir to get me home. She looked at Nasir then, and sure enough, he was scowling at her.

"Nasir can't stand me, but he works for Eze's family and will do his job, I'm sure." Nasir's flexing jaw was the only emotion her comment received. He would warm to her eventually, she was sure.

"I don't care who your roommate sends for you. I will be taking you home tonight. I promised your uncle, and besides that, I want to."

She sighed in exhaustion. It was too late, or early rather, for bickering. "Fine. You can give Nasir and me a ride."

"Not necessary. I will find my way."

Mags smiled. Eze's bodyguard could speak. "I insist."

Jonathan didn't look thrilled, but he led them across the street to the car.

Jonathan made a point of opening the front passenger door for Nasir before opening the back and helping her in and sliding next to her.

While Nasir gave the driver directions, Jonathan took her hand and placed it on his thigh, covering it with his own. "Jon," she warned. He didn't release her hand, and because she was weak where he was concerned, she didn't force the issue.

For the next ten minutes, they didn't speak, but she was hyper aware of his strong, hard thigh warm under her palm. She wanted desperately to press her fingertips against his pants to feel his body underneath. She didn't.

Mags felt disappointed when Eze's building came into view and cursed herself for the weakness. As she reached for the door handle, Jonathan said, "Wait." He linked his fingers through the hand that was already warmed from his body heat and opened the back door on his side, sliding out and bringing her with him.

He asked the driver to wait for him and walked her to the building's front entrance, where valets were waiting to park the other inhabitants' vehicles, though it was quiet this time of night.

Nasir stood stiffly several paces away. Pretending not to watch her and Jonathan. Mags felt exhaustion like a heavy, wet blanket across her shoulders.

She was still holding Jonathan's hand. Not what friends in their group had ever done, unless they were secretly seeing one another, which she and Jonathan were not.

Since he didn't seem capable of anything but staring at her, Mags pulled her hand from his and said, "Goodnight. Thank you for tonight." Still nothing. "You and Daniel are great friends."

"I'm not your friend," he grumbled and took back both of her hands.

"Okay," she drew the word out.

"Damn it! I mean, we are friends, but we're more than that, or I hope we are. I want us to be."

It was everything she wanted to hear. However, she only had to think of the many women she'd seen him out with to know his feelings were fleeting at best. She remained silent.

"Please, Mags. At least agree to meet me tomorrow." Before she could say no, he added, "I know I don't deserve it. I'm asking as someone who's known you since you were little. Meet me for lunch. Just lunch. I need to tell you some things. Explain them, I mean."

He groaned, shaking his head in exasperation. "Meet me at that bakery you like. I'll buy you one of those American muffins you like so much. An hour, Mags. That's all I'm asking for."

No matter how he'd made her feel in the past, she couldn't leave him hanging. "Not tomorrow, but Sunday, the girls and I are meeting for lunch with your mom and aunts. I'll meet you on my way to the gallery. Eight-thirty at Bácús."

Jonathan smiled and brought her hand to his mouth and pressed his lips to her fingers. "Thank you. I swear, you won't regret it."

She already did.

twenty-two

MAGS

MAGS SWORE as her tote bounced off her hip again. The repeated blows from a bag that had to equal her body weight had to be leaving bruises. She forced her steps to slow from a powerwalk speed to a fast saunter.

After all, she didn't need to hurry. She wasn't late for her meeting with Jonathan. The extra hustle in her step came from nerves.

She might have taken an extra minute on her appearance. Her wide-legged yoga pants, crew neck t-shirt, jacket, and tennis shoes were all in shades of taupe, casual but on trend. She wore tiny red rose earrings, and her long, wavy hair was held back by one of her favorite embroidered headbands, red and peach roses.

Hey, why not look cute and rep her business? Speaking of, the printers weren't far away from Bácús. She could swing by and grab the business cards that Gray helped her design. What was a few more pounds of paper pulling on her shoulder's tender flesh?

Someday, she would have a real shop where she'd have no need to tote half her sewing paraphernalia around.

Her shoe caught the edge of a raised stone in the ancient-as-hell footpath. "Christ, Mags," she cursed herself.

She'd known Jonathan O'Faolain her whole life. Where was all this nervous energy coming from?

She also knew how he kissed. "Not helping," she muttered under her breath.

She was determined to let him have his say. Whatever that might be. She'd convinced herself that he was on some sort of apology tour for that New Year's Eve blunder, except he'd been touching her. Women plastered to his side and handholding had been kept exclusively for his many, many, many other women.

The question was why he was trying to do that to her. The why of it was driving her mad. She rubbed her palm over the backs of her fingers. He'd kissed those fingers last night. He didn't do that with Bébhinn, Gray, or Blair. Ciar and Dagr would kick his ass if he tried, true, but he didn't kiss Blair's hands.

Her life had been way too dramatic lately. Even after Jonathan left her last night, the drama wasn't done. As Mags had let herself into the apartment complex lobby, she was startled when Nasir stepped from a shadowed alcove near the elevators.

She was used to his blank expression and silence, so when he spoke, she was properly surprised. He also appeared to be very angry.

"I am leaving in a few hours for home," he spat each word as though he was cursing her instead of discussing his travel plans.

She nodded in acknowledgment. Eze had told her that his father had recalled Nasir to Nigeria. When Mags asked him why they'd sent a bodyguard in the first place, when Eze had never had one before, he chuckled.

"I'm sure it was my mother's idea, and she got Father to go along with it. Nasir was here to spy on my life and report back. My mother worries," he added sheepishly. "Mother was very aware of my relationship with Nasir and probably hoped his handsome face might entice me back to Nigeria."

"And has it worked?"

"Oh, Nasir is an enticement, but I will not be altering my future plans for a person who struggles with fidelity," he said grimly.

"Has he tried to speak to you? Privately?"

"Yes. I'm well past such nonsense."

Eze's clenched jaw and brooding said otherwise. "You've been tweaking his nose since the day he got here. You've let him believe we are more than we are. Consider speaking to him, even if it is just to bring closure for you both."

When Eze began to tap his fingertips against his thighs, which he admitted was a way to calm his mind so he could concentrate on mental math, Mags knew the conversation was over. He wouldn't take her advice.

Nasir had had a similar reaction to her advice the night before. After he informed her of his plans to leave, Mags said, "Eze told me. Safe travels."

"You are cheating on him with the white-haired man, and Eze is too trusting of you to see it."

My, my, my. Nasir was definitely letting her have it. Mags was tired and in no mood to caudle. Before she stepped into the elevator, she faced him fully. "I don't think you give him enough credit, Nasir. He wasn't too trusting to see when you cheated."

The man's eyes rounded in surprised shock. "Cheaters always think everyone cheats." As she depressed the floor number and as the doors were sliding shut, she couldn't help but add, "Eze deserved better." She really despised cheaters.

Bácús was three blocks away.

She was running on little sleep. She'd spoken to her parents for almost an hour. Unsurprisingly, Jonathan and Daniel were their new heroes. Mags agreed.

Her parents were going to be home at the end of next week. They even said they had some exciting news to share, but they wouldn't tell her a thing until they were face-to-face.

They planned to invite everyone over for a big dinner and expected their daughters to come early to catch up.

As if she wouldn't be the first one there to greet them. Her parents planned on explaining to their family and friends about getting cancer again. Her mom sighed. "Not that my bald head won't give it away."

"You don't need hair to be beautiful, Mom. Dad thinks so too."

Mags told Eze before she left the flat that morning about her parents' homecoming. He insisted that he would buy her plane ticket to Scotland. She'd refused, of course. He refused to take no for an answer. They glared at one another until Jol butted in.

"Eze's family produces oil and owns a hotel chain. Let him buy you the damn ticket, Margaret."

"Fine but buy two tickets. My folks want to meet my room-mate." Mags had finally come clean about school, her move. She didn't, however, burden them with her finances or roughing it on the attic floor.

Bácús was two blocks away.

A frisson of unease zipped up her spine. She was afraid to hear what Jonathan had to say. If nothing else, the meeting should answer where in the hell his mind and intentions were.

She wanted to move past him and concentrate on her new life, which, with Eze's help, had taken a decidedly better path.

She lifted her chin and readjusted the tote straps, which dug into her neck and shoulder, when several things happened at once.

She heard the squealing of tires somewhere behind her, men shouting and a woman screaming, and a wide-eyed Nasir running at her with his arms outstretched.

twenty-three

JONATHAN

MAGS WASN'T COMING. She'd stood him up. It didn't seem her style. If she changed her mind, she would have at least shot him a text.

He texted twice and called once, but her phone was shut off, which was odd when she was in the middle of building a new business.

No, Margaret Morrow didn't hide. She hadn't hidden once when he had women hanging on his arm. She would look him in the eye and pretend he wasn't hurting her. He deserved to be stood up.

As he was picking up his discarded napkins and empty teacup, finally conceding after an hour that he should pack it in, his phone lit up with a call from an unknown number.

He answered. "O'Faolain."

A man with an accent asked, "Jonathan O'Faolain?"

"It is. Who is this?"

"Eze Otaji. I am...Margaret's friend."

Jonathan's heart rate accelerated—the bastard she was living with. "Where is she?"

"She is getting taken care of at the hospital. She asked me to call you. A car clipped her on her way to meet you, and one of my men was on-site and immediately took her to the emergency room. She appears to have only sustained a few new bumps and bruises, but her phone was broken."

Jonathan was running to a line of taxis before Eze finished speaking. "I'm on my way."

Jonathan didn't think he breathed during the fifteen-minute drive to the hospital. He was too upset to call or text any of their friends, just silently giving thanks that she'd wanted him to know.

While he'd been feeling sorry for himself, Mags had been hit by a car. "Goddamnit," he growled, pushing his way out of the car, he ran toward the sliding glass doors of the emergency wing.

He saw Eze immediately standing with another smaller man near the nurses' station. He remembered them both from the charity event. Shoving down all of his panic, he walked up to the large Nigerian and stuck his hand out. "Thank you for calling me."

Eze nodded. "Margaret asked it of me. The nurse told me that she is banged up from the fall and had the wind knocked out of her, but she will be just fine. The car hit the big bag she's always lugging around first. She is lucky."

Jonathan felt better at hearing the news, but he wouldn't relax until he spoke with her himself.

"As soon as the police finish with her statement, she's free to go home."

"Was the driver under the influence?"

"They don't know yet. The man drove on, then abandoned the car and ran away. The police are looking for him." Eze pinched the bridge of his nose before adding, "Nasir and some of the other witnesses saw the man purposely turn the wheel toward Margaret."

A young nurse, not much older than Mags, wheeled her out then. She wasn't smiling, but he didn't expect her to be.

"My driver is waiting to take us home," Eze said as he began to walk toward the exit.

When they stepped outside behind Mags' wheelchair, Jonathan saw a middle-aged woman staring intently at Mags—like creepily focused. There was a colorful scarf wrapped about her head with a few muddy blonde bits of hair sticking out, and she was wearing a sensible outfit of trousers and a cardigan.

Nothing about the woman was remarkable, except for the unnerving stare and the way her mouth kept moving, as if she were talking to herself. Clearly, she had mental issues, and Jonathan blew it off as they reached Eze's large sedan.

Jonathan looked at Mags. "I'm coming with you." Thankfully, no one took issue. When Eze's man hung back, Mags leaned forward from the backseat of the car.

"Nasir?"

Eze glanced at the other man, a look of irritation plain on his face. "Nasir has duties to see to."

Jonathan, who was sitting opposite Mags on the rear-facing bench, had to stop himself from catching Mags' hand before it landed on Eze's arm.

"Eze," she said softly. "Can he please come home with us? I would like to speak to Nasir before he goes back to Nigeria."

Eze's jaw clenched, but he bowed his head at Mags once before barking at the other man. "Nasir. With us."

Some strange dynamic was at work, but Jonathan couldn't

figure out what it was, and honestly, he didn't care to. Even though he was on his way to the flat that Mags shared with another man, he could only feel relief that she was going to be okay and that even during all the turmoil of the hit and run, she'd thought to have someone call him.

"Well, Eze, I bet you're rethinking our friendship," she chuckled softly. She was exhausted, probably from an adrenaline dump. "I seem to have become one of the clumsiest people on the planet."

"Hardly," Eze replied. "I am thankful we met and just think, cleaning up after your mishaps gives me plenty of time to consider mathematical theories."

That made Mags snort in amusement. "Asshole," she teased.

Jonathan felt like *he'd* been hit by a car when Eze pulled Mags against his side and patted her head where she lay it on his shoulder. They were very comfortable with one another.

He turned his head to look out the window and noticed Nasir watching the couple across from them. The man had the same look of longing he felt on his own face. *What the hell?* Did Mags have another man after her affections?

It didn't matter. He wouldn't cave or falter. He wouldn't walk away from Mags, not until he'd exhausted every groveling tactic man had ever created to get a woman's forgiveness.

Once they were let into Eze's flat, a woman named Jol, who he learned was married to Abeo, the driver, met them at the entrance and hustled Mags away to get her changed into more comfortable, clean clothes.

Eventually, Mags was led, under protestations, to the living room couch where a bundle of soft, fluffy blankets awaited. "Sit, Margaret, while I get your tea." Jol hovered over Mags until she was satisfied with the cocoon they'd made.

Jonathan was glad for the distraction. The silence between

the four men as they waited for Mags' reemergence had been wearing.

Mags glanced at the men. "Nasir." Upon hearing his name, the man's head jerked up from where he'd been studying the floor. "I can't tell you enough how thankful I am for you saving me. Had you not been there...had you not run so fast, I wouldn't have been so lucky."

"It was nothing." With his hands clasped behind his back, Nasir lowered his head slightly, accepting her thanks.

"It was definitely something to me," Mags insisted. "Would you come over here? I would like to speak to you in something lower than a bellow."

Hearing this, Jol called from the kitchen. "Boys," she commanded, "please come help me with the tea tray." Jonathan glanced back a few times and watched as Nasir stood stiffly before Mags. He couldn't hear anything she was saying, but whatever it was had the man's full attention.

Soon, Jonathan hoped to have her full attention.

twenty-four

MAGS

"YOU WEREN'T SUPPOSED to be following me." That wasn't a question. Mags knew he was supposed to be on a plane home.

"No."

"Regardless of your reason, I'm grateful. In fact, I think the whole ordeal was destined to be."

Mags watched Nasir's eyes widen at that. According to Eze, his family and their close circle, including servants and guards, were incredibly spiritual.

"I'm going to tell you something, some of which is mine to tell and some of which is not. I dislike subterfuge, so I'm going for it," she smiled then, because Nasir seemed so comically uncomfortable.

"For my part, I considered myself in love with Jonathan O'Faolain since I was about fifteen years old, but he ruined that. What's happening now...well, your guess is as good as mine.

"You and Eze had what he considered a relationship. You

shit all over that, and though I can't pretend to sympathize with you, your reasons are your own. However, coming here with a chip on your shoulder and a sense of entitlement over Eze's life is a touch too far, all things considered.

"You hurt him, and he's hurting you through me. He has become one of my closest friends, and so even though I feel wrong for speaking of him to you at all, I know what it feels like to have loved someone and had it thrown back in my face.

"You did that, Nasir. For the sake of a friendship I can only assume you two once shared, I thought you might want to, at the very least, apologize."

Mags expected chagrin. She didn't expect Nasir to drop to his knees and cover his face. Mags leaned forward, wincing as a few of her new bruises grumbled, and placed her hand on his shoulder.

After several heartbeats, Nasir dropped his hands. "I've loved Eze since we were boys. I loved him while he dated count-less girls. I loved him even when he had sex with them.

"And then one day, he held my hand. It was the best day of my life."

"Why then?" *Why did you become a cheater? Why did you hurt your best friend?*

"I didn't believe it would last. I didn't believe, because of the women, that he would or could commit to just me. I...I hurt him before he could hurt me, and I've never regretted anything more in my life."

Mags cupped Nasir's face, softly framing his anguish. "Eze is one of the most honorable people I know. You know that too. Explain, Nasir. Don't leave Dublin without making him hear you."

Nasir clasped his hands to his chest and dropped his fore-head to rest on the edge of her knees. She didn't dare move. Her eyes darted toward the kitchen, where she met first Jonathan's and then Eze's gaze, whose eyes were glassy.

Nasir stirred before standing. "You have honored me with your thoughts. I would be doubly honored to count you as my friend."

"Easily done. Now, I think it's time I spoke with Jonathan. He's probably used up his patience quota for the month." She chuckled, but her throat was suddenly dry.

Nasir turned but quickly spun back. "Margaret. Have you considered that Jonathan hurt you out of fear too?"

He didn't wait for her answer, which was good because she didn't have one. She watched with bated breath as Nasir approached Eze, but the view was blocked as Jonathan approached, holding Jol's tea tray.

Once the tray was settled on the table in front of the couch, Jonathan handed her a cup of tea and a small dish of pastries, which she set on the table at her elbow, taking only a small sip of the milky, steamy goodness. Her nerves were way too jumbled to handle food.

Jonathan sat close to her on the couch, turning his knees toward her so that they were face to face. "Thank you for having Eze call me. I was worried." He shrugged and grimaced before adding, "Well, my feelings were hurt at first, thinking you'd chosen not to meet even though I knew that isn't the type of person you are.

"And then Eze called. I think my heart only stopped racing a moment ago."

Mags watched all the emotions cross Jonathan's handsome face and knew he wasn't lying. Her brain knew that, anyway, her heart...not so much.

"At least my giant tote that everyone gives me such a hard time about saved me from the brunt of it." She was trying to lighten the mood, but Jonathan's lips didn't even twitch.

No small talk then. "Listen, Jon, I know you wanted to speak to me, but I have to tell you that I'm content with our friendship and my new business. My parents will be home next week, Blair, Gray, and Bébhinn are happy, Mirren's new artist is making a splash in the art world, and I plan on asking Eze for a small loan for materials since I'm not working any of my extra jobs besides cleaning the gallery." Her hands rose with her shoulders in an "I don't know what you need from me" gesture.

His jaw clenched, probably at hearing how her life was turning around and she wasn't in need of a savior, namely him. She'd finally been released from the repercussions of her unrequited love. He was so used to the hearts in her eyes when she looked at him that now that they were gone—though she admitted it was still a struggle to hide them—he couldn't fathom the new dynamic, that they were friends.

"If your pride has taken a hit because I no longer care to worship at your shrine, that isn't my problem."

"You have me all figured out, huh? You think I'm here for my ego? You think I want to regress to the days when I date women that I care nothing for. Don't get me wrong, Mags, I want you to look at me the way you used to because I finally realized that I've always looked right back at you with the same feelings.

"I don't deserve it, but I'm begging you for another chance. Let me prove to you that you're it for me."

Mags felt her heart implode, then explode. He was saying everything she'd wanted to hear since she was a teenager. The problem was, he'd burned her. He'd been burning her since their first—and only—kiss.

Jonathan was sincere, or he was as sincere as he knew how to be. It was only that he had no clue how badly he'd hurt her, how little trust she had where he was concerned.

She wanted to say yes badly. "No. No, Jonathan." At his

crushed look, she added, "It was never required that you feel about me how I felt about you. Never."

She took one of his hands and pressed it between her own. "You have always had a right to your feelings. As I've matured, I've had to understand that I had been unfair in my expectations.

"I think what hurt me most wasn't seeing one woman after another on your arm. It was that my pain and hurt could have ended almost three years ago had you only cared enough about our friendship to say, *Hey, Mags, sorry I kissed you. It didn't mean anything, and I hate that it hurt you when I went from you to another girl within minutes.*"

"It did mean something, damnit," he growled, placing his free hand over hers, making their hands sandwiched together. "I've been running from how much it meant ever since."

"And you had this epiphany around the time I finally walked away and found someone else?" She should feel guilty for using her friendship with Eze to poke at Jonathan.

"I admit that I felt you pulling back. It made me panic. I let you see me with even more women in the hopes that you would react the way you always had, with censure and disdain. To me, it meant you still cared.

"I can't believe that a man in my position, with the family that raised me, could be so blind and foolish, so callous and immature.

"You know how close Mom and her sisters are, how close Dad and Uncle Bran are, and how badly it wrecked us all to lose Grandpa. I don't think Aunt Rowan will ever fully recover from the loss. When you witness firsthand what it looks like for a person to lose their other half, it's fucking terrifying.

"You aren't some self-absorbed woman where social media likes hit like a drug high. You are real and loyal, caring and genuine. Your embroidery makes people happy. Your smile is the first thing I look for when I come into a room.

"When you're stressed, I am. When you're down, I am. When you used to call me out on my shit, it made me feel seen."

Mags' head was spinning. He thought all these things about her...then why? Why choose everyone but her?

Her confusion must show. "I have no excuse except for idiocy. I kept telling myself that I was too young for commitment, that it was way more fun to play the field, that society expected me to be a bit of a playboy.

"Had I been honest with myself, I would have admitted what I've always known. You are it for me."

"And you aren't bothered that I'm living with Eze?" That was a good test of his resolve.

"I'm bothered, but I also know that if you two had anything between you that he wouldn't have allowed this," he motioned between the two of them, "and you wouldn't have given me the time of day. I think you are friends only."

"He doesn't kiss me like a friend." Low blow, but then she'd been on the receiving end of many low hits from Jonathan.

She watched Jonathan close his eyes as if he were in pain. She knew how that felt. "That wasn't nice, I'm sorry."

"I deserve it. If you told me you'd fallen in love with Eze, I would hear you, but I would never stop fighting for you."

Mags' phone dinged. It was a text from Eze.

Eze: I sent Jol and Abeo to a spa for lunch and massages. Nasir and I have left as well. I would have told you, but I didn't want to interrupt.

Mags: Okay. Thank you.

Eze: It seems you had quite a lot to say to Nasir.

Mags smiled, imagining Eze's dry tone and frown as he typed.

> Mags: I did. Because you're my friend, and I love you. You can thank me later.

> Eze: To be determined.

She set her phone aside to find Jonathan watching her face intently. "That was Eze. Apparently, everyone snuck out to give us privacy."

His face relaxed at that, and he grinned. Before she surmised his intent, he peeled the blanket from her lap and scooped her up, repositioning her on his lap. Mags was so shocked that her mouth opened, but not so much as a peep emerged.

"Good. Now we can finish our conversation while you remember how to be comfortable with me again."

"And sitting in your lap will make me comfortable?"

"What better way to bridge the chasm between us than forced proximity. Plus, I have to prove to Mom, Raven, and Rowan that I am capable of wooing you without their help."

Her spine straightened, and her palms flattened against his chest, pushing her further away. "What do you mean your mom and aunts...their help," she spluttered. "What?"

Jonathan smiled one of his easy smiles, the one she hadn't seen in forever, clearly enjoying her shock. "As much as I hate to admit this to you, and I will deny it fully if you so much as breath it to our friends, especially Daniel, I was forced into a Byrne sister intervention."

"Oh my God, no way," Mags laughed.

"Apparently, they felt I needed help admitting my feelings for you and getting you to forgive me. I cannot stress enough how absolutely painful it was."

"And have you admitted to having feelings?" Why did she ask that? "Forget I asked," she shook her head in chagrin. Their conversation had gone from zero to one hundred without obeying any of the traffic signs like speed limit, stop, yield, and especially caution.

One of Jonathan's hands rubbed circles over her back. It felt so good, she couldn't bring herself to stop him.

"I know what I feel, and I'm trying and clearly not succeeding in telling you. Give me a chance, Mags," he pleaded, bending close enough that his breath fanned over her lips. "Give us a chance."

She could have easily put distance between them, but she wanted to give them a chance. She wanted his commitment. She wanted him to touch her and taste her.

She wanted him.

Slowly, she pivoted on her hips until both her knees straddled his thighs. His strong hands rested at her waist. "Mags," he breathed, not moving a muscle, probably afraid she'd change her mind.

"You know me, Jon, probably better than my parents and friends. Regardless of how you've hurt me in the past, if you truly mean what you've said today—"

"I do," he cut in.

"Then, I'm willing to see where this goes. But slowly," she amended.

"Anything, Christ, Mags, anything," he implored.

And maybe because she'd survived dead animals, falling down stairs, and a hit and run, living her life to the fullest had become paramount. Having the love of her life looking at her with such abject devotion made her want to throw caution to the wind and be reckless with her feelings.

"I think we should seal this pact with a kiss."

"Thank, Christ," he all but shouted, his hands sliding from

her waist to her back and neck, bringing their lips together, slowly and soft at first. The first moan that left her throat triggered Jonathan to plunder.

Tongues dueled, teeth scraped, and hands explored. Mags was helpless to still her hips, thrusting, rubbing, and finally grinding against the part of his anatomy that had remained a complete mystery even in her dreams.

Under his pants, he was hard, thick, and long, basically the trifecta of every woman's fantasy. Somewhere in the hazy, lust fields of her mind, she knew she needed to put the brakes on.

Slow! Slow! Slow!

"Mags! Fuck, Mags! We've got to stop. I'm going to—"

"I'm there! Oh, God, Jon." The mother of all orgasms seized her body, screaming and pulsing. Fire. Jonathan shouted a second after her final moan, his body shuddering under hers.

She pulled back. They stared at each other in what must be identical shocked expressions. "That was…"

"Unexpected as fuck," he finished.

"We just…" she left her scattered thought hanging.

"Came in our pants. Mine probably has more noticeable consequences," Jonathan said, grimacing as he adjusted his jeans.

Mags couldn't help it. She started giggling, the crazy interlude something she'd never expected. Her dreams over the years had them in similar positions, but reality had long since been a wet blanket, cold and smothering.

Now, her optimistic self saw only potential.

She showed him to the guest restroom to…clean up. They were now circling each other at the front door. Jonathan needed to get to work. She decided to work from home, having plenty of projects in her bag that had thankfully been completely salvaged after the accident.

Her roommate and the man who kept saving her ass asked

her to stay home and rest. She decided it wasn't a fight worth having and acquiesced.

Finally, Jonathan pulled her into his arms and held her tight. "You won't regret this, Mags. I swear, I'll never give you a reason to regret me."

"You know I can be difficult. I'm not perfect, Jon. If we try this, don't put me on a pedestal."

"Not if or try. We are doing this, and you're perfect to me, for me," he emphasized. "I hate leaving you, but I still have to stop home and change. Someone helped me make a mess."

"We got carried away," she smirked. "My guess it that it won't be the last time."

He kissed her chastely once and then twice more. "It can happen a million more times, I just want it to be when we're both naked, and I'm buried deep inside your body."

She rested her head on his chest and sighed. "I never thought we'd," she hesitated, "be here. I thought our first kiss was our last." She had to bite her lip to stop it from quivering.

"I have a lot to atone for. Just promise me that if pressed, you'll give the Byrne sisters a glowing report of my efforts."

She couldn't stop the burst of laughter. It felt amazing to laugh again with Jonathan.

"I don't want to ruin this moment, but I also don't want to get blindsided later," Jonathan started hesitantly. "You've agreed to try...us. Will you please not kiss or do anything with Eze or anyone else?"

She considered letting him sweat, but no matter what happened between her and Jonathan, at the end of it, they would always be in the same circle of friends. Eze was a part of that circle now, and she wanted them to be friends too.

"We matter to each other and have become close, but we're only good friends. The kiss we shared was to make Nasir jealous." At his surprise, she added, "They have history."

"So, you didn't feel anything when he kissed you? He didn't feel anything?"

Mags smiled and kissed the corner of his lips. "I never said that."

twenty-five

MIRREN MÒR MACGREGOR-MORROW CAMPBELL

MIRREN WAS BACK IN DUBLIN, having given her husband, Finn, and their two children, Dean and Mary, kisses and hugs goodbye. She'd only be gone two days and one night, but she hated being away from her family.

She'd been the manager for the Smiths' Edinburgh gallery since she was twenty-one. She was in her late thirties now and still managed that gallery, but the Smiths sent her all over the world in search of new talent.

Mirren had a knack for finding the extraordinary. Her husband and his twin sister, Fiona, were two of many over the years.

Anna Wilkes was Mirren's newest find. As it happened, Mirren and her daughter Mary had been perusing stalls at a Saturday market in Wales, where Finn had taken them for a short weekend of fun away from home. She and her daughter enjoyed looking at the booths with various bits and bobs, hand-made trinkets, crocheted hats and mittens, dog collars, farm-grown fruits and vegetables, and, as it happened, Anna's small table of oil paintings.

Anna had a way with making simple landscapes glow with something unearthly and very fine. She'd struck up a conversation with the artist, who said that she was born in a small coastal town in the south of Ireland but currently lived in Dublin, where she worked a couple of jobs to afford rent and paint.

Mirren frowned, thinking about that because it sounded too much like what her sister had been doing behind her back. She should have known that her baby sister would work herself to the bone before asking for help.

Anna traveled on weekends to various markets where she could show her art that were close enough for her to drive or take the ferry.

That had been a year ago. Mirren took several photos of her work and sent them to Kain and Lillias Smith, the brother and sister duo behind Smith Gallery's success. They agreed to sponsor Anna for a few months while she worked on pieces for a possible exhibit. Mirren had assessed her progress after four months.

Unsurprisingly, her work was masterful, and it had been full steam ahead. The exhibit was that evening, and Mirren was excited. She dropped her bags at Eze and Mags' flat and was heading to the gallery for last-minute adjustments when her phone began to ring.

The caller ID showed 'Unknown,' but, knowing her wonky service in Ireland, she picked up. "Hello."

"Is this Mirren MacGregor-Morrow?" A woman's voice tentatively asked.

"Mirren Campbell, actually, but yes."

"Oh, of course, you'll have gotten married. I got your name from," the woman hesitated, "an old police report."

That made the hair on Mirren's neck stand on end. "Who is this?"

"Forgive me. I'm old but not so old to have forgotten my manners," she chastised herself. "Julia Todd, Hannah Todd's mother."

"Jesus Christ," Mirren gasped. She hadn't heard that name in years.

"Exactly," Mrs. Todd replied grimly. "Hear me out, please. My daughter, as you know, was incarcerated in a high-security mental facility for all the horrible things she did, including what she did to me."

Hannah Todd was an artist who suffered from schizophrenia. She had stalked several artists she was competing against, including Mirren's sister-in-law, Fiona. Hannah even killed a man and held her mother captive, chained and half-starved, while forcing her to paint landscapes for the competition under Hannah's name.

"I was aware of that, yes, and though it's well overdue, Mrs. Todd, I am horribly sorry about what she put you through."

"That's kind of you to say. I'm not embarrassed to say that it took me years to overcome and even more years to forgive myself for not seeing what she was capable of. However, that isn't why I called. Hannah has been let out of the hospital."

Mirren got out of the Uber and leaned against the gallery's exterior, not wanting to enter while she was on the phone. Besides, she didn't think her wobbly knees would make the trek over the threshold.

"What do you mean? Like, she's free?"

"I only found out. I wasn't even informed. There was no hearing for competency. Nothing. Hannah's psychiatrist found her miraculously healed and let her walk free. I've lived in fear for days and knew I at least had to let you know since it was well documented that she blamed you for getting caught."

Mirren was taken aback. "How could this be? Probation?"

"I asked at the hospital and got nowhere. What medication is she on? *I couldn't say*, they told me. Who is she supposed to check in with? Where? When? *I couldn't say*, they said again. I've gone to the police. They promised to check on it." Julia Todd was beside herself, and well she should be.

"I couldn't in good conscience wait to warn you. I'm sure the police will find out what has happened. It's just, until then, we haven't a clue where my daughter is. After all these years, I hate to be an alarmist, but please make sure your family knows and takes precautions."

Mirren felt her heart thumping heavily beneath her cocktail dress, her fingers already itching to dial Finn, her parents, her sisters. She already knew she would call her father, Thomas MacGregor, who raised her.

She wouldn't breathe easy until she handed these concerns over to people who could do something about them, and her dad's security business was step one.

"Mrs. Todd," Mirren blew a gust of air, gathering her thoughts, "my father runs a security firm. If you wouldn't mind, I would feel better if they were involved. Dad's name is Thomas MacGregor. I'm going to give him your name and number with your permission.

"I think we would both feel safer with another party looking into what in the hell is going on," Mirren thought to add.

"Oh, Mrs. Campbell," Mrs. Todd sniffled.

"Mirren," she corrected.

"Julia, then. Yes, please, give your father my information. I have tried to tell myself that I'm overreacting, but I can't shake the feeling that something is very wrong. Hannah should never, ever be allowed to live outside hospital walls."

"I have an exhibit to see to in Dublin this evening, so I'm

going to ring off and start the ball rolling with Dad. I promise to keep in touch, Julia. I'm sure my father will tell you this same thing, but I think you should leave Edinburgh until your daughter's whereabouts are discovered. Do you have a friend you might visit?"

"Thank you, Mirren. Thank you so much for taking me seriously. I'll pack now. My best friend lives in a secure flat in London. I won't do anything until I hear from your father."

Mirren ended the call, a queer sense of déjà vu swirling around her ears. Surely, Julia was making too much of this. She would let her husband and dad know, of course, but she had to believe that this—whatever this mess was—would blow over.

twenty-six

HANNAH

SMITH GALLERY DUBLIN was lit up like a glittery beacon in the otherwise overcast, dreary sky. Hannah watched all the socialite darlings swagger into the posh gallery—that used to be her. She used to be invited to all the best events.

Hannah had pretended to peek at the art through the window while couples streamed past. She wore a simple black wrap dress, a faux fur swing coat, and a fake diamond and emerald necklace she'd picked up earlier at one of the shopping mall kiosks.

A size fourteen when she used to be a four.

Not a lot of calories are burned sucking men off.

One voice cackled. *Did you know we had you suck off that filthy druggie in the alley as part of his payment?*

She pretended not to hear them, though she winced. Hannah remembered after she came back from her lost hours that there'd been an awful taste in her mouth. She'd suspected.

One young woman with short hair and wearing a sharp,

fitted suit stopped to look at the artist's picture and bio posted outside for the event in a disgustingly reverent way.

Hannah decided to try to gain some intel. "I wonder if the artist works directly with Mirren Campbell. She's one of the best in the business." She made sure to keep her fancy, wide-brimmed hat tilted over half her face. The shadows would help hide her appearance in case someone was clever enough to look at the gallery's cameras.

The young woman tore her gaze from the flyer. "You know Mirren?"

"Oh yes. We ran in the same circles in Edinburgh. I came early tonight to see the exhibit because I have to leave town soon, and unfortunately, I missed seeing Mirren. Do you know if her younger sister, Margaret, will attend? I so wanted to meet her." In hell, Hannah thought.

"I don't know, but I'm sure she is. Would you like me to pass on a message if she does come? What was your name again?"

She didn't hesitate. "Hannah Keels. And no message, I'll be back in town for the next exhibit. Have a lovely evening. The artist is wonderful."

The voices snickered in her head at the name she gave. She loved it when she amused them.

"Anna deserves to be celebrated," the young woman remarked. "Safe travels."

She used to be a celebrated artist, Hannah thought, as she walked away.

Now you're just old, fat, and ugly.

Crazy murderers don't usually get fancy invites printed on perfumed cardstock.

"Fuck all of you," she hissed. "I'm not the one who botched a simple hit-and-run, am I?" She wouldn't take their abuse because they were angry that the girl bounced back yet again from one of their grand schemes.

"You fucked everything up now. Did you hide my identity when you gave that man drugs and sent him off in a stolen car? Because if they find him, we'll be back in that hospital before the sun rises.

"You complain about my subtle psychological plays, but your efforts in hiring drug addicts haven't worked out so well for you either."

The Morrow bitch has nine lives.

If we had a better body, we could have taken her out ourselves and fuck the middleman, but no, we have you.

Disgusting.

Dumb.

Untalented.

Good for nothing.

Freak.

Psychological plays? We're back speaking about the dead animals again. Christ save us. Did you hope she'd slip on the single droplet of blood and break her neck falling down the stairs?

"Fuck you," she growled, leaning against the closed shop window across the street from the gallery.

Quiet. The deadliest of her voices demanded. *This can't go on. Eventually, the gardaí will catch up to us. We need to prepare.*

"I have an idea," Hannah began, trying to sound remorseful for her outburst.

This is assuredly not going to be good.

Good for nothing cow.

Speak.

Gritting her teeth and ignoring the thousandth slur of the day, she offered up what she considered a last-ditch effort to hurt Mirren.

"I believe that all we can hope for now is to destroy the sister's livelihood. Hurting her physically hasn't worked out well, and we've run out of time. We will be caught if we stay here any longer.

"I say we trash the attic when we're assured she isn't there. I don't think we can count on her absence tonight, but soon. We'll leave some special messages for the bitch to find. Leave her financially devastated and scared of her own shadow.

"Then we skip town while we still have enough money to travel and pay a long overdue visit to my mother."

There was silence, which either meant they were thinking of the cruelest comments to pitch her way, or they were contemplating Hannah's strategy.

Fine, but you'll owe us blood for your habitual ineptness.

"Of course," she agreed readily. They agreed with her plan. Hannah glowed with pride.

twenty-seven

JONATHAN

MAGS WAS GOING to one of her sister's gallery exhibits. Without him. With Eze. "Damn it," Jonathan cursed. He had a project he should be working on for work and another project to look over for his father, but his concentration was shot.

Instead, he was brooding, staring blankly out the picture window of his and Daniels' townhouse. Thankfully, Daniel was over helping Blair fix one of her plant trellises and wasn't around to witness Jonathan's moping about.

He felt some relief knowing that Eze was interested in someone besides Mags, but that didn't mean the man couldn't change his mind or that he might decide to hedge his bets and pursue two relationships at once. Granted, Eze didn't appear to be a player, but Jonathan didn't know him well.

Mags had agreed to try with him, so there was that. She wanted to go slow. Fine. He would give her complete control and gladly.

Unable to stop himself, he pulled out his phone and found her contact.

> Jonathan: Send me a picture of you all dressed up.

He watched the waving dots with an intense focus that he should be expending on his work projects. "Damn," he breathed as a video loaded.

Her dress was an aquamarine blue, some silky material that touched her nowhere and everywhere at once. It looked like an old-fashioned slip that women used to wear under their clothes, except hers wasn't cotton and utilitarian.

She turned slowly in front of the full-length bathroom mirror, capturing the moment for the video, the soft fabric of her dress moving with her. Her hair was swept up in a loose bun at the nape of her neck, a few strands escaping just enough to make it look effortless.

Jonathan's chest tightened as he watched.

He could picture it too clearly—him standing right behind her, close enough to feel the warmth of her skin, his hands settling at her waist. His mouth would find that delicate curve where her neck met her shoulder, pressing a slow, lingering kiss there before trailing upward, then down along the line of her collarbone.

The strappy sandals were playful, but it was her nod to jewelry that really drew his eyes. She wore a wide, embroidered wrist cuff. He paused the video and zoomed in on the piece. It was an ocean scene, a pirate ship and mermaid included.

Classic Mags. She never did anything by halves.

> Jonathan: Stunning. You'll have men falling all over themselves and women begging you to make them cuffs. I hope you get a bunch of new clients tonight. I also hope you ignore every man there, including your date.

He hated that he sounded insecure, but the reality was... well, that he was. Mags was the first woman he'd ever wanted to date where the next day mattered—and the next, and the next, days, weeks, and even months after mattered.

Mags: You're being silly. I'm going to an art exhibition, not a dance club.

Jonathan: Let me pick you up after the event. Eze won't mind.

Mags: Nasir had to go back to Nigeria. Eze is grumpy but needs attention.

Jonathan grimaced at the attention bit, but he was far from deterred.

Jonathan: How about I pick you both up, and we go for a drink at Gray Eyes and then you let me drop Eze off and come home with me. I promise not to keep you out too late.

Mags: Scrap Gray Eyes. Eze said he has a math formula he would like to "delve deeper" into when he gets home.

Jonathan: Let me pick you up.

"Don't say no, Mags," he pleaded in the silent living room.

Mags: 9:00

twenty-eight

MAGS

"I'M happy one of us has reason to smile," Eze told Mags with little inflection as they sat in the back of his car. Abeo was driving and met her eyes in the rearview mirror, rolling his eyes dramatically. It was all Mags could do to stifle a giggle.

She patted Eze's arm in a patronizing "poor baby" gesture. She wasn't offended by Eze's mood. Love had a way of bringing out the best and the worst of anyone.

"Would your parents be okay if you had a serious relationship with Nasir?"

Eze clicked his tongue in annoyance, as if she were foolish for asking. Perhaps she was. "I am my parents' youngest son, and though they are loving to all of their children, as the youngest, I have more leeway, so to speak, in my...proclivities.

"My father loves me and simply chooses to believe I'm a profligate. My mother, however, understands that what I had with Nasir...well, it was love on my part."

"His too," Mags quickly defended the guard.

"Perhaps," Eze conceded. "In my country, same sex relationships are forbidden and even in recent years, punishable by death."

Mags sucked in a sharp breath. Eze nodded once in understanding. "My parents will turn a blind eye and always love me, but only if I uphold a strict level of circumspection."

"So," Mags surmised, "while you make England your home, your parents would happily agree to Nasir being your guard?"

"Assuredly."

"And will you invite him?"

"Perhaps," Eze answered with the vagueness and subterfuge of a career politician.

"Save me from a man's psyche," Mags replied, rolling her eyes, earning her a slight smile on her friend's lips.

"I told Jonathan he could pick me up tonight. Do you mind?"

"Of course not. I will mind, as I've told you before, if he treats you falsely."

"It's a gamble on my part, I know." As Abeo pulled up to the curb of the gallery, late because of Eze's online tutoring class, she added, "Jonathan is the one thing that I would regret for the rest of my life if I didn't, I don't know, try."

Eze nodded in understanding as he helped her from the sedan. Mags was excited to see the new exhibit and to watch her older sister do her professional thing.

She had always looked up to Mirren. Her sister was a badass in her profession, an amazing wife, and the best mother to Mags' twin niece and nephew.

Mags and Eze began the circuit, pausing before each piece to appreciate the artist's talent. She accidentally jostled a person at her elbow while admiring a painting of a shepherd finding a lost lamb in the shelter of a castle ruin.

While still studying the painting, she apologized for bumping them. "Isn't the artist a master of light. Just look at how the sun is infiltrating even the smallest crevices in the stone." Mags' eyes widened when she finally glanced right and recognized the person at her elbow that she'd been speaking to.

"Justin Turner!" Mags exclaimed. "My word, it's been ages." Mags hadn't seen them since she dropped out of school.

"Oh my God, I haven't seen you in ages. I had to take a break from uni. I miss seeing everyone."

Justin's cheeks pinkened as they returned Mags' bear hug. "It's Jina now, or again rather. It's good to see you too, Mags."

Justin, or Jina rather, had had a ginormous crush on Bébhinn forever ago when they were in the same hiking club.

"I'd be happy if we never bring up my Justin faze. Christ, but I was so ridiculously obvious when I was mooning over Bébhinn. It took a while, but once I learned to love myself, love being a woman who loves other women, yeah, I figured out I didn't need to change my name or pronouns to be, well, exactly who I'm supposed to be.

"Poor Bébhinn. Crushing on her is one of my biggest regrets, but also one of the best things that ever happened to me. No one should ever have to change who they are for anyone."

"Well said. I'm happy for you and never be embarrassed by the past," Mags bumped Jina's side, I've been mooning over the same man since I was fifteen. You got over your crush a lot faster than I have.

"Speaking of the men in my life," she turned around to find Eze still studying the castle ruin and clasped his forearm, "Jina, this is my good friend and flat mate, Eze Otaji. Eze, this is a friend from university, Jina Turner."

Once introductions were finished, Mags asked, "Do you have any work here tonight?" The focus was on one artist, but there were still pieces by other artists throughout that sold through Smith Gallery.

Jina rubbed the back of her neck and blushed again. "I don't have any pieces, no, but my girlfriend does. She's crazy talented. Tonight is in her honor."

"No way! My older sister, Mirren, is the one managing this gig," Mags bragged.

"You're joking," Jina huffed. "Anna speaks of nothing so much as your sister. I'm dying to meet her myself. Speaking of. There was some crazy loon who stopped me outside asking after a Mirren MacGregor. She must have meant your sister, Mirren Campbell. The woman even asked if Mirren's younger sister would be here. She had to have meant you."

"I guess, but that is odd, and Mir's been married for years. Surely, if the woman knew our family, she would know that. Did she say what she wanted?"

"She only wanted to know if I knew either sister, and if you guys were inside yet or not. She'd already walked through, but said she was leaving town, so she couldn't stay. Before she walked away, I asked her name. Hannah Keels, not sure of the spelling. I'm sure it was someone Mirren must know, so maybe don't tell her I said the woman was crazy," Jina laughed.

"Probably an artist wanting an easy in and pretending to know my sister. I could have saved them the trouble. There is no easy in with Mir. You're either amazing or you aren't. Your Anna must be tipping the amazing scale."

"Oh, she is. I would love to introduce you."

Mags looped her arm through Eze's as they followed Jina through the crowd, where she ended up at the shoulder of a beautiful woman, perhaps early thirties, and clearly Anna if Jina's broad smile was anything to go by.

Mags gave her sister a quick hug while Mirren introduced Anna to her and Eze. "It's very nice to meet you, Anna. Jina and I had mutual friends at uni. Eze and I haven't been through your full collection yet, but we're both truly blown away."

"That's lovely of you to say, but I think your sister deserves the credit, if only for believing in me. I would still—"

Anna abruptly cut herself off to grasp Mags' hand, turning her wrist this way and that. "Your bracelet is stunning. Jina," she gasped over her shoulder to her girlfriend, "did you see this? Where did you get it?"

Mirren grinned. "My sister is an artist as well, but instead of paint, her medium is embroidery floss. Our family is very proud of her. The PM's wife wore one of her pieces recently."

"Stop bragging me up," Mags shook her head, fighting the heat that wanted to bloom in her cheeks.

"But this is bragworthy, Mags. It's really beautiful," Jina said, taking her own close look. "I can't believe you can get that detail with thread."

"Oops," Mirren interrupted. "Duty calls, Anna. One of the servers just signaled me that one of your pieces has a potential buyer."

Anna let out a high-pitched squeal, promptly covering her mouth, "Oh Jesus, I'm so unprofessional."

"If I were an artist, I could assure you that I would crow the house down with every sale. My husband is way too stoic in that department," Mirren shook her head in disgust.

"I'll walk with you, babe. You've got this," Jina encouraged as they began to move away.

Anna turned back once to ask Mags to give Mirren several of her business cards. "I will." Mags barely held in her own squeal. Eze excused himself to visit a professor he knew, leaving the sisters alone. For the first time tonight, she noticed that Mirren appeared tense.

"Is something bothering you, Mir?"

Mirren massaged her temples and blew out an irritated sigh. "I hate to even tell you. It's so crazy. Hell, I feel like a nutter even entertaining it, but I received a call that bothered me."

"Jesus. What? Now you have to say."

"I've already called Dad. MacGregor, not Morrow."

She and Mirren had the same parents, but their Morrow father didn't know about Mirren until she was around sixteen. Thomas MacGregor, Gray's father, raised Mirren, and he would definitely be the father to turn to with things like weird phone calls.

Eze joined them once more. "Is it okay if Eze hears whatever you're about to tell me?"

"Yes, and probably the more people that are aware, the better. When you were only a child, before I married Finn, even, I represented Finn and Fiona for the Smiths. At the time, the Scottish National Gallery of Modern Art was holding a competition across several mediums, with the winners having their art displayed for a year.

"Fiona won in oil, and Finn in metal work."

"Of course they did," Mags grinned, very proud of her brother-in-law and his twin sister.

Mirren grinned but quickly sank back into her story. "Unfortunately, the competition made national news, not for the work but because several horrible things kept happening to the artists.

"Private things were revealed to the media, breaking a marriage apart, a fire destroyed half of another artist's collection, Fiona's past was unearthed, a car's brakes failed, injuring another. One artist was murdered," Mirren finished with a grimace.

"Christ, Mirren, that's frightening."

"Yes. Well, the culprit was none other than one of the competitors. Hannah Todd. Her half-brother, Lance, made the connection between the crimes and Hannah. Her mother was found chained in a painting room where she was forced to paint for her daughter. She was barely alive when they found her.

"She was arrested during Finn and Fiona's exhibit at the Smith Gallery in Edinburgh. She was deemed a schizophrenic and sent to a high-security mental institution.

"Julia Todd called me this morning. Hannah's mother."

Mags felt the hair on the back of her neck stand on end. Something felt off here. "That was so many years ago? Why would this woman contact you now?"

"Hannah was released. Her psychiatrist judged her redeemed and fit for society. She was released without a hearing. Her past crimes, including murder, were not revisited. Her mother is frantic.

"The hospital is being uncooperative. Julia contacted the police and filed a report. They've promised to make inquiries at the hospital and with her psychiatrist to ensure the law was followed in her release, but that might take ages.

"Julia doesn't believe her daughter is reformed. She doesn't trust that Hannah hasn't worked the system. She even believes Hannah would have found a way to slip her medications.

"Julia believes it's only a matter of time before Hannah strikes out, whether it's her or me. I'm sick with worry. Hannah is a complete psychopath. She's capable of anything. Dad and Uncle Coll are trying to find the woman's trail once she was released. They told Julia to move away until her location is found, and they have a chance to speak to the police in Edinburgh.

"She plays with her victims. You have to be careful, Mags. She might try to strike at my family. Promise me," Mirren demanded.

"Without question. Does Finn know?"

"I called him first. He'll protect the kids, and between Finn and Fiona's husband, they'll be safe."

Mags suddenly gasped, her mind beginning to connect dots. She clasped Mirren's hand. "Jina. Jina Turner, Anna's girlfriend. She said an odd woman asked after you tonight. And me."

"What? My God, surely it wasn't." Mirren thought for a moment. "This feels as crazy as it did all those years ago. If it's that woman, how in the hell would she know where to find you or me?"

Addressing Eze, Mirren said, "Margaret can't be alone until this woman is found."

"That is not a problem," Eze nodded in understanding. "I can bring some of my parents' security from Nigeria."

"Thank you, I might have you do that, but let me speak with my father first and see how many security teams they have available. I'll step into the back office and call him now. He and Coll will want access to the cameras here anyway."

Mirren clasped Mags' hand. "Prepare yourself, Mags. Dad might want you back in the townhouse where his own security system is already in place."

"Whatever Margaret's father prefers, however, I will be calling in enough men to shadow her until this situation is resolved." Eze gave Mags a look that said, "Don't argue."

"Jonathan was going to pick me up here at nine." At Mirren's raised brows, Mags shook her head. Later.

"Text Jonathan to meet us at my place," Eze stated. "I will message Abeo to make his way back here now. My flat is secure and can only be accessed via biometric authentication. We will figure the rest out once Mirren speaks to her father. This could be nothing, but it could be something. We'll treat it like something."

Mirren let out a deep, shaky breath and clasped Mags' hand and squeezed in comfort, then turned to go to the back office to call her dad. Before Eze called Abeo and his family, she said, "Have them send Nasir. He'll have just gotten home, but he'll come back if you request it."

Eze gave her his standard dark, steely glare, but he didn't say no.

Mags walked over and sat on one of the padded chairs lining the wall.

> Mags: Change of plans.

> Jonathan: Please don't tell me you're cancelling.

> Mags: I'm not. I want to see you, but you'll have to meet me at Eze's place. I'll explain everything then. We're leaving the exhibit early. Meet me when you can.

twenty-nine

JONATHAN

"THAT IS," Jonathan started slowly after Mags explained everything that her sister had told her.

"A lot. Yeah, I know. The woman should not have been let out. It's a bit of a waiting game until Uncle Coll and Thomas see what they find. Honestly, I'm not worried. It's just so weird."

"What about that woman who spoke to your friend outside the gallery?"

"I agree that was suspect, but there might very well be a logical explanation, like what I initially thought, which was that it was some undiscovered artist trying to make an impression on Mir.

"Still, all we can do is go on with our lives and hope either MacGregor Security or the police find her."

Before Eze retired to his room, he told Jonathan that Mags' Uncle Coll had called. They were short on manpower at the moment, as many security detail teams were out of the country, and took Eze up on his offer for people.

Coll also asked that Mags stay with Eze in case she was

considering moving back to the townhouse, which was exactly what Jonathan had wanted her to do. However, Coll and Mags were right, there was no reason to bring any unwanted attention to Blair, who still lived in the adjoining townhouse next to his and Daniel's just in case the woman was following both her and her sister.

"I'm meeting the girls for lunch tomorrow at Murphy's. What do you have going on?"

"For starters, I'll be taking you to Murphy's. You're not to be on your own, or have you forgotten already?"

"Ugh, I haven't forgotten. And what will you be doing while the girls and I gossip about you boys?" she asked, her eyes sparkling.

"All the work that I should have done today but couldn't concentrate on because of some sassy little brunette." She rolled her eyes, but she couldn't hide that she was pleased.

"You look stunning in that dress, Mags, but why don't you go change. Being in Eze's flat wasn't exactly what I had in mind for tonight, but we can still relax together. Watch a movie, maybe." After all, they'd made out once on the very couch he was eyeing now.

Mags stood, and he did his best not to notice how the blue silky material of her dress touched her body. He stayed still, praying she didn't notice that a certain part of him really appreciated the view.

"I have a counteroffer," she said, and was it his imagination, or did her voice sound huskier than a moment ago? "How about you come with me to my room. I'll change, and we can snuggle in bed, and you can tell me all about your new architectural design projects while we pick out a movie."

"I thought architecture bored you. You used to walk off if I brought up anything to do with work." Well, he managed to sound like a whining ass.

"I've always been interested in your work. I just couldn't stand you knowing. It's been ages since I've been included in your career, or rather, I believed you didn't want to include me." she added, moving closer to his legs.

"I've been a fool. Worse than that." How he hated knowing how careless he'd been with Mags' feelings.

She had come near enough now that the hem of her dress grazed his legs. "You do possess a few redeeming traits."

There was no hiding the effect she had on him now—every part of his body keyed in, focused entirely on Mags. She had his full attention, his body's full attention, effortless as ever.

He pushed to his feet, rising to his full height over her smaller frame, the shift in proximity charged with quiet intensity.

"I choose your idea," he said, his voice lower now, steadier. "Let's go."

Fifteen minutes later, Mags came out of the bathroom in a short and tee combo, her hair brushed and loose, and her face pink from washing. He'd already dimmed the lights, and the golden glow touched every inch of her glistening skin.

He sat on the edge of the bed like a sad hound, still fully dressed, as if he couldn't quite figure out how far "keeping things PG" was supposed to go. Clothes? No clothes? If he was being honest with himself, he hoped things might get as crazy as the last time they'd had their hands on each other.

"You still have your shoes on," she pointed out.

Jonathan looked up just as Mags—barefoot and entirely too distracting—closed the distance between them. She stepped in close, until she stood between his knees, her presence pulling all his focus.

"Surely you want to get comfortable too," she added.

His hands moved before he could stop them, settling on the backs of her bare thighs. His grip tightened slightly, thumbs hovering, tempted to explore further but holding just shy of it.

He cleared his throat, forcing out, "You said we'd take it slow."

She leaned forward, her posture softening until her mouth hovered just near his. "You're right," she murmured. "I'm sorry. It's just...being like this with you has kind of been a long time coming."

When she started to pull back, hesitant, he didn't let her get far. His hands slid upward, from her thighs to her waist, drawing her back in and stopping her retreat.

"Hey," he said quietly.

Then, softer—"Give me a kiss first."

He guided her closer until she settled across his lap, her weight grounding and impossible to ignore. His hands steadied at her waist as he tipped his head toward hers, his voice dropping just enough to betray him.

"We can slow down after that."

thirty

MAGS

MAGS WAS aware that she was yet again breaking the rules that she herself had set, but she dared any woman to stand so close to the white-headed Adonis and not cave.

The O'Faolain men had some damn fine genes, she thought as her ass found a seat on his jean-clad thighs. Jonathan touched her lips gently in a sweet kiss, telling her, "You're the loveliest woman, Margaret Colleen Morrow."

Mags kissed him back, a longer exploration. "And you're the loveliest man, Jonathan Sean O'Faolain."

He took her mouth again, and Mags couldn't help the moan she shared around his tongue. Breaking contact again, she said, "Feel free to lose the shirt. We haven't gotten to the slow-down portion of the evening yet."

"Only if you want to lose yours," Jonathan's sexy smile teased.

Mags fiddled with the hem of her t-shirt. "I've been told my breasts are perfection. Are you sure you can handle seeing them in all their naked glory?"

In answer, he pulled his shirt over his head, and Mags froze mid-flirt. Yes, she had seen Jonathan without his shirt on over the years, whether it was group swimming or watching the boys play sports, but not like this.

Never this close, touchably close, which she took immediate advantage of. She ran her fingers across his smooth, pale, broad shoulders. If her hands shook, she chose to ignore them, refusing to be embarrassed about what a pleasure it was to touch him.

Finally.

"Your body is beautiful, Jon," she said softly, her tone almost reverent as her hands continued to wander.

His chest was strong and well-defined beneath her touch, and he couldn't help the sharp intake of breath when her fingers traced lightly over his skin, sending a shiver through him.

"Mags, you're killing me."

"Don't die. We aren't slowing down yet," she reminded again, knowing very well that she was playing with fire.

The moment her hands glided over his abs, his muscles tensed and rippled. His waistband was really in the way. She tapped her short nail on the head of the metal button.

Mags was so fixated on learning his body that when Jonathan said, "Take your shirt off," she startled.

It wasn't that she was a shy or reserved woman. She had made herself orgasm not very many days ago from the same position she was in now. Deciding that living dangerously was a whole hell of a lot more satisfying, she lifted the hem and peeled the shirt from her body, tossing it to the floor.

Her long, brown waves landed against her chest, allowing only the barest hint of her nipples to peak through.

"Christ," he uttered as he reverently swept her hair behind her. He stood with one hand supporting her ass before turning and placing her in the middle of the bed, crawling up her body until it was him straddling her thighs.

Then it was his turn to explore her body. With a single finger, he traced the outline of her breasts, her tiny, dark areolas and nipples puckered, begging for attention.

He smoothed his thumbs over the peaks. "I can't believe I'm touching you this way." He bent and let his warm breath wash over the tip. "Can I taste these, or is that too fast?" he growled.

"Not too fast," Mags heard the unsaid, "Please do," as she arched her back.

He had both hands cupped at her breasts, and when his mouth closed over one tip, sucking her flesh deep into his mouth, she gasped at the sensation. He was ravenous as his tongue licked and laved both breasts until she was writhing and begging for more when it should have been for less.

"Jonathan," she panted, running her hands more frantically over his bared skin, stopping when her explorations found the button of his jeans once more.

His ministrations paused when he felt her trace his zipper and everything that it constricted under the metal teeth. "Would it be too fast if you took your pants off? For comfort," she added.

He nipped the side of her right breast before climbing to his feet and shedding the denim. She tried not to gape at the barely constrained monster tethered only by a pair of Tom Ford briefs.

When he came back to bed, he didn't immediately resume his position at her breasts. Instead, he kneeled at her feet, his hands caressing her calves, his eyes caressing the rest of her.

"My God, you're beautiful, lying naked underneath me. Almost naked," he said, touching her shorts. "Can I take these off?"

"That's not very slow of you." She tried for wit, but the breathless quality of her voice was disturbingly blatant.

Mags mentally shrugged. Slow had never been her thing.

"Fine, but tit for tat," she watched his eyes widen as she snapped the waistband of his briefs.

Jonathan ran one finger between her breasts and stopped, keeping only the slightest pressure at the base of her sternum.

"Are we done going slow?" he asked, a shag of white hair partially covering the left eye on his handsome face.

"I believe you regret hurting me, and if our families have taught me anything, second chances are necessary." She shrugged, adding, "Bigger the risk, bigger the reward."

"That's my girl." Thumbs already hooked in his underwear, he asked, "Together?"

Mags took a deep breath, feeling her lungs expand and stretch against her skin. She hooked her fingers, too, but her eyes never left his.

It wasn't just about sex. They were starting something that would either work and soar or crash and burn. Both had consequences; either would change them. Jonathan would change her. He already had.

"Together," she nodded. And then they were slipping out of the last barrier that separated their bodies.

Mags was by no means a virgin—she'd only had one lover, but that one was a repeat offender—she'd seen penises, personally and on television, but Jonathan was...blessed.

While she was busy ogling the unwrapped present, he was intent upon studying her in return. "No woman is so beautiful as you, Mags."

She stretched under his perusal, lifting her hips until the inside of her thighs slid up his muscular legs, barely stopping before her center touched his balls.

He brought his hands under her to grasp her ass and close the gap. When her heat met his, they moaned in tandem.

"Surely, no woman is more perfectly made."

He kissed her deeply then, while sending her body spiraling from sensation. Bent over her like he was, he was able to pump his sex through her wet folds.

It was too much and not enough, but through the intoxication of near orgasm, doubts about their sustainability roared to life.

Would she regret this? Regret him?

Would he pull away from her like he had all those years ago?

She wasn't brave enough to tell him what her true feelings were, too much of a coward to chance him not returning them.

She knew he cared for her. They were friends. That was undeniable, but...

Jonathan's thrusts stalled. "Mags? Where did you go?"

She would like to lie because she hated sounding insecure, but she wouldn't. "I," she halted before trying again. "I was wondering how long it would take before you got bored and moved on to another woman like you've always done in the past."

He reared back, looking angry and hurt, pinning her hands above her head. "Listen to me, Margaret Morrow. I won't grow bored," he practically growled. "I won't move on. I never had you in my arms."

She was quick to remind, "You did. Once."

"And I fucked that up, yes. I handled my feelings and yours in the worst way. You were only seventeen—"

"Almost eighteen at the time," she interrupted.

"Almost eighteen," he conceded, "and my dad would have ripped me a new one had I touched you like I'd really wanted to."

She could only nod, acknowledging the point. Still...

"Mags," he said in a stern voice, tugging her hands higher until her chest arched, causing her breasts to press against his chest, "I need this chance. I'm not talking about sex, though I'm dying for it. I mean that I need you to believe in me again. We can stop the physical tonight, just don't stop our new start."

Whatever tension had been building drained from her neck and shoulders. Jonathan might have proved his ability to be a prick in the past, but he wasn't a liar. She needed to remember that.

"I want the new start too. I also want the physical. Continue your perusal of my awesome body," she grinned, hooking her heels over his ass.

thirty-one

MAGS

WHEN THEY KISSED, it started slow—unhurried, almost tentative—but the heat between them built quickly, catching and spreading until it was impossible to ignore. Soon, the air felt warmer, charged, their breaths uneven as they lost themselves in it.

Mags drew in a shaky breath, her forehead brushing his as Jonathan murmured her name, the sound low and strained.

Their hands moved constantly, exploring, holding, pulling each other closer as if neither could get enough. Every touch seemed to spark something deeper, her body alive with sensation, every nerve tuned to him.

"I need to be inside you," he groaned as he pushed first one and then two fingers inside her body.

She sucked in a sharp breath at the fullness. It was nothing compared to what the thick shaft dragging across her inner thigh would feel like. Still, it was heaven. Her hips were already half frantic, thrusting up to meet him.

"Con...condom?" she asked, barely getting the word out

when he pushed his fingers deeper and curled them just enough to make her eyes roll back.

Jonathan's ministrations stalled, and his eyes widened. "Fuck. Fuck. Fuck," he cursed. "Are you on—" he cut himself off, wincing.

"I'm on the pill, and I've only ever used a condom," she offered.

"I've never gone without one."

He looked so desperate, it was precious. "First time for both of us then."

She could feel the slight tremor in his hands as he straightened and ran his hands from her neck to her hips.

Lining his sex up with her center, he slicked his head back and forth. He made a "Ahh" sound while she said, "Oh, God."

"This feels...I've never felt," he tried again, "...this first time might be...fast."

Mags' mouth dried at the feel of him against her entrance. "It might not fit," she gulped. Some women might have been embarrassed speaking their fears aloud, but when you'd known a person as long as she'd known Jonathan, honesty was comfortable. Plus, it was a *big* fear.

He huffed in amusement, which seemed to relax his stiff shoulders. "It will. I've imagined all the ways that I will fit into you perfectly. Okay, here we go," he grunted as he started to feed his engorged sex into her body inch by inch.

And then words failed them both. It was pure sensation, agony, and ecstasy. Her back bowed, his hips thrust, slow at first and then when he felt her body give, faster and faster until the headboard rapped against the wall sounding like a symphony of steel drums.

Jonathan reared up and watched himself moving in her, transfixed. "So, beautiful. So perfect. Christ, Mags, you're strangling me," he growled before placing his palm above their connection and pressing until her sensitive flesh screamed for release.

"Don't stop, Jon. Oh God, I'm going to come! Don't stop!" she begged.

The minute her release slammed through her core, Jonathan's hoarse, "Fuck," preceded his release.

"Never felt anything like that," he mumbled against her neck, where his head had dropped.

He reached a hand under her back, and as he slowly lay on his side, he moved her to lie against his chest, his penis, still semi-hard, still inside her.

"We'll make a mess this way unless you let me up to use the restroom."

"I want the mess," he stated, giving her ass a slap for good measure. "Besides, I'm far from done with you."

Mags smiled against his chest, so much for slow. She had no regrets.

"How do you feel now that we've," she faltered, not sure how to describe the encounter, "known each other in the Biblical sense." She had to place a hand over her mouth to stifle a giggle, enjoying Jonathan's look of astonishment.

"Biblical sense, huh? I didn't feel very holy, Mags, I can assure you. That was fucking plain and simple. Only it was fucking a woman who I never plan on letting go."

Her heart thumped hard at that. Some women might not consider his words romantic, but between two people who'd grown up together and knowing that he'd never had nor wanted a serious relationship before, they were pure poetry to her.

She felt her face burn when she recalled how loud their headboard had been. Speaking into Jonathan's shoulder, she moaned, "The headboard. Oh God, do you think everyone heard?"

His shoulders were shaking before she finished asking. "Definitely," he choked out, clearly enjoying her mortification.

"Jackass," she cursed him, lightly slapping his chest. "You're such an old-fashioned chest beater. I bet you loved Eze knowing exactly what we were up to."

"You did mention kissing him."

Her mouth dropped open in amazement at how men's brains worked. "That's your reasoning?"

He shrugged. "Yes."

Men are simple creatures.

"Can I ask you something?" he asked while idly tracing figure eights over her back.

"Of course." She felt him tense beneath her cheek and tensed in response.

In response, he flattened his hand on her back and pulled her tighter against his body. "Well, umm. Okay, this is dumb," he admitted, running his free hand over his face. "Forget it."

"It's not dumb, if it bothers you. What?"

"I'm ashamed to admit this. Christ," he cursed, giving his head a shake. "Fine. I held out hope that you had never been with a guy since we kissed."

That got her attention. She sat up and propped her head on her hand so that she could get a better look at his face. "Let me get this straight. You practically majored in being a manwhore, and you expected me to remain untouched?"

"I've told you that I'm a selfish idiot where you're concerned. I'm sorry. I knew I shouldn't have said anything."

She sat up and crossed her legs, pulling the sheet over her lap. "Would you like to swap stories about our previous partners? Because I can assure you that I'm not interested in hearing about yours, and mine only consists of one man."

"One?" he asked, so hopeful that Mags hated to crush his almost-a-virgin picture he was creating of her.

"Yes. One. We've been hooking up every now and again since I turned eighteen."

Rory was someone she'd met in the grocery store of all places. She had moved into the O'Faolain townhouse by then. Rory was buying flowers for a date, and Mags had intervened.

"Who are the flowers for, if you don't mind my asking?" Rory had been wearing sharp business casual, sexy dark hair perfectly trimmed over the ears, blue eyes, and a great smile with definite dimple potential.

He put down the vase of red roses before answering. "First date," he shrugged.

"Don't get the roses. The sunflower and daisy bouquet says you're fun without taking yourself so seriously. She'll look at them tomorrow morning and smile."

Mags smiled and walked away. She'd been halfway across the parking lot where Bébhinn was waiting in her old Jeep when she heard a man shout, "Hey, flower lady."

They ended up exchanging numbers and became great friends. Within a couple of months of meeting for coffees and friendly text exchanges, she'd accepted an invitation for dinner at his house.

She lost her virginity that night, but not her heart. That organ had unfortunately belonged to someone else. Rory was still in love with his high school sweetheart. It turned out that even though they were both emotionally unavailable, the sex had been amazing. He was a generous lover and hadn't minded her inexperience.

They both still went on dates, hers were platonic, his were not. They weren't exclusive, but they did respect one another.

"You've been...intimate with one man for almost three years." It was more of a statement than a query. "Do you still see him? Have feelings for him?"

"Rory and I are friends. Do you think you'll ever be in a situation where one of your exes is present, where you'll speak to them?"

His jaw clenched. "I don't want you to ever endure another moment around one of my dates," he said barely above a whisper. "I don't want anyone else around either of us."

Mags hid her smile. His O'Faolain obstinacy was beginning to show. She really didn't wish to tell him about Rory, but he thought the relationship was more than sex, and it wasn't.

"I met him not long after that New Year's Eve night. I was still smarting from your rejection, and I saw you not long after with another girl hanging off your arm at Murphy's, so when Rory asked me if I was interested in something simple, no strings attached, I agreed.

"Admittedly, he didn't know that I was barely eighteen and a virgin since he was older and already in his career. Still, it worked for us."

Jonathan looked so pained, she couldn't help touching his cheekbone and the hollow beneath. "I made a choice for myself, right or wrong."

"And what's your choice now?" he asked, capturing her hand under his own and leaning his face into her palm.

"If you don't know the answer to that after what we just got up to, there's no hope for you, boy," she teased.

"You're right," he said, nodding his acceptance.

He looked a little lost, and Mags understood that feeling more than she wanted to admit. Every time he'd shown up with someone new on his arm, it had carved small, quiet doubts into her confidence.

She pushed the sheet back, letting her gaze travel over him —broad shoulders tapering into lean, defined lines, muscle shifting subtly beneath his skin. There was something almost sculptural about him, like he'd been carved with care, softened only by the warm undertone he'd inherited from his mother.

Stunning.

The O'Faolain men really were a blessed lot.

Before he could say a word, she moved, swinging herself over his hips, settling there with deliberate ease. His sharp intake of breath sent a flicker of satisfaction through her.

His hands reacted instantly, finding her waist, guiding her closer—like he couldn't help himself.

"You make me crazy, Margaret Morrow." His voice had dropped, rougher now, threaded with something urgent, almost pleading, as his gaze locked onto hers.

"How crazy?" she asked.

"I'm fucking furious that I didn't keep you in my arms that night. I want to hunt down that Rory and ruin him. I want you to have never chosen him, taken him to your bed, and into your body.

"I want you to have only ever been mine. I need promises from you as selfish as that sounds." During his entire impassioned speech, he never stopped gliding his shaft between her parted thighs, making her wetter and wetter.

Bending, she kissed him slowly, surely, and hopefully, with everything she was feeling. She inched down his body, moaning as his sex moved from between her legs to her stomach and higher.

Mags kept kissing and sucking and taking nibbles from his flesh until she was equal with his belly button, which she licked and explored as she had every part of his upper body so far.

When she continued to shift down, Jonathan finally realized her intention. His breathing became ragged and she felt his hips lifting involuntarily against her chest.

"I need—" he started.

"Need what?"

"Your mouth. On me. Christ, Mags, I'm begging."

thirty-two

JONATHAN

MAGS tackled sex like she did everything else, fearlessly, passionately, and uninhibited. She had just gone to the bathroom to pee, "Which I don't need an audience for," she'd said over her shoulder as she strutted naked from the bedroom.

Jonathan rolled onto his back, staring up at the ceiling as the memory of the night before came rushing in.

He'd never felt that kind of satisfaction before. Usually it was simple—an hour or two, mutual release, a polite goodbye, making sure the woman got home safe. Contractual. Contained. No strings.

This had been anything but. There weren't simply strings between him and Mags, there were knotted ropes and chains. Solid. Unbreakable. Forever.

One singular woman had changed the trajectory of his life.

The way she looked at him, like she wasn't holding anything back. Like she wanted him, not just the moment. That was what unraveled him. What stripped away that control he'd always prided himself on.

Mags had gotten under his skin, into his head, and his mind was a cacophony of plans for the future.

He and Mags had been insatiable, especially after she'd taken him into her mouth. Things had become...frenzied. It wasn't the sexual act alone that had him blowing like a virgin. He'd had plenty of women over the years to know the difference. It was seeing Mags work him over that was the mind fuck. She broke his legendary control and left his body and mind at her mercy.

He shouldn't be entertaining sliding into her body again but one glance between his legs had his mind conjuring her silky-smooth body wrapped around him, all wet and soapy and steaming hot.

Joining Mags in the shower was quickly overtaking every other thought in his usually sharp mind.

He should be working.

Mags. Sex.

His colleagues were counting on him.

Mags. Sex.

Her body was probably tender.

Sex. Sex. Sex.

Jonathan slid off the bed and padded toward the bathroom. The sound of water and Mags' off-key humming met his ears as soon as he opened the door.

The glass shower door was covered in steam. It opened both ways, so he pulled the door toward him and caught Mags rinsing soap suds from her body.

Mags squeaked in surprise as he stepped into the spray with her, shutting the door behind him. "What the hell, Jon!"

Laughing, he wrapped his arms around her warm body and hugged her tight to his body. "I was lonely," he admitted, grinning.

Reaching a hand between them, she stroked the length of

his sex. "I don't think you were lonely at all. I think you were having a conversation with your dick."

"That too," he admitted. He slid one of his hands down her stomach until he could lightly caress her folds.

"Tell me you're not too sore," he pleaded as he pressed two fingers deep between her legs while playing with her breasts, massaging the weights, pinching and tugging at her nipples until she was panting. Her head tipped back and leaned against the tile, the water running down her body as he worked her over.

Her hips were thrusting, meeting his fingers and taking them deeper. She flicked her eyes open, saying, "I'm sore, but I don't give a damn."

Forty-five minutes and three orgasms later, two of which were hers, they were dressed and leaning against the kitchen island, sipping a cup of tea while continuously grinning at each other, when Eze and Nasir walked in the front door.

Eze had texted Mags two hours ago that he was picking Nasir up from the airport. The security guard apparently took a flight back to Dublin an hour after landing in Nigeria.

Nasir didn't speak, taking a solitary position near a wall in the connecting living room despite the fact that he must be exhausted. The man nodded at him and Mags, which, according to her, meant they were practically best friends now.

Eze cleared his throat, his grim demeanor on high definition. He eyed them both long enough to cause Jonathan to side-eye Mags in a "What the hell is going on here?" way. She grinned, not in the least concerned by Eze's silence.

Another five minutes passed, during which the sipping of tea and shuffling of feet were the only noise in the house. Eze finally cleared his throat and, in a completely deadpan voice, he asked, "Margaret, shall I have Jol inquire after a carpenter to fix your bedframe?

"From the rather egregious noises coming from your room last night, I can only assume there is structural damage of some kind."

Mags started giggling. "Eze, you ass." She looked at Jonathan and shook her head in exasperation. "Take me to my lunch date with the girls, Jon, and then go get your work done. Maybe tonight we can destroy the furniture at your place."

Jonathan found a parking spot near Murphy's and insisted on walking Mags to the door, even though she insisted it wasn't necessary.

They stood close outside the pub's entrance. He leaned into her and gave her a quick kiss. "I don't want to leave you," Jonathan admitted, and even he could hear the wonder in his voice.

Mags' wide smile dropped, and she clasped his hands tighter. "I hoped it wasn't just me feeling that way."

"I know you have to work after lunch, but can I pick you up for drinks tonight? I know your family wants you to stay at Eze's until that woman is found. I'll take you there after we go out."

She moved close, running her hands around his sides and resting her palms on his lower back. "And will you sleep over again?"

"I didn't want to presume," he hedged, her laughter cutting him off before he could continue.

"Since when, you arrogant ass? I've never known you to not take what you wanted," she said, jabbing her finger in his side.

"I wanted you for years, and I didn't make a move." He kissed her because he couldn't help himself. Months of wanting to touch had made him insatiable. "I'll stay over, but Eze might have something to say about that."

Mags laughed but soon sobered, suddenly looking ill at ease. Jonanthan tightened his fingers, worried she might try to move away from him.

"What's going on?" When she only fiddled with the tail of his t-shirt, he said, "Mags. What are you thinking?"

She blushed, but true to her personality, she swallowed and lifted her chin. "I'm going to Scotland this weekend. Mom and Dad will finally be home. This is probably too soon, and I'll have to cancel on Eze, but I thought," she hesitated, "you might want to come with me."

"It isn't too soon," he confirmed with finality. "I'll make travel arrangements this afternoon."

"I can—"

"Let me take care of this small thing," he interrupted.

thirty-three

MAGS

MAGS WAS SO HAPPY, she practically skipped through the front door of Murphy's Pub. Slow might work for some couples, but it didn't suit her or Jonathan. He might not be as rash as her personality led her to be, but he was a risk-taker, and way more willing to gamble than his best friend and cousin, Daniel.

She couldn't help the grin practically splitting her face when she saw her best friends at a high-top table near the bar. Before she joined them, she stood on the bar's foot rail to lean far enough to give the pub's owners and brothers, Ciaran and Cormac, hugs and kisses. Ciaran was Ciar's father and a father figure to her and all of her friends.

She headed toward her friends, rum and Coke in hand. At her approach, the table quieted, and three sets of eyes zeroed in, clocking each step. Gray, Bébhinn, and Blair all watched her with identical knowing expressions.

"Jeez, guys, did I miss something?" She asked as she hopped up on the free chair at the table.

"I don't know. Did you?" Gray replied dryly.

"Okay," Mags began, "you bitches are being way too shady right now." Blair simply pursed her lips while her brows winged high.

Bébhinn took a sip of her lemon water before leaning her elbows on the table and resting her chin on her linked fingers. "If you insist on playing dumb, I can fill you in."

Taking a sip of her own drink, she waved a hand in Bébhinn's direction. "Be my guest. Please."

"Gladly. Blair learned from her mother, who learned from your uncle Coll, and Gray learned from her mother, who learned from her husband, and I learned from my mother, who learned from Catriona, Josephine, and your mother, Mags, that a possible psychopath who's been locked up for over fifteen years may or may not have it out for your sister, and may or may not be coming for you as well since she might have been sighted in Dublin."

"And you didn't bother to text or call your best friends with that information," Gray finished.

Mags had the good grace to wince in apology. "In my defense, it literally just happened last night. I knew we were meeting today and planned to tell you all about it. I momentarily forgot how our families share information at the speed of light," she defended.

"We know," Gray grinned. "We just wanted to give you shit but damn, that is one wackadoo lady. Blair's dad and my dad were there the night that the police arrested her all those years ago. It's pretty wild."

"I know, right. Normally, I would blow it off because it just seems too weird to be a serious issue, but Mirren was upset, and it takes a lot to shake my sister. I promised to be careful, but decided not to put too much of my brainpower into it. With

Uncle Coll and your dad, Gray, I know they'll figure out where she's hiding sooner than later."

"I looked up the newspaper article from the time of the lady's arrest. Mirren was managing your brother-in-law and his sister's exhibits. Crazy shit," Bébhinn said, shivering.

Blair, silent up until then, signed, "Now that we've addressed the psycho on the loose, can we discuss why I was a witness to Jonathan's tongue having explicit sex with your throat outside?"

Fire, hot and swift, enveloped Mags' skin from head to toe. "I was going to tell you about that too!" she defended. "It's... new."

"Blair said it didn't look like your first or even your hundredth kiss," Bébhinn said, tapping the top of Mags' icy glass.

"Give us the details, or we're calling Jonathan," Gray threatened.

"Jesus, fine, you weirdos. Last night wasn't our first night messing around, but it was our first sleepover, and the first time we had sex."

"Yes!" Gray laughed, her eyes sparkling in approval.

"Hallelujah!" Bébhinn clapped her hands in excitement.

"About fucking time," Blair swore, grinning ear to ear. "More importantly, was he as good as his reputation makes him out to be?"

Where her best friends were concerned, Mags never held back the details of her sex life. They all knew about Rory and had even met him on occasion.

"Beyond," Mags answered Blair's question while grinning and patting her hot cheeks. "I was adamant that I wanted to go slow. I told him I would give us a try, but *slowly*. "And then he took his shirt off," she said, and shrugged.

The table erupted in laughter. They decided on sharing

appetizers instead of ordering full meals, and Gray slipped away to give her father-in-law the order. When she joined them again, she said, "Just so you know, it doesn't get any better. Ciar takes his shirt off, and my panties hit the floor.

"That man's body," she closed her eyes and sighed, "is an addiction."

Blair covered her face with both hands before signing, "Please tell me you two are using protection. None of us is ready for a third baby from you guys yet."

Gray's amusement fizzed from her as she shook her head dramatically. "Birth control pills. No exception. We decided to wait a few years to see if we were definitely done making babies, and if our minds don't change, Ciar said he'd get snipped."

"Two is a lovely number. A boy and a girl is pretty perfect. I can't wait to find out what Dagr and I have cooking." Bébhinn said, smiling softly while she rubbed the slight swell of her belly. "But yeah, I'm still completely distracted by Dagr. Christ, his ass," she giggled. "Chef's kiss."

Another round of laughter erupted when Bébhinn started blowing kisses. "You know," Mags began, growing serious, "it isn't just the sex or his body or his handsome face, despite the tension between Jon and me in the past, there was always a level of...closeness, I guess. His girlfriends hurt me, but I could never let the idea of us go."

"Did he go all caveman on you and demand to know about past lovers? Ciar was relentless," Gray shared.

Mags chuckled. "I think he truly thought he'd be taking my virginity. Don't get me wrong, I wish it had been him, but with the hell he's put me through with his revolving door of women, he can hardly blame me."

"I would damn well hope not!" Bébhinn slapped the table for emphasis.

"You and Dagr kind of ripped the band aids off at the start. I still can't believe you each had to deal with an ex on one of your first official dates. Still, it took all the dramatics out of it," Blair offered.

"Agreed. It was a horror show when Ciar came face to face with Cannon. Humiliating doesn't begin to describe the horror of that lunch, which I still blame you for, Mags." Gray glared at her friend across the table.

"I did you a favor, and you know it," Mags laughed. "Jonathan did try to subtly ask about my sex life. Ridiculous! As if we all haven't had front row seats to his one-night stands for years!"

"Let me guess," Gray smirked, "when you told him, he forbade all contact like a medieval warlord?"

Mags felt her jaw drop. "Exactly. He did exactly that. I reminded him that we'd have trouble going to the damn toilet without running into one of his conquests. Give me a break. Tell me Ciar loosened up now that you're married and have two children."

At Gray's silence, Mags swore. "Fuck me," she groaned.

"So," Bébhinn began slowly, "are you two exclusive? Like, has he agreed to that?"

"He said I was it for him, that he didn't want anyone else, and well, you guys know how I feel about him."

Blair clapped her hands and grinned. "It took a while, but you're finally there. I'm so happy for you, Mags."

Bébhinn held up her glass of water, and they all clinked glasses. Mags felt a surge of warmth for her friends and their support. She could only hope that she and Jonathan didn't screw things up.

"Clearly, Jonathan knows you weren't a virgin after last night, but does he know it was only one man and who that man is?" Blair asked.

Mags groaned. "He knows there was only one. He knows his name is Rory and that we've been seeing each other for a few years." She held her hands up like "What more is there?"

Bébhinn raised her brows in a knowing look. "Does he know that Rory is thirty-seven and is a partner of a successful commercial architecture business? The very business that I've heard the men in my family discussing will give Jonathan the most competition once he opens up his firm next year?"

Mags deflated. "Yeah, that didn't come up, but honestly," she defended, "it was never serious."

Blair touched Mags' hand to get her attention. "The few times I was around him when we all went out, I have to say that the man had hearts in his eyes when he looked at you."

Mags was taken aback. She didn't outright deny that Rory might have felt a certain way about her because Blair notoriously saw things in people that most missed. She just didn't want it to be true.

"I hope he didn't. We were always open about where we stood with each other." She popped a grilled shrimp in her mouth and used the time to think over the Rory thing while she chewed.

"I should probably reach out to him and let him know that I won't be meeting him anymore."

"But that's a problem for another day," Gray said, bumping Mags' side while shoving a chip in her mouth. "Tell us when you and Jonathan are having sex again."

Blair signed, "Yes, do. You know I live vicariously through you guys, which is really sad when I hear that in my head."

Mags shook her head in exasperation but gladly spent the next thirty minutes telling the girls some of the romantic gestures Jonathan had made, his apologies for the past, and their tentative plans for the future.

"Speaking of," Mags said, clenching her teeth and grimacing, "I asked Jon if he wanted to go home with me to see my folks this weekend even though we're so new."

"And he said?" Bébhinn asked, her hands clasped against her chest.

"He said yes and then immediately took charge of the travel arrangements."

"Of course he did. He's an O'Faolain, they don't know any other way," Bébhinn shrugged. "That he didn't hesitate to go with you to see your family tells me he truly has changed."

"Yeah," Mags agreed. "I was nervous to ask, but I admit that when he instantly wanted to come, I was pretty pleased."

"I wish I could go home too," Blair frowned. "I want to see Aunt Aileen. My parents are super disappointed, but they understand."

Mags clasped one of Blair's hands. "Your interview with the head of Oklahoma State University's plant pathology is too important to miss. The woman is flying to Dublin to meet with you. We're all so proud of you."

"My grumpy father-in-law is still mad he couldn't convince you to join his cause in Wales, but he still has hopes of bringing you around after you *Sew your wild oats in America*."

Blair rolled her eyes but grinned at Ulf's antics. Talk turned to the Chamber of Commerce dinner hosted by Gray Eyes next week. She couldn't wait. As a new business owner, the networking potential would be crazy.

Plus, it would be the first event she and Jonathan showed up as an official couple, which was equal parts amazing and terrifying.

"I created an embroidered fan for Eze's mother for her birthday. I refused payment, of course, but he threw such a mantrum, I told him I would use his credit card to order a dress for the Chamber event. It came in a few days ago. I love it."

"Does he know that you're a bargain-shopping queen and spent next to nothing for the dress?" Bébhinn asked.

Mags laughed as her eye caught sight of Nasir standing stiffly by the pub's front door. "I'm counting on that man over there," she nodded her head toward the unsmiling Nigerian, "to keep Eze occupied."

"Ahh," Gray said, eyeing the bodyguard, "the ex. I presume."

"He's very handsome. Does he still not like you?" Blair asked.

"We had a nice talk. We're good," Mags assured.

Everyone threw some money on the table, preparing to go their separate ways. Bébhinn seemed to hesitate. Clearly, she had something to say but was holding back, which wasn't like her.

Blair signed, "Are you feeling alright, Bébhinn?"

"You'll think I'm being hormonal, and I probably am, but I just want to say that I like that we're back to talking again. Not just about nonsense but the tough stuff. Like we used to. Secrets never used to be who we were, and I hope we all try to keep our relationships open to the type of support we can offer one another. Cheers," Bébhinn held her glass of water up.

"Cheers," Gray seconded.

"Cheers," Blair signed, holding up the last bit of whatever dark lager she'd ordered.

"Cheers and Amen," Mags held her almost empty glass up in solidarity before she stood and grabbed her heavy tote hanging on the back of her chair and slung it over her shoulder. "I need to get to work, guys. If I don't see you before, I'll see you at Gray Eyes next week."

"With more details," Gray demanded.

"Of course," Mags winked over her shoulder before turning toward Nasir.

thirty-four

HANNAH

WASN'T Mirren's little sister living her best life? "What a happy little bitch," Hannah sneered, where she sat in one of the two-seat tables that were tucked away in one of the pub's shadowy walls.

She'd still been close enough to hear most of the trivial bullshit Margaret Morrow and her friends ran on about, careful not to draw unwanted attention.

The only attention you'd draw in a pub like this is from the Ugly Police.

"Just you wait," Hannah whispered under her breath while pretending to read a book for anyone who might look her way. The girls left the pub five minutes ago, so she could relax her guard. "Once we get our revenge on Mirren and we take care of Mom, I'm going to take us to a beach somewhere and swim and run on the beach. I'll get my looks back, don't you worry about that."

Don't bore us with your pathetic fiction, Cow.

I can't decide if I'm going to stay. One of the voices threatened.

You're a boring shell, Hannah. A husk of what you used to be...what you used to be capable of.

We used to get intoxicated off your blood and tears, your anger and violence. Now...

Hannah felt the pinch of panic. They weren't just goading her. Hannah felt it in her bones that they may finally be finished with her.

She had to do something. She had to prove that she was still worthy. Sweat broke out across her skin, only thinking about not having her...family, for lack of a better word. She would die without their guidance, even though they made her so mad at times. What families didn't quarrel?

She might have to rethink her plans for little Margaret. If her family wanted blood, fear, and pain, she would give it to them.

thirty-five

PATRICK

RIVER THOUGHT she could get by with telling him that their son was in love with someone, without giving any details. His wife should have remembered that she was married to an O'Faolain, and challenges were their favorite pastime.

For several days, either by himself or with his brother Bran, they'd stalked their wives. They followed them to work, to lunch, shopping, the spa, Raven's gynecologist appointment, and Rowan's bikini wax. They waited outside the rooms for both of those, of course, until finally, finally, they caved.

Because Patrick and his brothers knew that where the Byrne sisters were concerned, it was all of them or nothing. Ulf was in town for a few days—don't get him started about how bizarre it was to find out that he and Bran had been living without their oldest brother their whole lives—and consented to tag along to meet the women for lunch.

As the three men walked into the pizzeria, Patrick's eyes instantly found his wife seated on one side of a six-top table between her sisters. Even though they were all giving the men evil eyes, it still made his heart clench to see the sisters side-by-side.

They had all been stunning when they'd first met in Oklahoma, all of them in their twenties, except for his dad. Now that the sisters were in their forties, they still stopped traffic, especially when they were all together, like they were now.

Their Native American and Irish heritage had created three siblings so similar in appearance that many mistook them for triplets, but for their husbands, his late father included, their wives were spectacularly unique.

Still, when they were set on something, their hive mind was formidable, which was why they were so annoyed that they'd given in.

Patrick hid his smile. He was smart like that, going to her side and kissing her until she finally sighed against his lips and kissed him back.

"Asshole," she whispered as she pulled back. Her voice didn't hold any bite, though.

One kiss, and he was ready to ditch lunch. Revelations about Jonathan could wait. He and River had always been like that. One touch ignited instant lust.

Before he pulled back, he whispered back to her, "I'm not hungry for pizza any longer. Let me take you home."

"Christ, Patrick," River breathed heavily, but soon enough, she shook off the haze and poked him in his hard stomach—a little lower would have been convenient—and told him to "Sit down."

Smirking, he made his way to his seat, noting that Raven looked slightly mussed as well. Bran must have greeted his wife similarly. And then he noticed Rowan. She was studiously watching the cooks through the open window, tossing dough into the air, pretending like she wasn't missing his father fiercely at that moment.

Damn it. He never wanted to make her uncomfortable. There was nothing for it but to pretend everything was normal. River and Raven glanced at their sister and winced, immediately concentrating on the plateware in front of them.

He glanced at his brothers, both of whom could see that Rowan was struggling. Ulf, in his taciturn way, grumbled, "I have places to be. Have you ladies ordered the food yet?"

Rowan focused on the table once more and rolled her eyes at Ulf. "We have." Realizing the table was quiet, she added, "I'm so excited. After lunch, I'm meeting Bébhinn for baby shopping."

Raven and River were instantly clapping their hands in glee and asking about the shops they'd be hitting up. That was all well and good, but this lunch wasn't meant for pleasantries. He wanted answers. Patrick cleared his throat to get their attention.

"River, I think you have something to tell me. Specifically, who in the hell has my son been mooning over for weeks now, and why is he being such an ass?"

"Margaret Morrow," River stated.

"Mags?" Patrick asked. That took him completely by surprise.

"According to Bébhinn, who just had lunch with Mags, Blair, and Gray, Mags and Jonathan are an official couple as of last night," Rowan said with a smile, clearly thrilled with the news.

"Christ, your son," Bran said to Patrick, shaking his head. "He'd better know what he's about. That girl's father, Charles, might be laidback, but her uncle, Coll, won't be so easy to get around. Come to that, Mags is Mirren's little sister, and MacGregor will surely have something to say about Jon. His reputation with women is not winning over any fathers."

"Hey," River interjected, taking exception to Bran's description of her son. "Jonathan is sweet and kind, and one of the most intelligent young men I know. Any family would be lucky to have him."

Patrick took his wife's hand across the table. "We know that, sweetheart, but Jon might have sewn a few too many wild oats, and unlike Dagr," he glanced at his oldest brother and glared, "our son's stomping ground was Dublin."

River pursed her lips but didn't deny the facts. "How sure are you that Mags is the one?" Bran asked.

"He's been running from her for almost three years," River answered.

"She's the one," Raven seconded.

"Margaret is his final play," Rowan agreed with finality.

thirty-six

MAGS

WORK HAD GONE WELL TODAY. The sunshine had been weak most of the afternoon, but whatever golden tendrils there were managed to heat the glass of her workshop and shine on the intricate pattern she'd spent several uninterrupted hours working on.

Sitting back in her worn-out office chair, Mags sighed with satisfaction. This was one of her largest pieces, and she hoped to deliver it to her client before the Chamber of Commerce party next week.

She'd already given Eze his mother's fan, which he planned on flying home in a few weeks to deliver personally on her birthday.

She'd gotten a few orders for embroidered cuffs thanks to Jina's artist girlfriend, Anna. Mags' heart thumped, barely able to contain her happiness.

What reasons were there not to be pleased?

Her embroidery business might actually have a chance at something great. Jonathan O'Faolain was her boyfriend, and

"

most importantly, her mother was cancer-free and coming home.

"She better stay that way," she threatened the empty room. Her mom's cancer had been a weight dragging her soul down for months, and now that it was over, hopefully for good, she felt as light as the clouds skittering in the breeze outside her window.

Nasir should be picking her up any minute to head back to Eze's, where her bags were already packed for Scotland. Jonathan was picking her up. However, they weren't going straight to the airport.

"God," Mags moaned and rubbed her eyes. Before they headed to the airport, Jonathan had told her only that morning that his family hoped they could stop by the O'Faolain building and have a drink.

The thing was, she shouldn't be nervous. She'd known his family her whole life. One of her best friends was an O'Faolain for heaven's sake. She'd set aside her worries about whether they would accept her dating Jonathan so that she could work, but now that her hands were at ease, her nerves were back.

Her phone pinged.

Jonathan: Stop worrying.

She grinned and shook her head. He made her ridiculously happy, and she'd come to realize that they never would have made it had they gotten together when they were younger. They both needed the time to grow up, and even though she would never admit it to him, he needed to date all those women, and she'd needed Rory. Otherwise, how would they have ever discovered that nothing was better than what they had together?

Mags: Easy for you to say. They're your family.

Jonathan: They loved you before you were
mine.

Her body warmed with his words. *They loved you before you were mine.* God, but she loved being his.

Her phone pinged again. Nasir was outside waiting to get her safely home. She messaged Jonathan back while she threw all of her hundreds of bits and bobs into her giant tote.

Mags: You're mine now too. Are you nervous
about seeing my family?

Jonathan: Point taken. I'm picking you up early.
I miss you. Get your ass home so I can make
out with you in the back of the car.

Mags: Yes, sir – except for the making out part.
I WILL NOT show up at your parents' house
with swollen lips.

Jonathan: We'll see. 😉

She carried that warmth with her all the way back to Eze's flat—through the quiet ride, through her shower, through the simple act of changing clothes. It lingered, steady and grounding, even now as she wrapped her arms around her roomie in the foyer.

"I'll be back in a few days. I'll miss you," she said, squeezing him tight. Somewhere along the way, Eze had stopped being just a friend and become something essential—someone she relied on without even thinking about it.

He only grunted in response, not one who was comfortable

with an overshare of emotion and instead gave her a solid thump on the back.

Mags pulled away with a grin. "Do something for me?" she asked, tilting her head.

"Of course," he growled, and she had to bite back a smile. He had a soft spot for her, no matter how much he pretended otherwise.

"Forgive Nasir." She lifted a hand before he could interrupt. "No—listen. He messed up, yeah. But so did you. You never said how you felt."

His expression darkened, but he didn't argue.

"Say it now," she pressed gently. "While I'm gone. Tonight."

She leaned in, pressing a quick kiss to his cheek before he could deflect again. Then she grabbed her weekend bag, flashing him one last look.

"Think about it," she tossed over her shoulder as she headed out, leaving him standing there—brooding, stubborn, and, hopefully, considering every word.

Jonathan was already waiting in the lobby when she arrived. The second he saw her, he stepped forward, taking her bag without hesitation and sliding the tote from her shoulder onto his with a quiet grunt that earned him a sheepish smile.

He followed her into the Uber, giving the driver the address before the door had even fully shut.

"I missed you today," he admitted, his voice softer now as he pulled her into his side.

The presence of the driver didn't seem to register for Jonathan as his hand slipped into her hair, fingers threading through the loose waves as he tilted her face toward his and kissed her, like he'd been dying to taste her all day.

Stopping him wasn't really an option.

Not when he touched her like that. Not when her body

answered so easily, leaning into him, wanting him just as much. It was a losing battle, and she knew it.

Still, she managed—barely—to pull back, breath uneven, lips tingling.

"Jon," she murmured, her voice a little breathless. "You've destroyed my lip gloss."

He looked entirely unapologetic.

Shaking her head, she reached for her bag, rummaging through it in a hurry. If she was about to meet his family, she needed to look like she hadn't just been thoroughly kissed in the back of a car.

"Mags," he growled, placing a firm hand on her thigh and squeezing. "You drive me crazy."

"Well, think of other things. They're your family, so you don't need to worry about first impressions, and thank God," she shot her boyfriend a sharp look, "but I still need to, and you will not lead me astray again tonight. Until we're alone again, that is," she grinned as she touched up her lips.

Jonathan snorted. "My family knows how much you mean to me. You have nothing to worry about."

Mags wondered how much she meant to him. They'd never said the words, though, if his dick could speak, it would surely say the L word, she thought with a sniff of irritation.

He clasped the hand not holding the lip glass and said, "After this trip, I would like to discuss our future."

Inside, she was crowing in delight, but instead of letting him know how badly she craved discussing what he saw for them, she teased, "I'll pencil you in."

He didn't laugh, only took her chin, moving her head until she was staring into his eyes. "Pencil me in for getting you naked. Often. Make a notation that I'll use every part of my body to make every part of yours know how important our meetings are."

Mags felt her body shiver, and without consciously telling her hand to move, she found it running up his thigh, needing to feel his…

"We've reached your destination," the driver announced. "And not a moment too soon," the woman added, chuckling, which had Mags' cheeks burning and Jonathan laughing.

"Thanks for the ride," he said as he opened things up.

"No. Thank you," she said, still laughing.

Mags couldn't stay embarrassed. They'd brought that on themselves, after all. She and Jonathan laughed all the way to the front door of his family's four-story monster of a home. The massive front door soon loomed before them, instantly filling her with nerves again.

She whispered an "Oh God" as Jonathan opened things up. *Christ have mercy.* His mom and two sisters were in the front to greet them, with his father, Patrick, and his brother, Bran, standing behind the sisters.

River cried, "Mags!" before pulling her into a hug and away from Jonathan's side and straight into a Byrne sister huddle. She caught Jonathan's eye over his mom's shoulder. His shrug had her head shaking.

River led her over to a table set up with finger foods and pitchers of water and tea. "I'm so glad you two could stop by before you go home."

"We were all relieved to hear that your mother beat cancer a second time," Raven said, patting Mag's hand.

"I hope she expects an ass-chewing from her brother, Thomas, Cat, and Jo," Rowan huffed. "I know she had to have had her reasons, but…well, I would have wanted to know."

River sighed and leaned back in her chair, sipping a lemon water on ice. "We all love your mom, Margaret. We would have helped in any way…in every way."

"Perhaps that's why she didn't tell, Riv. She wanted to do it alone. With Charles, of course," Raven said thoughtfully.

Rowan sat forward and captured Mags' attention. "Aileen had her reasons, and we all respect that. You, on the other hand, had no reason to leave the townhouse. You should have come to one of us while your parents were away. You should have never let finances come between our love and care for you.

"Hugh would have been devastated to find out that you didn't feel as though you could stay outside of being a student."

As soon as Rowan spoke Hugh's name, her eyes became glassy, and then, like dominoes, River and Raven were blinking rapidly. Mags felt her own eyes become misty and desperately hoped to salvage the situation.

"He would have blistered my ears before personally moving my things back into the townhouse, and then he would have called every man in my family.

"Bébhinn is exactly like her father, and it was because of that that I kept things from her. I admit, I panicked and made mistakes, but I was trying to do my best by my parents, and I didn't want to worry my friends.

"You three will be happy to know that I've since seen the error of my ways. I won't keep secrets from my friends again." Mags was happy to see that the sad moment had passed and the sisters were smiling again.

Mags had never considered what it would be like to have River as the mother of her boyfriend. A person really did get three Byrnes for the price of one.

Raven stood and grabbed the small plates. "Should we grab some snacks and join the men at the bar?"

Mags chuckled as she started loading her plate. "This spread is like an ultimate girl dinner buffet. My favorite." The sisters laughed, agreeing. "Before I forget, Rowan. I think I'm going to make a soft fabric book for the baby with lots of embroidery and fun interactive pages, perfect for little hands. I just wasn't sure if Bébhinn had decided yet on nursery colors."

"Oh, Mags, she'll love that. Truly. The two base colors will be tans and greens, with shades of blue for a boy or shades of rose for a girl. Muted earth tones for sure."

"My favorite colors to work with. Yay!" As the ladies walked toward Jonathan, Patrick, and Bran, Daniel walked through the front door to join the party.

When she reached Jonathan's side, he instantly wrapped his arm around her waist and bent to give her a kiss.

"That's going to take some getting used to. Christ, Jon, you two together still seem weird as hell," Daniel groused, joining them at the bar.

Mags laughed. "As weird as your dad's sister marrying his nephew?"

"Have mercy, Mags." Daniel mock shuddered as his father handed him a drink. "You win."

"Are you ready to face Mags' family, Jon?" his father asked, nodding his head her way, his eyes twinkling.

Luckily for her, Jonathan took after his father, which meant that as these men aged, they became more handsome. No wonder the Byrne sisters were obsessed with their husbands. She remembered Rowan then and winced. Mags was already so attached to Jonathan. What must it have been like to lose the love of your life after twenty years together?

Jonathan moved Mags so that her back could lean against his front, his hands gently moved over the tops of her shoulders, sending a shiver of awareness through her body that was completely inappropriate in front of their current audience.

"Mags and I have known each other for years. I doubt her family will come for me too hard," Jonathan announced casually.

His uncle Bran snorted with amusement. Mags admitted that Jonathan might be slightly overconfident where the men in her family were concerned. In an attempt to stand up for her boyfriend, she said, "Dad will be thrilled about us, I think." She patted the hand at her collarbone.

"I imagine Thomas MacGregor, Coll Barr, and probably even their boys, Lochlann and Laith, won't be greeting you with open arms," Patrick huffed, shaking his head at his son's attitude.

"Well, they won't yet anyway," Mags piped up. "I haven't told my family. Gray and Blair promised to keep it from their parents until I could surprise everyone." Her cheeks pinkened at the look of shock and horror on the Byrne sisters' faces, and the laughter on the men's.

Not all of the men.

Jonathan's hands flexed before he slowly turned her to face him and asked, "You didn't tell *any* of them?" The whites around his eyes seem to grow as he must have seen the truth on her face.

"Umm, I thought it would be best to, you know...surprise!" She threw some jazz hands up and smiled—or grimaced. She couldn't tell because her face felt slightly numb. Perhaps waiting had been a mistake.

"Would it make you feel better if I texted my parents?"

"Not even your parents?" he asked, exasperated.

"Well, honestly," she started, shifting her weight from foot to foot, "I figured the explosion that was coming from Coll and Thomas about mom keeping the cancer and treatments a secret from everyone would surely overshadow the fact that you and I are um...are—"

"Dating?" Jonathan finished stonily. "Exclusively? That we practically live with each other? Are you embarrassed to tell them because it's me?"

The room was suddenly quiet and stiflingly hot. Mags might have misjudged not telling her family, but his accusation that she was embarrassed by him pissed her right off.

"That," she poked him hard in the chest, "was a ridiculous thing to ask, and I won't bother with answering something so foolish. Truthfully, I've been so happy—with you—or I was up until this moment, that I didn't prioritize how my family would react, because to be perfectly honest, your opinion and my opinion is the most important thing to me."

She backed up a few steps and held her hand up when he looked to be about to speak. "Let me rectify this, Jon."

She dialed her dad first, and when he answered, she asked him to put her on speaker. If Jonathan's eyes got any wider, they would be in danger of popping from his head.

Once her parents were both on, she said, "Hey, I just wanted to tell you guys that I'm bringing my boyfriend home for the weekend. It's Jonathan O'Faolain." After shocked surprise and congratulations were made, she lifted her eyebrows in challenge at said boyfriend and finished with, "We'll stay in my old bedroom. Because we sleep together. Every night." Her dad laughed and said he couldn't wait to hear the story behind such a thoughtful announcement and that he'd see her in a few hours.

She dialed Catriona Barr next. "Hey, Aunt Cat, I just wanted to let you know I'm bringing my boyfriend home for the weekend. It's Jonathan O'Faolain. I can't wait to see you at the cookout tomorrow." After Catriona's exclamations of amazement, Mags heard cursing from her uncle Coll in the background. "Love you, bye."

She never took her eyes off Jonathan, who looked slightly ill. Some of his family were doing a poor job of controlling their laughter at her back.

Finally, she called Josephine, her sister Mirren's stepmom

and Gray's mom. "Hey, Jo, I just wanted to..." She gave the same spiel before signing off with love yous.

She placed both hands on her hips and frowned at her boyfriend. "I suggest, Jon, that you never call my feelings for you into question again."

"I won't."

thirty-seven

JONATHAN

JONATHAN'S FAMILY would never let him live down getting his ass handed to him by Mags, but Christ, had she been glorious while she'd done it.

He should not have doubted her. And he sure as hell shouldn't have doubted her in front of an audience. Lesson learned. A huge lesson learned.

They were in a hired car on their way to Bunchrew, Mags' hometown. It lay three miles west of Inverness on the Beauly Firth. The area possessed a distinct appeal; during the infrequent family gatherings he attended there, he developed a genuine appreciation for the countryside.

Funnily enough, it reminded him of some of the small towns surrounding his father's hometown of Tulsa, Oklahoma, in the United States. Everyone knew everyone and their business. He smiled, thinking about some of the stories he'd heard about Mags as a child. She'd been a hellion for the poor teachers of Bunchrew, including her mother.

When they landed, a text from Aileen had come through.

The family decided to have an evening at MacGregor's house. According to Mags' mother, the family had insisted.

It looked like Mags' earlier revelation calls had impacted their plans upon landing. Mags was quiet on the drive to her parents'. They were going there first to drop their bags and for her to reconnect with her parents after so many months apart.

Aileen was nervous about meeting the family. They all believed that the big news of the evening was Mags bringing a boyfriend home, but really, it was about Aileen not telling them about her cancer.

She was nervous, but Aileen swore she was glad not to wait another night to tell them. Jonathan clasped one of Mags' hands and pulled it into his lap.

"Had I not gotten butthurt about you waiting to tell your family about us, your mom wouldn't be rushed into a confession. I'm sorry, Mags. Truly."

She pulled her gaze from the window, less than a minute from her parents' home. She leaned into his side and kissed his jaw in a sweet kiss. He let his fingers feather over her cheek, humbled to have her by his side.

"I might be cross with you, Jon, for doubting me," she said, a teasing smile tugging at her lips, "but you've already proven you know better now."

He huffed a quiet breath but didn't interrupt.

"As for tonight," she continued, her tone softening, "I actually think Mom's relieved. Nervous, yeah—but relieved. Honestly, all the secrecy probably made it worse for her."

She shifted slightly toward him, more thoughtful now. "They only got in a couple of hours ago, and she admitted that putting it off had been weighing on her. The family didn't understand what was going on, and that bothered her. So...this? Tonight? It's probably exactly what she needed."

Jonathan nodded, his expression easing. "Your family's too

close-knit to hold onto anger for long. If anyone grumbles, it'll just be because they love her."

"That's what I think too." She paused, just for a second, then pushed forward, her voice quieter but more deliberate. "Jon...I need you to believe something."

His attention sharpened immediately.

"I didn't keep us a secret because I was ashamed. Or unsure. Or anything like that—even for a moment." Her gaze held his steadily. "You matter to me. And I don't take this—us—for granted. Not even a little."

The words hit him harder than he expected. After everything—after the doubt, the second-guessing—this was what undid him. He blinked, jaw tightening slightly as emotion crept up on him.

"Christ," he muttered under his breath, dragging a hand through his hair. "My questioning you...that wasn't really about you." He looked back at her, honesty laid bare. "That was me questioning myself."

She didn't look away.

"I haven't always been someone worth trusting," he went on, voice lower now. "But I'm not screwing this up. Not with you." His gaze held hers, steady and certain. "If I ever do something that makes you doubt me—even a little—I want you to tell me. Right away. I mean that. I'm in this. Fully."

Her expression softened, something warm and sure settling in her eyes.

"And if I'm the one who messes up?" she asked quietly. "You'll tell me too?"

"I will," he said without hesitation.

From the moment the car dropped them at Charles and Aileen's house, they had exactly twenty-two minutes to drop their bags, for Mags to hug and cry over her parents, and load back into Charles' old Land Rover and head to MacGregor's.

Jonathan cursed himself yet again for insisting that her family needed to know of his arrival. Surprise might have been the better option.

Charles met his eyes in the rearview mirror and grinned. Aileen looked at her husband and sighed dramatically. "Really, Charles. Do you have to find everything so damn amusing?"

"I can't help it," he shrugged before chuckling. "Coll and Thomas are going to be pissed at us—"

"Me," Aileen interrupted. "They'll be pissed at me. I was the one who didn't want to tell anyone."

"Oh, they'll include me, my love." Charles patted his wife's leg to let her know he didn't mind, and it was clear he really didn't. "Like I was saying, they'll be pissed as bears woken from hibernation. Cat and Jo will be hurt. That's up to you to fix. What's got me tickled is that Mags and Jonathan have offered us a perfect diversion.

"If things get too heated because of your months of lying—"

"You're pushing your luck, Charles."

Mags snorted, quickly covering her nose and mouth before she interrupted her parents' extremely amusing conversation.

Ignoring his wife, Charles continued. "When things look to be taking a turn for the worse, Jonathan, here," he pointed his thumb over his shoulder in Jonathan's direction, "will kiss Margaret and voila, we'll be forgotten."

Mags did laugh then. "Brilliant, Dad, but I prefer Jon's face blood-free."

Charles' fist hadn't even made contact with MacGregor's front door before it was pulled open, and Catriona and Josephine were outside on the wraparound porch, pulling Aileen into a group hug.

The women were all smiles and laughter until they noticed Aileen's headscarf. It was like witnessing a toy's battery die. One moment animation, the next absolute stillness.

"Aileen," Josephine whispered. Gray's mother reached out and rubbed Aileen's scarf between her fingers. "I don't understand."

A single tear rolled down Catriona's cheek. "Oh, Aileen. Why didn't you tell us?"

"Let's go inside," Aileen urged, "and I'll explain."

Emotions, of course, were running high, and it took Aileen half an hour to explain when she'd found out about the cancer, her treatments, and why she chose to leave her family in the dark.

The first thing Mags' uncle Coll said was, "You fucking bastard," to Charles. "You let my sister go through that alone. Without me."

Charles had some sort of superpower. He never reacted to aggression like most people would, more Zen than a Buddhist monk.

"She was never alone, Coll. Ever. I'm sure you would rather hug your sister and tell her you love her instead of cussing me out," Charles said evenly.

Coll actually flinched before rushing his sister and wrapping her in a giant hug, clutching her to his chest and sniffling in her hair. Aileen, for her part, hugged him just as tight, patting his back like a parent would a child's.

When he finally set her back on her feet, Thomas took his place and received a similar treatment. The women were next, while Aileen explained the last few months, the doctors, the treatments, and finally told them that she was cancer-free.

At one point, Aileen explained that "Charles didn't have a choice to know and to worry, but I did have a choice to keep that from you. Had things not gone my way, I would have told you."

"That wasn't your call to make," Coll said stubbornly.

"Actually, it was, brother," Aileen said serenely, quite used to her sibling.

MacGregor stood next to his best friend, frowning. "Coll, you'll need to put trackers in everything Aileen owns, car, phone, tablet—maybe even herself. If we can't trust her to tell us things, we'll find them out on our own," he added stubbornly.

When Aileen gasped in outrage, Mags stifled a giggle.

"Charles," Aileen demanded, "Tell these overgrown baboons that they have no right to track me." To which her husband only shrugged.

"For the love of God," Aileen threw her hands up, "to think that I missed you two."

Charles, as calm as ever, put his hands up in front of his chest. "I love you, which was why I went along with your wishes, but I did warn you that there would be consequences." He then pointed one finger at Coll and one at Thomas and said, "Meet your consequences."

After a few more minutes, Jonathan and Mags poured themselves drinks and sat at the large kitchen table with Lochlann and Laith, both young boys had managed to stare at him with looks of distrust while still watching their parents' reunion with Charles and Aileen. Mirren, Mags' sister, wouldn't be there until the morning.

After half an hour, Coll and Thomas stepped away from the women and made eye contact with Jonathan. He prayed his face remained impassive—Coll Barr and Thomas MacGregor were intense sonofabitches.

Without breaking the stare-off, MacGregor asked Margaret, "How long have you and O'Faolain dated?"

Unperturbed by the accusatory tone, she grinned and linked her hand with the hand Jonathan had resting on the tabletop. "Not long. We're very serious, however."

Jonathan barely swallowed his groan. She was baiting them.

"Gray and Blair never told their mothers," Coll growled.

"I asked them not to. Surprise!"

Christ Almighty.

"Patrick didn't call us," Coll continued, his frown growing deeper if that was possible.

"We only just shared the news, and Dad knew I was joining Mags this weekend. I'm sure he thought, as two adults, Mags and I could handle sharing the news on our own." Jonathan let a hint of his irritation sound in his reply. He wasn't some pimply teenager for crying out loud.

Attempting to divert the interrogation, he glanced at Lochlann and Laith. "Ciar asked if you two were still coming to stay in Dublin over the Christmas holiday this year." Before the boys could answer, he added, "He also wanted you to know, Lochlann, that Gray was looking forward to it."

Jonathan had to bite his lip to keep from laughing. Neither boy looked thrilled to spend some of their holiday in a home with two small children, but at the mention of Loch's big sister, it was clear the boy would give in, which meant his best friend would as well.

Sighing in defeat, Lochlann crossed his arms over his chest in irritation, not unlike his father, but said, "We are."

"Where do you plan on sleeping for the next two nights? Coll and I have space for you." Clearly, there was no side-tracking the men in Mags' family.

Mags didn't let him answer. "Thank you for the offer, but Jon and I sleep together."

Fuck my life. Did Mags want him to get his ass beaten?

"Charles," MacGregor barked, "surely you don't mean to let your young daughter sleep in the same bed with a man. In your house."

Before her dad could intervene, Mags shot back with "Gray is less than a year older than me and has two children. I hardly think you're in a position to cast disparagements. Also, you aren't my father. *My* father doesn't mind."

"Oh shit," Josephine muttered.

"Mirren is my daughter as much as she's Charles', which means you're partly mine too." The big man swung his head to Charles. "Isn't that right?"

Charles, always the peacemaker, said, "You are Mirren's father as much as I am, of course, Thomas, and Margaret has always been fortunate to have you as well. And Mags, I do mind. Very much. However, once we're home, if both of you can convince me that this is permanent, for both of you, then you'll have my blessing."

Everyone remained silent for a moment. Charles may not bark or bite, but he wasn't a pushover either.

Clearly, the evenings gauntlet wasn't over yet.

Mags looked startled by her father's decree, saying quietly, "Of course, Dad."

Somewhat mollified, Thomas lifted his brows in an "I told you so" move to which Jonathan had to squelch any hint of amusement, well used to close-knit families and their antics.

Charles cleared his throat and gave him and Mags an amused smile before announcing, "I forgot to mention that I met with a Netflix representative a few weeks ago. It seems they are interested in turning my historicals into a miniseries.

"I have to fly back in a few months when I finish the second book to meet with them again."

And just like that, mine and Mags' sleeping arrangements,

as well as Aileen's cancer subterfuge, were forgotten amidst the shouts, screams, and congratulations.

Charles Morrow was a smart sonofabitch. He'd been saving that nugget for just the right moment.

An hour later, they were bundled into the back of Charles' Land Rover. Jonathan couldn't help tugging on the neck of his shirt, wondering what "convincing" Charles might entail and disappointed that the one man capable of shredding tension wouldn't be coming to his rescue again.

thirty-eight

MAGS

MAGS PUT on a cheerful face for the drive home, but inside, she was reeling. The moment her dad had announced that he wasn't fine with her and Jonathan sleeping together, her world had tilted ever so slightly off its axis.

She couldn't place her finger on exactly what her father's tone of voice had broadcast. It definitely wasn't anger or disappointment but... She bit her lower lip, intent on unearthing the serious note that had been unmistakable.

Sensing her mood, Jonathan brought one of her hands to his mouth and kissed her knuckles. "Stop worrying, Mags," he whispered in her ear. "If your dad isn't satisfied with our answers tonight, then we keep trying until he is. Not sleeping in the same room doesn't make us any less together."

She let out a shuddering breath but nodded. He was right, and this level of insecurity didn't suit her. She may not be the smoothest talker, but what she did have was mettle. She wouldn't flatten under pressure. She might explode, but she wouldn't back down, especially when it was something as important as her feelings for Jonathan.

Not that she had shared those feelings with him. Or him with her.

Perhaps her unease stemmed from not knowing what Jonathan's answers would be to her father's questions. Hell, she didn't know what her answers were going to be.

Sighing internally, Mags knew exactly how she felt. Her indecision was whether or not she'd be truthful. Or would the truth scare Jonathan?

They were so new, and she was cautious.

Perhaps too cautious. "You're right. We'll figure it out."

"Together," he said with enough conviction that Mags' chest warmed.

Firming her resolve, she made up her mind to face this family moment as she had all other obstacles, which calmed her nerves.

Once they were seated on the living room's comfy couches, her dad handed out drinks, water all the way around for the tired group. He sat forward, her mom by his side. "I understand that your mom and I have been gone for a while, so I'd like to know when you two...started things," he said, choking a bit on the last words.

Right to it then. Mags glanced at Jonathan, who took the hint and answered. "We've only been officially dating for a few weeks. It took a while to convince your daughter to trust me."

Mags winced. Her dad was a researcher, and trust, or the lack thereof, was just the type of rabbit hole he would enjoy digging in.

"Why wouldn't she trust you?"

She hated being right.

Jonathan winced, but Mags knew him well enough to know that he would never be anything but a hundred percent honest.

"I hurt Mags at a New Year's Eve party almost three years ago."

Her mom's eyes widened, but her dad looked furious. "What the hell do you mean you hurt her? Physically?"

That put Mags' back up. "Christ, Dad. I expect chest-beating and jumping to conclusions from Uncle Colly and Thomas, but not from you. You owe Jon an apology for even thinking he would raise a hand against me, let alone saying it out loud." She was so angry her body vibrated with it. Jonathan put a hand on her leg in an attempt to calm her. *Good fucking luck.*

As quickly as the anger had come, it flowed out of her dad. He shook his head and rubbed his face roughly. "Margaret is right. I apologize, Jonathan. I didn't think it was violence, but I did jump to...I don't know, unwanted sexual advances, which is just as bad. I'm truly sorry.

"I wouldn't change being with your mother these past few months. Not for anything. However, I find myself out of sorts. Being so far from my girls has been hard. Hearing that you've started a new business, live with a man I've never met, have a new boyfriend, and that there might be a delusional killer after one or both of my children is a lot to take in."

Her mom put an arm around her husband and hugged him tight to her side. "I'm sorry, Charles. I asked a lot of you, and by not telling our family, I made you shoulder my treatments alone."

Several tears streaked down her mom's face, gutting Mags and her father if the sick look on his face was any indication.

"Aileen," her dad said softly, forcing her chin up to meet his eyes. "Where you go, I go. Nothing less. Don't insult our marriage by indicating that supporting you isn't my top priority. Is that clear?"

In a watery voice, her mom answered, "It is."

He nodded but kept his arm tightly around his wife. "The conduct I've exhibited this evening, Jonathan, is regrettable and doesn't reflect my usual character. The truth is, I feel like Margaret grew up, and I missed it. It's a father's regret and probably not an unusual one.

"But back to my original inquiry, how did you hurt my daughter?"

Jonathan had stayed quiet while her parents hashed out their feelings, but the spotlight was back on him. He sat forward, squeezing her leg once more before folding his hands at his knees.

"I kissed Mags during the New Year's countdown almost three years ago. I knew she liked me, and I liked her even though she was a few months shy of eighteen. I knew I'd screwed up by seeking her out, and like an idiot, I tried to make her believe that our kiss meant nothing and immediately left her side to kiss someone else.

"I regretted it immediately, but the damage was done. She's barely tolerated me since, wrecked an ungodly number of my dates, and enjoyed using her sharp tongue to flay me. Well, up until I begged her to give me another chance."

Her parents found his retelling amusing. "Traitors," she muttered. That made them laugh harder.

Her mom sat straighter, adjusting her scarf. "Do you love each other? That's really all your dad and I care about."

Mags's mouth went dry. Her lips stuck to her teeth, making her resemble a dog begging for treats. "That is an extremely private question," Mags replied, a chiding tone in place.

"No more personal than my youngest daughter sleeping with a man she's only been dating a few weeks and under my roof." Her dad wasn't angry, but his typical good-natured smile was absent.

Matching her father's serious mien, Mags made sure to

meet her parents' eyes straight on. "Jon and I haven't discussed our feelings to that extent." She made the mistake of looking left. Jonathan was frowning.

"We haven't discussed our feelings, but that doesn't mean we don't have them. I have them," Jonathan declared.

It was Mags' turn for widened eyes and a slackened jaw. Did he mean...was he admitting...?

Completely ignoring her parents, Jonathan twisted on the couch to face her. "Don't you have feelings, Mags? For me."

She'd been wanting this, to know exactly how he was feeling, but he hadn't said anything specific yet. "I do." There. Committed yet noncommittal.

If anything, his frown grew more pronounced in response to her answer while the moonlight accentuated the creases on his face, setting off both his white hair and the amber tones of his eyes. Her heart momentarily faltered before racing uncontrollably in her chest.

They could have been on a deserted island or a crowded London street—or in her childhood home sitting across from her parents—and it wouldn't have mattered. They were locked in a battle of wills. The question was, did it matter who said I love you first?

Jonathan made the question moot. Without hesitation, he took both her hands and held them between their knees. "I should have told you before now, but I've been afraid. I love you, Mags.

Well. Well then. That simplified things. "I love you too... have loved you for years."

Her parents stood and announced they were off to bed. She and Jonathan never took their eyes from one another.

"That's good."

"Very good," she replied just as evenly.

The house was quiet in that fragile, late-night way that made every small sound feel amplified.

The lamp in the corner of the living room cast a low amber glow over the couch where Jonathan and Mags sat sideways, knee to knee. Upstairs, a floorboard creaked once, then settled. Her parents' bedroom door had clicked shut several minutes ago.

Still, neither of them had moved.

Jonathan's white hair caught the warm light, almost silver against the dim room. His amber eyes flicked toward the hallway, then back to her. "I can't believe you love me, that you still love after all the bullshit," he murmured.

Mags huffed a quiet laugh, her bright hazel eyes sparkling. "No one's more surprised than me," she teased.

"I want us to live together." His voice dropped. "I don't want to be apart, and I would rather not sleep at Eze's."

She shifted slightly until their thighs were touching. The contact felt louder than it should have. Heat slid through her stomach.

"You're nervous," she teased.

"I'm in your parents' house," he replied, gaze steady on hers. "That seems like an appropriate response, especially since I want them to like me."

Her smile softened. "They're asleep or on their way."

"Mm." His hand rested on the couch cushion near hers, close but not touching. "That's not the reassuring detail you think it is."

The air between them thickened, charged. She could feel the warmth radiating from him. Feel the way he was holding himself back. She had no plan to abstain. His admitting that he loved her had made her want him desperately. She wanted the words again while he took her body.

"You're thinking too much."

"And you," he said quietly, "aren't thinking enough. We can surely wait until we're back in Dublin."

But his hand moved.

Slowly.

His fingers brushed hers—just barely. A question. A warning.

She didn't pull away.

Instead, she slid her hand over his, lacing their fingers together. "You know, I'm not good with waiting," she whispered.

The shift in him was immediate.

Jonathan's jaw tightened, amber eyes darkening as he leaned closer. His free hand came up, brushing a loose wave of brown hair away from her face. His knuckles skimmed her cheek, then lingered.

"You're going to get me in trouble," he said softly.

Mags' lips curved. "With who?"

"We might have satisfied your parents' questions tonight, but that doesn't mean they'd appreciate us christening their couch." His jaw tightened when she slid her hand high on his thigh. "Mags," he groaned, "you're making this hard."

She brushed her fingertips against his quickly swelling sex. "I can tell."

"Let's at least go to your room. Babe," he gritted as her palm fitted flush against his fly.

And then he kissed her.

It wasn't rushed. It wasn't careless. It was slow and deliberate—Jonathan's mouth warm against hers, testing, deepening when she sighed into him. Mags' fingers tightened in his shirt, pulling him closer. The kiss turned hungry in seconds, restraint unraveling thread by thread.

His hand slid to her waist, thumb grazing the curve of her hip beneath her shirt. She gasped softly, and both of them froze.

Silence.

They listened.

Nothing but the hum of the refrigerator and the distant ticking of the hallway clock.

Jonathan exhaled against her lips. "Still time to stop."

"Do you want to?" she asked.

His answer was another kiss—deeper now, his hand slipping beneath the hem of her shirt, palm warm against bare skin. Her breath hitched as his fingers traced upward along her spine.

She shifted onto his lap without breaking the kiss, straddling him carefully. The couch dipped beneath their combined weight, springs creaking faintly.

They both stilled again.

Jonathan pressed his forehead to hers, fighting a grin. "That's not subtle."

"You're the one who said stop thinking."

A quiet laugh left him, low and rough. "I believe you have that backwards." His hands settled on her hips, firm now, guiding her closer. She could feel how much he wanted her. The realization sent heat rushing through her.

"Mags," he murmured, thumb brushing beneath the edge of her waistband. A question again.

She nodded.

His restraint snapped.

The kisses turned desperate, open-mouthed, breathless. He trailed his mouth along her jaw, down the curve of her neck, drawing a soft moan from her that she quickly smothered against his shoulder. His hands moved with growing confidence—exploring, memorizing, pulling her body flush against his.

Fabric shifted. Buttons slipped free. Her fingers tangled in his white hair as he lifted her slightly, positioning her more securely against him. The couch gave another small creak that made them both freeze—then laugh quietly, breathless with nerves and adrenaline.

"Your parents are going to hear," he whispered against her skin.

"Trust me, we're better off out here. My room and my parents' room share vents. I grew up blaring music or a fan at night," she whispered back.

His amber eyes met hers, an incredulous shake of his head, before he clasped her face, a hungry predator hovered close.

"God, I love when you look at me like that," she breathed.

That was what undid him.

He moved carefully but decisively, lowering her back against the couch cushions, bracing himself above her.

Their movements were quiet but intense, gasps swallowed into skin, fingers gripping tight. The world narrowed to the sound of their breathing, the brush of skin against skin, the careful rhythm they found together.

When he finally joined with her, it was slow—measured, eyes locked on hers. She clutched his shoulders, trying not to cry out as pleasure rolled through her in waves.

He kissed her to muffle the sound.

The couch shifted beneath them in a steady, restrained rhythm. Every small creak made their hearts race faster, made the moment sharper, more electric. The risk of being overheard shrank underneath the way her body responded to his.

"Mags..." he breathed, voice rough and unsteady.

"I'm here," she whispered back, fingers digging into his back as she met his movements.

It built and built and built until restraint dissolved completely. She bit down on his shoulder to keep from moaning too loud as she shattered beneath him. He followed seconds later, burying his face against her neck to stifle his own sound.

And then—

Silence.

The house remained undisturbed.

They stayed tangled together on the couch, breathing hard, hearts hammering.

Jonathan lifted his head, hair falling into his eyes. "We are never doing that here again."

Mags smiled lazily up at him, hazel eyes glowing. "You say that now."

He laughed quietly, pressing one last slow kiss to her lips.

Upstairs, a floorboard creaked again.

They both froze.

"Okay," he muttered, "we are definitely never doing that here again."

Mags spent the short flight from Inverness to Dublin reminiscing over the weekend. The cookout was a lot of fun. Josephine and Catriona fussed over her mom, and even though Mags knew her mom would have preferred to brush the whole cancer scare under the rug, she knew her best friends had every right to express their feelings.

Even though it hadn't been that long since she'd hung out with her sister, Mirren, it had been amazing to enjoy each other's company without their mom's health looming so large over their heads.

There were no more sightings of the crazy artist from Edinburgh, though the family was still taking the threat seriously. The video surveillance outside the museum had shown Jina speaking to a woman with a large, angled hat, but the woman's face had been obscured, the angle always just slightly off.

"I spoke to MacGregor, Barr, and your father. I told them

that we wanted to move in together," Jonathan said matter-of-factly as the plane began its descent. He did have the humility to grimace before tacking on "I may have taken a bit of license with your wants."

Mags patted his knee closest to her. "You took a bit of license with your life, babe. Of course, I want us together. What did the guys say?"

Jonathan chuckled and shook his head. "Your uncle and MacGregor were so angry they couldn't make their jaws unhinge, which I'm thankful for, but your dad wasn't opposed; he only wanted us to wait to make any big changes until after that crazy woman is found. I completely understand, but we can still start planning in the meantime. I had some ideas," he threw out, pretending a nonchalance he didn't own.

"Oh, really? And what exactly are your ideas?" Mags asked, nudging his side.

"Only if you approve," he started, "and I'm open to suggestions."

Mags felt excitement bubbling up from her stomach. The fact that Jonathan had put so much thought into their future was intoxicating. "I'm listening."

"I thought I might ask Daniel if he would find another place to live. Well, Blair, too, but I would rent her a place anywhere in the city, no problem. I thought you might enjoy redecorating one of the townhouses as our home, and the connected townhouse could be your business.

"Women, and men, of course, could have a space to come for fittings and whatever else is necessary for your embroidery."

Mags stayed silent for several minutes, through the flight attendant's 'prepare for landing' speech and the final trash collection.

And then, heart bursting, she said, "That's brilliant."

thirty-nine

HANNAH

"OKAY, HANNAH," the nurse announced briskly, "this won't hurt. Just a small prick on the end of your finger."

The woman's bedside manner left little to be desired. Of course, Hannah's expectations were low, having lived through the nightmare of a waiting room in the shitty medical clinic she'd found online. They accepted uninsured patients as long as they paid with cash up front.

She'd come down with something the evening after she'd spied Mirren's sister at the pub, which meant she hadn't felt well enough to pay the girl's attic workshop a visit while she was out of town. A perfect opportunity ruined.

And the voices hadn't let up once about her inadequacies since.

Why would we? As if you weren't disgusting enough, you went and got swollen balls over your neck and surrounding your fat, filthy minge.

Hannah winced at the vulgar image. It was true, though. She thought it was just a cold until her lymph nodes in her neck and groin area popped up. Still... "It could still be just a cold," she mumbled.

The nurse, thinking Hannah was speaking to her, said: "One would think, except for the number of swollen lymph nodes combined with a fever, stomach rash, and oral thrush."

"Yes, but—" Hannah began to downplay the current situation when the nurse interrupted.

"You've admitted to unprotected sex. I know you're frightened, but you need to prepare yourself for the possibility of a positive HIV test."

Swallowing a moan of sickened dread, the nurse took that moment to prick her finger. The small sting created a well of blood to pool.

"This is a simple, rapid test. I'll let you know the results within twenty to thirty minutes." She opened the door with a "Sit tight" thrown over her shoulder.

Hannah sighed and leaned her back against the plastic chair's back. This was an absolute nightmare. She only had a few loose ends to tie up after she made Mirren's little sister pay, which would be way worse than if she'd done something to Mirren personally.

She was supposed to work on gathering more funds and finding a sunny beach somewhere to live out the rest of her life.

HIV positive—the insult of it all.

I bet it was that unfortunate time you blew that homeless drug addict while his equally disgusting back-alley buddy took your back hole.

If only you could have seen how pathetic you looked, screaming in pain around the man's filthy dick.

We made you stay still.

Froze your body like a broken elevator.

I bet your ass blood and his spit were the perfect HIV incubator, wasn't it slut?

Did you know that happened—that someone took you there?

Hannah clenched her jaw and kept her eyes closed. Appearing weak would not help her cause. Of course, she'd known that she'd been hurt. She'd been sore for days, which was probably when her body had enjoyed incubating the disease—if that's what she had.

Her health was in the shitter. Add her current problem to the already declining state of her body, and her diminishing funds...she was well and truly fucked. Her family would jump ship if she faltered worse than she already had.

She needed to prove that she still had something they found amusing or worth their time. Violence and blood would prevail.

As the Americans so liked to shout from the tallest building, "Fuck around and find out." The voices would find out she still was worth their time. Hannah Todd or Hannah Keels, rather, still had some life left in her.

The nurse breezed in holding a piece of paper. "Test results are positive, I'm afraid."

Fuck my life.

Fuck our lives.

Fuck this diseased bitch.

"I'm not done yet," she whispered.

forty

MAGS

"I GOT two more of my pieces delivered to clients this afternoon. I'm not gonna lie, making money for my embroidery will never get old," Mags told Jonathan, who was on speaker phone as she dashed around her bathroom getting dolled up for the Chamber event at Gray Eyes that evening.

"You deserve the success. You work so hard, and you're so talented. I'm proud of you," Jonathan told her.

Mags glanced at herself in the mirror, seeing the soft look in her eyes. She was so far gone for that man.

"You earned a kiss for that," she teased.

He snorted before coming back with, "I don't have to earn your affection. You want my mouth and a whole lot more than that, touching you every chance you can."

"Which is why I'm glad you aren't here while I'm getting dressed. I want to look stunning without the orgasm afterglow."

"Why? It's your best look. Hang on, Dan's yelling for me."

Mags heard muted voices and laughter before Jonathan

resumed the call. "I'm back. He needed my signature on a couple of documents from our meeting earlier today. Now, where were we? Oh, right, we were discussing all the orgasms I'm going to give you later. Ouch," Jonathan barked.

"What happened?"

"Daniel hit me and told me to get out of his room, the prick. Just because he's celibate doesn't mean I am."

"Speaking of, Ciar might be joining the celibate club, just not by choice," Mags chuckled.

"Do tell. I love nothing more than gossip about that big, Russian ass."

"Ciar's just as much Irish as Russian," Mags defended.

"Yeah, but he gets all his prickish ways from his Russian side. I'm all Irish and don't act anything like him," Jonathan sniffed over the phone like a priss.

"Need I remind you that you are actually three-quarters American, and your arrogant pride proves it. Blair and I are one hundred percent Scottish, and you don't see us yammering on about it."

"You just did, but fine. Now tell me what Ciar did so I can make fun of him tonight."

She shook her head in exasperation, even though he couldn't see her. "Gray called right before you did. When she modeled the dress she was wearing tonight, which is stunning by the way, Ciar asked her if she thought it might be a little revealing for a mother of two small children."

"Christ," Jonathan swore. He wasn't married or a father, but he knew how out of line that was. "I'm not defending him—"

"I should hope not," Mags cut in.

"Not his finest moment, true, but you and I both know that Gray is stunning inside and out, right?"

"Damn straight, she is," Mags huffed.

"Have you, or Gray, for that matter, considered that he

knows that there will be a ton of men at the party, and he doesn't want any of them to see his wife in something that makes her look more gorgeous than she already is?"

Mags tapped her upper lip thoughtfully. "I hate when you're right."

Laughing, he said, "Better text Gray and tell her to let Ciar explain his stupid comment. He does have a point, though. What are you wearing?"

Mags, Mirren, and their mother had gone shopping after the cookout last weekend at one of her favorite secondhand designer-clothing stores. It had a few tears where the rings held the fabric together and a stain on the hem, but it fit her like a glove and—hello—she was pretty handy with a needle.

"A long black dress. The neckline barely shows my collarbone, and the hem brushes my ankles." If she purposely left out that the dress hugged her body like a second skin and that the sides, from below her armpit to the floor, were held together with beautiful gold rings, showing a perfect amount of creamy, white flesh and side boob, well, it was a simple oversight. Surely.

"That dress should be fucking illegal, Mags," Jonathan growled in her ear while they were ushered into Gray Eyes.

He had her practically surgically sewn to his side, probably trying to hide some of her body, but it wasn't like she didn't have two sides. When he picked her up at Eze's, it had been extremely satisfying to watch his eyes nearly pop from his head.

He twirled her around in the lobby before backing her against a column and kissing her senseless, the doormen be damned.

That had been thirty minutes ago, and since then and now,

he'd asked her no less than forty times if she was sure she wouldn't be too cold.

After he asked the last time, and she snarled, "I don't know, Ciar, do you think I'll be too cold?" he accepted defeat and became her new trench coat.

They saw their friends gathered at one of the back bars and waved, but before they could join them, Jonathan stopped walking, and since they were literally joined at the hip, she stopped too.

He touched her cheek gently. "I'm sorry for being such an ass, Mags. You're stunning. I'm proud that you're mine. I just want to pummel every shady little shit that looks at you like I do."

Mags' posture relaxed. "No one looks at me like you do, Jon, and if they do, I'd never notice. I love you."

"I love you, too, but if you tell Gray about this, I will spank your ass until you can't sit down."

Mags grinned as they started walking again. "I'm afraid your punishment just makes me want to tell her even more." She giggled when he cursed.

The cocktail hour had been all about mingling and meeting other business owners. She vowed to herself that eventually she would be successful enough to speak at one of these illustrious events.

Normally, an O'Faolain would speak at an event like this, especially given all the philanthropic ventures the family undertook for the Dublin community and surrounding villages, but since Hugh's passing, his sons and grandsons had taken a step back. Everyone knew them, respected and even feared them if they happened to want the same business or property one of the 'Wolves' wanted, but foremost, they were respected.

Mags and Jonathan were about to follow their group to the tables set up for that night's event when a beautiful blonde, taller than Christ in 6-inch stilettos and hair braided and bedazzled enough to be seen from Heaven.

Fine. That might have been an exaggeration. She was tall and runway-ready, though, with a supercilious expression sucking in her already sunken cheeks.

The negative opinion formed the second she stepped between her and Jonathan, turning her slender back to Mags' face.

"Jonathan O'Faolain," she purred like a fat cat hacking up a hairball. "I haven't seen you in weeks."

Weeks. Not months.

Mags had to blink rapidly to expel the red shell of fury trying to cover her eyes. *Wait for an explanation, Mags.*

"We were supposed to go to Aspen, and you never called me back." Pouty voice engaged. "I bought six more pairs of your favorite lace panties that you enjoy ripping off me so much."

Mags was about to step around the stilt walker and excuse herself with as much dignity as she could drum up when the woman stepped closer to Jonathan.

"Say you'll come by my place tonight. My sister's in town, and the three of us had so much fun together last time."

"Sorry, Deirdre, not tonight. I'm busy."

And that was all she could handle. *Not tonight. I'm busy! He should have said, I'm in a relationship, or I'm never going to your place again.*

Furious now, Mags sidestepped the woman until she could see Jonathan. Granted, he looked furious. Unfortunately for him and their relationship, his words didn't match his face.

He swallowed firmly when their eyes met. "I'm going to go grab a seat with my friends." Emphasis on "my."

He was quick to grab her elbow, and had they not been at an important event, she would have used that elbow to thump him in the ribs.

"I'll take you," he declared before turning to his ex-what-ever. "I should have mentioned before, but I'm exclusively dating Mags now—forever, I hope. My past is very much staying there. Good evening."

His declaration should have soothed Mags' ruffled feathers. He eventually made it right, but one minute or an hour later was still too late. He should have announced to the woman exactly who was standing behind her. He should never have let her stand at any woman's back.

Mags didn't bother to look at the lady again, even when she huffed and parted with, "Whatever."

As they pulled away, Jonathan slowed. "Mags. Please let me—"

"Explain? No need. You already threw out a couple of good explanations. You're busy *tonight*, was my favorite. Plus, the back of her dress is lovely. I got to study it for a while."

"Jesus, Mags, please. I was thrown. Seeing someone that I'd slept with while we're basically on our first date was bad enough, but then she brought up...specifics. I froze, and not because I was tempted. She means nothing to me and vice versa. It was only sex, I swear it. I froze because my past was hurting you again.

"You had to listen to those things, and I hated it. Please say you forgive me. If something like that happens again, and I hope like hell it doesn't, I swear I'll handle it better. Tell me I haven't ruined the whole evening," he begged.

Mags had already softened once she heard the sincerity in his voice, and even though she wasn't completely over it—hello, threesome—she patted his arm and attempted a smile. After all, the likelihood of running into one of his exes had been a matter of when, not if. It happened. She needed to Google how to bleach the last few minutes from her memories and move on.

When she started to move, he clasped her fingers and flattened them against his chest. "I love you, Mags."

"I know. Perhaps start with that next time a woman solicits you." She raised her brows and tilted her head, but the smile that curled her lips was genuine, and Jonathan smiled too.

"I'll do that, brat." He tugged her toward their table, where their friends were already eating appetizers.

For the next hour and a half, she and her friends enjoyed good food and amazing Chamber speakers. It was a packed house, and the only seats left at their table were across from one another. The good news was that Mags had been able to drive Jonathan wild with her bare feet under the table. His looks of retribution sent burning anticipation through her body.

At the end of the evening, their small group decided to have one more drink to celebrate the great evening before they paired off for home. Ciar and Gray would go home to their two children, Dagr and Bébhinn, to snuggle her precious baby bump, Daniel would escort Blair back to the twin townhouses, and Jonathan would come home with her to Eze's.

She and Blair followed the group, deep in conversation about the possibility of her accepting an offer to pursue a plant pathology PhD from Oklahoma State University in the States, as they snaked their way through the crowd, heading to the same bar they'd started the evening, when she heard a man calling her name.

Mags tapped Blair's cheek to make sure she would look at her face and mouthed an "Oh, shit. Rory." That was all she got out before a metaphorical bag of shit exploded over her head.

Rory, her tall, dark, and handsome 'casual partner,' hailed her from across the pub. Before she could so much as clutch her imagined pearls, Jonathan was at her side and waving at the man barreling toward them.

What the hell was this nightmare?

She locked eyes with Rory at the same time Jonathan stepped forward and clapped him hard on the back, as men are wont to do.

"Phipps," Jonathan exclaimed enthusiastically. Phipps was Rory's last name. "Good to see you, man. Well done on Silverton. Hell of a project, but that old man will be a trial to impress."

Rory grinned, his dimples creasing his lean cheeks. He glanced at me once more before focusing on Jonathan, returning her boyfriend's banter.

"Your firm should be thanking me personally for winning that bid, Jon. Silverton is," Rory hesitated, attempting professionalism, "worse than my partners and I imagined.

"Speaking of nightmares, I hear the O'Faolains are gearing up to open their own architectural firm. Tell me the rumors are just that."

"I'm afraid I'm not at liberty to say," Jonathan answered, his smirk totally giving him away.

If she weren't so paralyzed with fear of the inevitable outcome of this meeting, she would preen over how proud she was of Jonathan's accomplishments. He was a phenomenal architect because he was foremost an artist.

"Well," Rory started, putting the shadow of a swinging guillotine blade over her throat, "it was good to see you, man, but I'm afraid I'm here to see the woman who haunts my every thought and convince her to finally be mine."

Rory stepped around Jonathan and had his arms around her back before she could so much as blink. "Maggie," Rory growled against her lips.

forty-one

HANNAH

THE HIV MEDS hadn't done crap to make her feel better. The nurse said to give them a week. All Hannah wanted was to go to bed and stay there for a month. Her body ached, and she was past exhausted.

Despite her drooping eyelids—drooping everything, really—her body had a jittery unease that worsened by the hour, especially as midnight approached.

The voices were threatening to leave her again, but this time, something about their matter-of-fact attitudes was chilling and made her believe they meant it this time.

Diseased whore.

Ugly.

Ruined.

Talentless.

Fat.

Crone.

Their words echoed around her throbbing skull, making her wince and stumble on the uneven cobbles.

That was her life now, stumbling along. Wretched. A wretch.

Hannah felt her nose drip and tears sting her eyes as she continued the now familiar route to the workshop above the gallery.

Mirren's workspace…soon to be left in ruin. That thought alone was the only bright spot in her otherwise miserable life.

Her family, the voices, had initially wanted Hannah to destroy the space, focusing on razing the girl's current work projects and stock, but because she needed to impress them now more than ever, she suggested something bigger.

Grander.

Deadly.

We went with your idea, you stupid idiot, perhaps consider not bouncing the damn bomb off your fat, fucking hip.

I don't know… If she blows herself up, it's a win-win for us.

The second we're done here, you'd better waddle as fast as you can to a train heading to Edinburgh.

We need money, and let's be clear, you don't have a future on your back.

Hannah doesn't have a future on her feet.

Hannah pulled the bag containing the explosive secured in a box closer to her side, minimizing the danger. She convinced the voices that destroying Mirren's sister's work wasn't enough. That would only set her back. What was needed was destruction and pain. Blood.

Fortunately, Hannah had been spending enough time in Dublin's underworld of drugs and degradation that she heard of an ex-military drug runner who loved nothing more than building bombs. It had taken the rest of the money her dear old psychiatrist had gifted her. She had only enough for train and ferry fare. Needs must.

Her shoulders hunched further over her ears, the comments taking their pound of flesh as intended.

She would prove her worth tonight.

Set the bomb.

Travel to Edinburgh.

Take every coin her mother had managed to hoard during her miserable life.

Find a beach for her little family.

Make the voices proud.

Live.

forty-two

JONATHAN

THIS HAD TO BE A JOKE. Rory Phipps was Mags'...no. "No fucking way." Jonathan hadn't realized he said that out loud until Daniel stood at his shoulder, giving him a "What the hell" look.

Blair and Daniel were the only two of their group close enough to witness the bullshit. Blair's eyes were wide, and her lips were clearly mouthing "Shit" over and over again.

Jonathan's mind was reeling. He'd met Rory Phipps, along with other Dublin architects, a handful of times over the last few years. He had drinks with the motherfucker who had taken Mags' virginity—with the man who taught her all the things she now did for him.

No way was he going to let Rory Fucking Phipps touch his girlfriend another second. Clasping the top of Rory's shoulder, he yanked him back and away from Mags.

Rory lost his balance and stumbled into Jonathan, who now stood at his back. He didn't dare look at Mags, knowing she'd be pissed at the display.

Rory spun on his heel, eyes widening when he realized Jonathan was the perpetrator.

"What the hell, O'Faolain?" At the same time, he reached behind him and grasped Mags' hands.

Over his shoulder, that piece of shit, Rory said, "Maggie, love, go get a drink with Blair. I'll be right behind you once I figure out what the hell is going on."

Maggie love. If Jonathan wasn't seeing red already...

He did look at Mags then, and for her part, he was relieved to see that she was trying to shake off Rory's hand.

"Rory, I should have told—"

Like an ass, Jonathan interrupted her. "That she is mine and only mine. Touch her again, Phipps, and you'll find out architecture isn't the only thing I'm good at."

"What the hell is your problem?" Rory demanded.

"Jon," Mags said, frowning at him, probably hoping he wouldn't escalate things further. Not likely.

Rory looked from Mags to him and back again. "Maggie?" Rory turned his back to Jonathan, but before he could drag the man away from Mags again, Daniel stepped between them and put a restraining hand on his chest.

"Don't touch him again, Jon. Christ. People are starting to take notice. I doubt you want to impress our fathers with your mugshot in the Daily."

Jonathan forced himself to breathe deeply, allowing the ringing in his ears to fade. Mags was in the middle of explaining their relationship, which the prick didn't deserve. They were over. That's all he needed to know.

"I'm sorry, Rory, I should have reached out. Jon and I are dating. It's serious."

Mags sounded calm, but her fiery, red cheeks spoke of her internal chaos.

"But Maggie, I don't understand. I've wanted us to be serious from the beginning. You have to know that I lo—"

Mags threw up a hand between her and Rory. "Don't say it."

"Why not? You know it's true," he pleaded.

From the stunned look on Mags' face, she hadn't known, which soothed some of his anger, but not nearly enough to allow her ex...lover near her.

"You only said there was someone from your past that you weren't over. I thought...I hoped that eventually—"

Jonathan watched the man's shoulders stiffen. The bastard finally caught up.

"It's him? O'Faolain is who you've always wanted? Fuck me, Maggie. He's like a world-class whore. You deserve better."

Jonathan had spun Rory around before he was conscious of deciding to touch him. He leaned in so only those standing close could hear. "*Was* a whore, Phipps. I will never be that man again. And you're one to talk. You were never exclusive with her."

Hearing a man who was respected in Dublin call him a whore had acid churning in his stomach. It sickened him that others might have perceived him that way—that he might have actually been that way.

"I had two women besides Maggie in the very beginning. Two," he reiterated, poking Jonathan in the chest with his middle and pointer fingers. "I realized quickly that she was the only woman I wanted. It took me one month to figure that out. What did it take you? Two years? Three years?"

Despite his better judgment screaming at him to walk away and take Mags with him, he couldn't help the knee-jerk reaction to have the last word.

"I love Mags, and unlike with you, she loves me back. Don't ever approach her again, or you'll find out quickly why no one wants to go up against an O'Faolain." He leaned close so he could whisper in Rory's ear. "Talk to her again, touch her, contact her, and I will bury your business and leave your reputation in ashes."

When he straightened, Mags was looking at him in horror before she clenched her jaw and turned to Blair. She must have mouthed something to Blair so that she could read Mags' lips, knowing that if she signed, Jonathan would know what was said.

Mags gave him one last look. Her fury building with every heartbeat. His heart seized when her gaze landed on Rory, who was still stiffly standing at Jonathan's shoulder.

Don't speak to him, Mags. Please.

She only shook her head in defeat before whirling away and heading for the exit. Daniel's rough shove between his shoulder blades had him moving. He followed her, weaving between guests stepping outside right after her.

"Mags, please stop. Talk to me." Now that Rory Phipps was no longer a visual threat, he winced at his behavior, feeling chagrined by his loss of control. His family would not be impressed. Hell, he was disgusted.

Keeping her back to him, she said, "And why would I do that, Jon?"

The wobble in her voice killed him. She walked to the covered area where guests could wait for their rides out of the weather. Thankfully, only one other older couple was waiting, and a valet was hailing them, leaving him and Mags alone.

"I overreacted."

Silence.

"I embarrassed you," he tried again.

Nothing.

He fisted his hair and squeezed the back of his neck before letting his hands fall loosely at his sides.

"Mags."

"Enough," Mags finally said, her voice holding a finality he hadn't heard from her before. "I've put up with your women for years, Jon, years. A few of them have even made cutting remarks at my expense.

"You held them, touched them, kissed them—all in front of me. You've been very clear that you enjoyed your love-them-and-leave-them lifestyle. Hell, even tonight I had to listen to the woman talk about your threesome with her and her sister.

"Did I like hearing that? Hell no. Did I get in her face and threaten her? No, even though it took you a long moment to tell her you were in a relationship.

"And yet," she shook her head, still looking at the bustling road before her, "you disrespected Rory, my one and *only* lover before you. You disrespected me. If you believed we were exclusive, you would never have behaved the way you did tonight.

"I think you are projecting your feelings. I think you are struggling with only having one woman on your arm." She stopped abruptly. Her head bowed as her arms wrapped protectively around her waist. "I don't want to say anything I'll regret, so I'm going home. Without you. I need space."

Every word was a blow to his middle, curving his spine. Every verbal lash she wielded was deserved except for his level of commitment. His jealous display was childish, yes, but he trusted her, them, implicitly.

Did his actions tonight prove that? No.

"Please give me a chance to explain. Let me come with you." Her brittle stance was worrying. And then, because he was escalating to panic, he added, "You aren't supposed to travel alone."

Blair and Daniel stepped out of Gray Eyes at that moment. "I'm not," was all Mags said before walking away, leaving him to drown in regrets.

forty-three

JONATHAN

JONATHAN HAD COME to understand that his anger over Mags' connection with Rory came from a far less comfortable place than he'd first assumed.

It wasn't about trusting her—he did. Completely. Mags had never been careless with people's feelings, never disloyal, never anything less than steady and sure in who she was.

It had everything to do with him. He felt inadequate. He had been disloyal to Mags for years. Jonathan couldn't believe she wouldn't regret giving him a chance because the truth was, he didn't deserve it.

His bad behavior stemmed from fear.

After sitting up all night in the quiet of his living room, contemplating his shit behavior, reliving a montage of his worst moments, he had come to a conclusion. He wouldn't let last night dictate their future. He would apologize, grovel, whatever it would take.

With that in mind, he walked to his bedroom, stripped last

night's clothes from his body, showered, and dressed as quickly as possible, and drove to Eze's flat.

Jol, the housekeeper, answered the early morning bell. He might have felt bad about the hour, but he knew from staying over that Eze was an early riser.

Mags, on the other hand, would have her head burrowed under a mound of pillows to keep even a hint of light from penetrating her lids.

Jol allowed him to come in, giving him a brief frown when she left him in the kitchen while she went to get the man of the house.

As expected, Eze was dressed and carrying a briefcase, clearly about to leave for the university, with Nasir walking several paces behind his employer before quietly taking up space against a wall where he could face Jonathan.

It looked like Jol wasn't the only person in the household annoyed with Jonathan, if Nasir's scowl was any indication. Undoubtedly, Mags had thoroughly won over the Nigerian security guard.

"What brings you, Jonathan?" Eze asked.

Jonathan took a fortifying breath before answering. "I would like to speak to Mags."

Eze's expression didn't change, only raising one brow in question as he accepted a cup of tea from Jol.

He forced himself to continue even though Eze was not happy. "Mags and I had a bit of a misunderstanding last night, and I would like to rectify that."

"You and Margaret are both quite articulate in expressing yourselves. A misunderstanding?" Eze's deep voice held a hint of disbelief.

Nosey asshole.

"I fucked up and want to apologize," Jonathan growled back.

"I see. She's in her room. Abeo will drive me this morning. Nasir will wait to take Margaret to work." With that, Mags' friend set his tea down and left.

Without hesitation, Jonathan headed to Mags' room. Before he could round the corner to the hallway where the bedrooms lay, Nasir said in his stiff, condescending way, "Miss Morrow's eyes were red-rimmed last night."

Jonathan barely kept himself from flinching. Eze's and Nasir's disapproval made his nerves jangling worse than ever, but it didn't matter. He wasn't turning around. He wasn't backing down.

His father had fought for his mother. Jonathan would do the same for Mags.

He didn't bother knocking. He knew she'd still be asleep—and if he was being honest, there was a good chance she wouldn't let him in if he gave her the choice.

Still, the moment he stepped inside and saw her, something in his chest eased.

Mags was curled into the bed like it was a nest, tangled in no fewer than ten pillows, with two fluffy ones framing her head like bookends. Her hair was a complete mess, strands sticking out in every direction.

A smile broke through his nerves before he could stop it.

God, he loved her.

He crossed the room quietly and sat on the edge of the mattress, careful not to jostle her too much. Reaching out, he tugged the top pillow out from under her head in one quick motion—like ripping off a Band-Aid.

At least, that was the hope.

"Why?" she croaked.

Her sleep roughened voice made him smile. "Mags. It's me." He knew the instant her sleepy brain realized who was sitting on her bed when her body stilled and stiffened.

Mags knocked off the rest of the pillows and blanket wrapped about her head and upper body, sitting up slowly and turning to face him.

She didn't respond right away. Instead, she shifted back, putting space between them until her shoulders met the headboard. Her arms crossed over her chest, a clear barrier, even as the movement subtly changed the line of her body beneath the soft fabric of her sleep tank.

Jonathan noticed.

Of course he did.

And just as quickly, he forced his gaze upward, locking onto her face instead.

Jonathan cleared his throat and shifted nervously on the mattress. There was nothing for it but to start.

Her feet were the closest part of her to him, so he wrapped one hand around her foot, needing to be touching her, connected in any way he could.

"I spent the night reflecting on my reaction to meeting Rory —well, I already knew him," he corrected, "but not as the man who…that you… had a relationship with.

"He wasn't a one-night stand, Mags, and even though you said you never loved him, there had to be some feelings on your side. That is the realization that came to me when he was professing his feelings towards you.

"I felt like I'd been stabbed, robbed of something essential. I wish I'd been your first," he moved up the bed so he could cup her cheeks and look directly in her eyes, "for everything. Everything! And I fucked that up. I wasn't there, and you gave your firsts to him.

"I lost it. My brain, my fucking common sense, abandoned me. There is no excuse. I did this to us. I don't have the right to feel hurt or wounded or whatever," he waved his hand in front of his face, "but I am. I was."

"Not anymore?" she asked softly, the first time she'd spoken since he'd started.

"I am." He exhaled heavily, relieved to admit that. "I also know I love you, and you love me. You're committed to me, and no one is more loyal than you, Margaret Morrow.

"I was up all night regretting my part in hurting you—regretting a whole shitload of things really. The truth is, Rory's been the better man to you for a long time. I panicked when I realized you had every right to pick him over me."

When she looked like she would argue, he quickly added, "But then I remembered you love me. You already chose me, and I acted like an ass for no reason.

"Tell me that we can put it behind us, and I'll promise to never...well, maybe not never, but I promise to try not to get jealous. No," he shook his head, "that's not right either. I promise that when I do get jealous, I'll try not to let it show."

Mags snorted in amusement and used her knee to bat his side. "That promise got weaker by the second," she grinned, "but I accept your apology because I love you even when you're an ass. Before you start patting yourself on the back for your half-assed apology, you need to know that I will be contacting Rory and apologizing. Not just for last night but for not contacting him sooner and telling him that he and I are finished."

He felt the ugly burn of jealousy wash over him. So much for turning over a new leaf. "We'll go together."

"Absolutely not."

"I'm the one who needs to apologize." He didn't mention to Mags that he was still thinking of making Rory's firm uneasy for a while—after all, friendly competition was fair game.

All she said was, "O'Faolains—can't live with them, can't live without them."

Jonathan kneeled on the mattress, and before his intentions registered, he grasped her hips and yanked her toward him until she was flat on her back with him between her legs.

"How about I remind you why you want to live with me?" he asked, while simultaneously reaching for her tank and panty set. His left hand dragged her tank over her head while his right pulled her panties below her knees.

"Look at you, baby, so pretty and all mine." Seeing her bare breasts and sex had every part of his body hardening. He stood on the bed, his clothes joining hers on the floor in under five seconds.

Jonathan stood long enough to take in Mags' beautiful body sprawled below him. He let out a low breath as the morning light spilled across the rumpled sheets and over her skin. For a moment, he simply looked at her, so thankful that she'd forgiven him.

Margaret Morrow was a siren.

Not just for the obvious reasons, the curve of her waist, the sleepy warmth in her eyes, or the way her hair fanned across the pillow, but also the quiet familiarity of her. The way she watched him was like she already knew every thought crossing his mind.

He loved having her eyes on him. As she took in his physique, her teeth snagged her bottom lip. She followed his hand intently as he brushed over his abs to firmly grasp his erection, slowly stroking his length.

As her eyes traced him, her fingers began to lightly touch and swirl over her collarbones and between her breasts. It was his turn to be fascinated.

He kneeled between her spread thighs, his thumbs tracing slow circles along her hips, his sex desperate to sink into her body.

"See?" he murmured, voice rough with lust and love.

"You're already reconsidering that whole *can't live with them* idea."

Mags huffed a quiet, breathless laugh and sat up, her hands sliding up his arms until they rested around his shoulders. "You're ridiculously confident for someone who just broke into his girlfriend's flat before coffee. Very cocky, Mr. O'Faolain."

Jonathan leaned down, brushing his nose against hers.

He led one of her hands to his aching erection, moaning when she stroked him base to tip. Very, very cocky," he hissed.

Her fingers slipped into his hair, tugging just enough to make his chest tighten. The teasing spark in her eyes softened into something warmer, deeper—the look she only gave him after all the joking fell away.

"Jonathan," she said quietly.

The way she said his name did things to him. Always had.

His hand moved to her cheek, thumb stroking along her jaw before he kissed her—slow at first, unhurried, like the morning belonged only to them. The kiss deepened naturally, the kind that came from knowing someone completely. No hesitation. No second-guessing.

They were new and insatiable, but with their history, there was also comfortable familiarity and trust. And love.

Mags arched slightly against his chest, brushing her tight nipples over his skin. "Are you ready for me?" Jonathan asked before watching two of his fingers disappear inside her body, moaning as she moaned.

"You're wet, baby. I bet I can make you come all over my fingers. Should I try, Mags?" He asked, groaning as her hips started meeting his strokes faster and faster.

"Don't. Stop. Jon!" she screamed as her body bucked and pulsed, squeezed. He watched, amused, as she sighed in contentment and fell back on the mattress, groaning louder when his fingers slid out.

"It's not naptime yet, baby," Jonathan chuckled, bending over her lax body to kiss and bite at her neck, earning more satisfied sighs.

"You still with me?" he asked softly.

Her answering smile was lazy and certain.

"Always."

That was all he needed.

Jonathan gathered her closer, kissing her again as the quiet morning wrapped around them—the soft rustle of sheets, her laughter mixing with his, the sunlight creeping higher across the bed.

"Mmm," she whimpered as the kiss became more demanding, his length sliding insistently between her wet folds.

She turned her head to break the kiss, panting and demanded, "Roll us over, Jon. I think you've been in control long enough."

"Say no more." Burrowing his hands beneath her body, he fisted her ass tight and rolled. Her squeal of delight made him chuckle.

Once she was situated over his lap, her hot center driving him crazy as she shifted her hips up and down, enough to tease, she announced, "We're calling in sick today. I'm decreeing it." She raised her fists in the air and whooped in excitement, driving her further against his sex.

Grasping her hips to keep her still, he growled, "I'll call in sick for a week, baby, but for the love of God, let me in your body already. You're killing me."

She leaned down and placed a quick kiss on his lips, his neck, then his chest, flicking her tongue over his nipples.

"Mags," he groaned, running his fingers through her hair until he gripped a bunch of strands, trying to move her mouth back to his lips, but she shook him off.

Jonathan felt his abdominal muscles ripple and tense as she

kept the brush of her lips moving ever south over the ridges and planes of his stomach.

"You have a stunning body, Jon," she hummed against his V-line, swiping her tongue closer and closer to his sex, the head already rubbing her cheek.

"Mags, Christ, please," he begged.

Jonathan was so turned on that by the time her hot mouth closed around his length, he was a gasping fool.

His hand hovered above the back of her hand, wanting desperately to take control, but if he did that, the moment would be over before it'd barely begun, and this wasn't ending until he was deep inside her body.

"That's it, baby. Your mouth is heaven."

Minutes later, Jonathan was pulling Mags up his body, rolling them once more. He couldn't wait another moment before sliding home.

He pushed fully into her heat in one thrust, taking her mouth at the same time to swallow her scream.

He grinned against her lips, wondering how many times he could make her come during their vacation day.

"You have the best ideas, Mags," he panted as he pulled out as far as he could without leaving her warmth completely.

Mags gasped at his slow, friction-building in-and-out glide. "Christ, baby, you feel so good, it drives me insane."

Her gasps and groans punctuated the list she was reciting. "Sex. Coffee. Sex. Lunch. Sex. Shower. Sex. Work from bed. Sex. Dinner. Sex. Shower. Sleep. Morning sex."

"I love how your mind works."

forty-four

HANNAH

"NOTHING TO DO about the broken lock," Hannah murmured to herself, earning a wary look from the woman sitting next to her on the train. She had managed to jimmy the antique lock of Mirren's sister's attic workshop before and easily, but she must have jammed the screwdriver too hard last night.

There was a definite clank of broken metal when she'd used the palm of her hand to hammer the handle of the tool. The bruise was already turning purple and smarted when she tried to carry her travel pack.

We should have already been at your mom's, but you took too long at the girl's shop.

Then we had to listen to you puke your guts up all night.

And then, the second the puke dried on your crusty lips, you ordered a fucking pizza instead of packing your bag.

Diseased cow.

"The meds make me sick," she hissed the rejoinder, earning more nervous glances from her traveling neighbors.

She'd been forced to check into a dive motel near Busáras, wanting to be able to easily walk to the bus station the next day to buy a ticket.

Unfortunately, she only became more ill, her stomach emptying the hot, cheesy pizza she'd enjoyed way more going down than coming up.

By ten o'clock the following morning, she'd been forced to call the doctor's clinic she'd gone to for blood tests and beg them to call Hannah in some nausea medication to an apothecary near the bus station.

She'd then spent even more money to have them delivered to the motel, as well as paying a second driver to deliver some water and crackers to ease the vomiting.

She'd lain in the midst of the creaky bed's rumpled, dingy sheets throughout the rest of the day, listening to the voices mentally flay her.

Her hope was that the little bitch was already a bloody spray decorating the colorful embroidery floss and stacks of creamy cottons.

Maybe you wouldn't have worn your sloppy body out if you hadn't taken so long to plant the bomb.

Yes, she had been sick and tired after planting the bomb, but it wasn't like she learned how to rig a bomb at her fancy boarding school. The man she'd purchased the explosive from had given her rudimentary instructions at best.

What about the wasted time you spent picking out an embroidered memento?

Hannah felt her cheeks heat. The girl did make pretty things, and it had been a very long time since she'd owned anything so fine.

The bus seat was uncomfortable, and she pressed a hand to her distended belly. The usually soft paunch had grown larger and harder, resembling nothing short of a misshapen pregnancy.

She felt her mouth screw up in distaste, feeling when the voices took control of her facial muscles.

The nurse had assured her that the side effects of the HIV medicines would last only a few weeks.

Only.

She'd been living in hell for so long. What was a few more weeks?

Soon, she would be happy. Soon.

<h1 style="text-align:center">forty-five</h1>

COLL BARR

"THOMAS," Coll barked into the phone, "we got a hit."

Coll and Thomas' security firm had put feelers out on Hannah Todd since the moment the woman's mother contacted his niece, Mirren.

Thomas had gone to Edinburgh to question the psychiatric hospital where Hannah Todd had spent so many years of her life, the woman clearly fooling the staff about her progress. Thomas hadn't approached the staff or her doctor directly.

Yet.

But it looked like that was about to change.

"What did you find?"

Coll ignored his best friend's terseness. Both men were frustrated that a woman who might possibly mean their family harm had become a ghost.

"She's on the move. Back to Edinburgh, I imagine. Bus, train, and ferry tickets were purchased under Hannah Keels."

"She screwed up," Thomas stated, relief evident in his voice.

"Yes. Finally." According to one of the gallery's patrons, the night of Mirren's artist's show, the artist's girlfriend spoke to a woman matching Hannah Todd's description.

It had been a stroke of luck that Todd had given Jina Turner the alias. Coll had put that and several variants of her name and family's names into the search engine that would notify Coll or a member of one of his teams when one of the names was used. It had felt like a needle in a haystack.

Until now.

Thomas exhaled a harsh breath. "I'm calling a detective I know on the force here. I'll have him meet me at the hospital. I think it's time to speak to Dr. Portman. I looked over Todd's finances, info that her mother provided. The woman wouldn't have had enough from the stipend her mother allotted to her psychotic daughter to live, when you consider food, rent, and transportation."

"Someone gave her money and circumvented the review of her mental health to release her. Portman is the likeliest person. It would be unlikely that a nurse would have the ready cash."

"I agree. It's the *why* of it all that flummoxes me," Thomas admitted.

"I have no doubt when Dr. Portman is sitting across from you, his secrets will spill out right along with the piss in his pants."

Another question that still alluded them was why the crazy woman had gone to Dublin. Surely, she hadn't known one of Mirren's artists would be putting on an exhibition. That would mean that Todd had been tracking Mirren's career, which, after so many years, was creepy as all hell.

Dangerous.

To their knowledge, Todd had never attempted to make contact with Mirren or, for that matter, Margaret.

"You've got people ready to apprehend Todd?"

"Of course. We've got a tail on her now with orders to stop her if she veers off course. Otherwise, we want the woman to make it to Edinburgh on her own. It will make it much easier for the local police to arrest her.

"Her little adventure is over."

forty-six

MAGS

AFTER SPENDING all of yesterday with Jonathan, talking about anything and everything, ordering take-away, and having sex until her quivering limbs had threatened to crumble if Mags so much as tried anything more strenuous than drinking tea, she was having breakfast toast with Eze and Nasir.

Jonathan left early that morning to make up for some of the work he'd blown off the day before at her request—worth it— but not before he held her against the entryway's wall and almost kissed her jeans back off.

They only broke apart when Eze cleared his throat. Right behind them. Jonathan laughed, completely unrepentant.

"Take care of my girl today," Jonathan said, clapping Eze on the shoulder as he walked toward the front door.

Eze never cracked a smile, nothing new, and replied, "Nasir will do his best."

Jonathan stopped again before opening the door. "I love you, Mags."

"You better," she teased. "I love you, too, babe."

"Call me when you're done for the day, and I'll come pick you up."

"You won't be able to pick her up if you never leave." Eze was already walking away and spoke over his shoulder.

His deadpan tone cracked Mags up. Jonathan was grinning too, giving her a loose salute before leaving.

Her lips still tingled just thinking about it.

She reached for her tea, trying to focus, but it was no use. Every time she closed her eyes, she could feel the weight of Jonathan's hands, the warmth of him, the way he looked at her like she was the only thing that mattered.

Mags felt her cheeks flush, which appeared to have become a permanent issue when she thought of her boyfriend.

She forced her attention to her emails and smiled when she had two new potential clients inquiring about making appointments.

Mags was about to read the emails to Eze and Nasir, the latter still refusing to sit at the kitchen table with her and Eze so that he could guard them from who knows what, when Nasir's phone rang.

Nasir grimaced at the noise. "Answer the phone, Nas," Eze said, exasperated with his longtime friend's complete adherence to social roles.

Mags rolled her eyes at Eze, who shook his head. Her mom called in at the same moment Nasir answered, "Mr. Barr."

"Mom? What's going on? Uncle Coll just called Nasir."

"Good news, sweetheart. Coll and Thomas tracked down that crazy woman."

"No way, that's amazing. Mirr must be so relieved." Her sister tried not to let on, but the woman had frightened Mirren years ago when she'd gone after several artists. Her husband, Finn, had had their family on lockdown for the past weeks.

"She is. Finn definitely is," her mom replied. "I wanted to call you girls and let Thomas and your uncle call Eze's guard and Jonathan."

Mags grinned even though her mom couldn't see. "Oh my, Thomas must have drawn the short stick."

"Men can truly be babies," her mom growled. "Your dad and I love Jon. The other men will come around eventually."

"I'm not worried, Mom. I love Jon, and he loves me. Thomas and Uncle Coll will come around, and if they don't, I'll sic Mirren on them."

"God help them if that happens," her mom laughed. "I'll let you go. I love you, Mags. Have a great day."

Once they were both off the phone, Mags glanced at the security guard who was back guarding the room from would-be intruders. "Poor Nasir won't know what to do with his days now that he doesn't have to follow me around," Mags teased.

Nasir pretended to ignore her, but she saw his eyes surreptitiously roll. Before she could tease the man further her phone vibrated. A text from Jonathan.

Jonathan: MacGregor called. I'm so relieved, babe.

Mags: I know! So happy for my sister. That crazy woman needs to be locked away again. I can't wait to hear the story of how she got out in the first place.

Jonathan: MacGregor said he would keep us informed. Which means the grouchy bastard will tell Dad, and Dad will call me.

Mags: I'd better get ready. The more work I get done today the sooner you can wine and dine me later.

She couldn't quite hide the flinch that tightened her mouth.

She did need to get to work—but there was a stop to make first. One Jonathan didn't know about.

The thought sat uneasily in her chest. She hated keeping things from him, hated the idea of even a small deception between them. But if he knew she was meeting Rory for coffee before heading to the gallery, it would turn into something bigger than it needed to be.

He'd be upset. Protective. Maybe even try to stop her.

And that...wasn't something she would accept.

Rory deserved an apology. From her. Especially after what he'd confessed. It hadn't been fair to leave things as they were —not after nearly three years together. She might never have loved him the way he'd wanted, the way she loved Jonathan, but she had cared. Deeply enough that walking away without closure felt wrong.

Still, the secrecy bothered her.

If she'd told Jonathan, he would have insisted on being there—or worse, tried to forbid it altogether. Neither option sat well with her. This was something she needed to do on her own.

Even if it meant facing the consequences later.

Jonathan: Love you, babe. You realize that with that woman being found, you don't have to live with Eze anymore.

Mags: Mentally packing my bags now. Daniel better find a two-bedroom for him and Blair. 😊 See you later!

She sighed as she set her phone on the table next to her abandoned toast, catching Eze giving her a disapproving look.

"You shouldn't keep secrets."

She leaned her head back in frustration. "Ugh, why did I tell you? You keep plenty of secrets," she replied with snark.

Eze merely raised his supercilious brows. "Not from those I love." He glanced over his shoulder at Nasir, who for one moment looked as though Eze had handed him the whole world with those five words.

Mags huffed in irritation, knowing he was right. "Fine. I'll tell Jon tonight over drinks. He can't be mad at something that's already done and dusted." Eze didn't bother to look up from the equation he was diligently working on. A clear sign of censure.

Mags stood and gathered her breakfast things and moved to the kitchen, ignoring Eze's continuing disapproval.

"I'll miss you today, Nasir, but I'm glad they found the woman." After rinsing her mug, she hoisted her heavy tote lounging like a fat cat on the counter and headed out. "Behave today, boys," she teased, tapping Nasir's back on the way out. The stoic bodyguard's choked cough made her smile.

***

"Thank you for meeting me, Rory," Mags said while giving her ex an awkward side hug.

Mags arrived a few minutes early and already had coffee and scones waiting on a small two-person table. Her nerves had kicked in on the walk to the bakery, cursing Eze for making her doubt the merit of her plan.

She would be so pissed if Jonathan met an ex-girlfriend without telling her first, and even though she had nothing but good intentions, she'd finally come to the conclusion that she wasn't being fair to Jonathan. She would definitely call him the moment she left the bakery and ask for forgiveness.

"I'm glad you reached out," Rory said solemnly.

"I was happy to. I've already got our coffee and a bite. I hope you don't mind."

"You always know what I like best."

Regrets, thy name is Margaret.

For his part, Rory smiled warmly and hugged her to his chest. If the embrace lasted a pinch too long, she chose to swallow the familiarity and invited him to sit.

Once they'd taken a sip of their coffee, Rory watched her silently, his lips thinning in discomfort. Mags rubbed her palms over her jeans, cursing herself for the awkward situation she was currently regretting.

"I won't keep you long. I'm sure you have a busy day, as do I." She inwardly grimaced at how stilted she sounded. "Because of our long...friendship, I wanted to personally apologize for what happened at the Chamber event."

He took her by surprise when he covered her hand that was resting on the table by her scone. She tensed and immediately pulled back and placed it back in her lap.

He looked hurt but apologized. "Damn it. I'm sorry. It's just...fuck, Maggie, I thought...I thought we were bound for more."

"I'm sorry you felt that way. I'm sorry that you were blind-sided. Rory, I—"

"Don't say you're sorry again. I should have told you how I felt. I should have made sure you knew that you had another option besides..." he stopped speaking, his jaw clenched.

His anger was understandable. Jonathan had really taken a bad moment and made it one hundred times worse. Still, she'd been transparent with Rory before sleeping with him the very first time, and she'd been quite a bit younger and much more naïve than she was now.

"There was never, never," she emphasized, "another option. Not for me."

He looked like he'd been punched, and Mags felt terrible for hurting him again but not for speaking the truth.

Rory turned his attention to the foot traffic outside the bakery's bay window. She let Rory get his emotions back under control before she spoke.

"Rory," she began, gently tapping the top of his hand that was clenching his coffee with two creams and one sugar, "I have always and will always consider you a close friend. If I hadn't already loved...if I hadn't...damn, Ro, I might—"

"Stop, Maggie. Don't try to make me feel better. This," he gestured between the two of them, "won't break me, it just fucking sucks right now. And Jon is an asshole who doesn't deserve you."

His attempt at a smirk made her smile. A little.

"He wasn't at his best, I admit, but in his defense, I never told him who you were, and he was caught off guard. Jon can be a bit over—"

"Bearing," Rory finished.

"Overprotective, but both are probably true. He is an—"

"O'Faolain."

"Most definitely." Mags smiled sadly at Rory and got to her feet. "I need to get to work, and I imagine you do too. I hope you find the one woman you can't live without. I would love to meet her."

Rory stood facing her. Before he could hug her, she stuck her hand out. They shook, though he didn't look particularly happy about it. If Jonathan asked her if she hugged him goodbye—and he would—she could happily tell him no.

Not that that one thing would make the call she was about to place easier.

He answered on the first ring. "Miss me already?"

"You wish." It wasn't good to start out on a lie, so she quickly recanted. "I do."

He must have heard something in her voice because he asked, "What's bothering you, Mags? Do you need me to come back to Eze's?"

"No. No, nothing like that. I'm almost to the gallery. I just," she paused, wishing she could have a do-over where she hadn't chosen to lie to her boyfriend. "I met Rory for coffee without telling you, and I completely regret it. I'm sorry."

She expected an explosion.

She got silence.

So much silence that she finally had to break it. "Jon? Are you there?"

"I am."

The oxygen felt sucked from her lungs. She'd hurt him, that was clear. Mags stopped a block from her workshop and leaned against one of the many solid brick walls.

"I was wrong to do it. I thought I knew better. Eze warned me that I was screwing up." Mags smacked her forehead instantly regretting bringing Eze into it.

"Eze knew, then?"

"Only after you left this morning. Listen, Jon. I did want to apologize to Rory, in my own way. I was afraid that if you went, it might escalate again. He doesn't deserve your anger, and neither do I. Not over him. You and I were not together.

"However, if the roles were reversed and you met a woman from your past without my knowledge or consent, I would be angry. Beyond angry.

"I screwed up, and I'm truly sorry. Please say you forgive me." The sun was barely straining its way through the clouds today, making the blustery wind especially cutting, but she was sweating through her layers.

Finally, he asked, "Did you touch him?"

Oh, shit. Mag's shook her head. She knew he would ask. "A brief side hug upon meeting and a handshake at the end. That's it. I don't want another man touching me in a romantic way except you, which you should know very well."

She was beginning to get annoyed. She deserved his censor after she'd lied by omission about meeting Rory, but really, her dedication to Jonathan, to their relationship, should be without question.

Wouldn't you want to know if he'd touched a woman that he'd slept with, even briefly? Damn it. Yes!

The internal honesty prompted her to say, "He touched my hand once, and I quickly removed it and placed it in my lap. I told him that you were it for me and always had been. He wasn't happy, but he did understand and accepted my decision."

Mags heard the squeak of his office chair. She could picture him leaning his head back and closing his eyes.

"I know you love me." Mags' sigh of relief lasted until "Which means that you shouldn't do things that you know will hurt me."

Mags couldn't stay still. She felt so sick and miserable. She already knew her creativity was shot for the day and would be shot until she saw Jonathan, and she saw with her own eyes that he forgave her.

"You're right," was all she managed as she dragged her feet toward the gallery's back entrance.

"But I did that to you and so much worse. Was this, I don't know, payback? Did you want me to have to picture you with a man who knows you as intimately as I do?"

Her foot tripped over a loose stone, and she barely managed not to drop her coffee. She'd made it to the gallery and leaned against the doorframe.

She almost wished he were angry. This wounded man made her body ache. "I would never set out to hurt you that way, and yes, you've hurt me countless times, but we weren't together then. We are now, and I would never do anything to jeopardize that.

"And before you say it, I realize now that that is exactly what my actions this morning look like, but that wasn't ever my intention. And Rory never knew me as intimately as you do because he never had my heart."

She entered the bottom landing, studying the steep set of stairs as if it were Mt. Niesen in Switzerland, the bag on her back the weight of the world.

Nothing was right when she and Jonathan were at odds.

Jonathan let out a long, shuddering breath. "I'm being a fool. Christ, Mags, I just can't stand to think of any man that isn't me touching you."

A smile started to tug on her lips as she put her foot on the first creaky stair.

"If I'd gone with you, I would have probably punched the asshole. You probably knew this and avoided another scene."

"I might have considered the possibility. Still, I shouldn't have kept it from you." She was glad he was coming around, but that didn't negate the fact that she'd lied.

"Can we agree that no matter how foolish we think the other might react to something, we tell each other anyway?"

"Completely agree."

"And even if you see Phipps in public by chance again, you ignore him completely?"

"Jon," Maggie growled, though it soon turned into a husky laugh. "You're impossible."

She reached the landing outside the attic door and was surprised to see that the brass lock was slightly askew, and the door wasn't entirely closed.

"That's weird," she murmured, gingerly touching the knob.

"What's weird?" Jon asked.

"My door lock looks, I don't know, broken maybe, and the door is not completely closed."

"What the hell! Get out of there, Mags, now! Someone might have broken in. Get outside now and wait. I'm coming."

She heard a door slam and assumed it was Jonathan rushing out of his office. "Stop, Jon, for heaven's sake. Everything's old in this building. The foundation probably shifted and broke it. I'll just give a quick peek to make sure my things are okay.

"You can stay on the phone." Gingerly, she placed one finger against the heavy door and slowly pushed.

"Don't go inside, damn it! I mean it, babe. I'm on my way."

And at a million miles an hour if his heavy pants were anything to go by. "Jon, I mean it. Go back to your office. I'm looking inside now, and not one thing is out of place."

"I'm still coming."

Stubborn as always. She creaked the door a few more inches open and stepped through. Her foot brushed something that had been hidden by a shadow. A brilliant arc of color and a deafening boom were the last things she remembered as her body was lifted like a feather in the wind.

forty-seven

HANNAH

"WOULD you like a bottle of water, Ms. Todd?"

"Yes, please. Thank you," Hannah answered meekly, twirling the pretty embroidered bracelet she'd lifted from Mirren's sister. It was so lovely.

"Can you tell me what you were doing in Dublin?" the second detective asked.

The bomb worked. That's all she'd been whispering to the voices since her arrest. Well, she wasn't arrested per se as much as detained for questioning. After all, she was just a former mental patient.

"I don't understand, Detective." She touched her throat in a bid to appear flustered and unsure. Helpless.

You fucking better win an Oscar for this performance, bitch.

There are no freedoms in prison, Hannah! We had it good at the hospital.

Everything that has gone wrong since our release is your fault.

You are slow, ugly, and stupid, and then you strapped us with a whore's disease that kept us in Dublin long enough to get caught.

This is your fault and only yours.

Look at where you've landed us. Jail!

Hannah shook her head no. Afraid they were right. Clearly, the bomb went off because she'd seen two of the men related to Mirren, who had been there the night she'd first been arrested all those years ago in Edinburgh. They were standing in the hallway outside this room, speaking to the detectives who were now questioning her.

It always came back to Mirren.

That bitch.

If they were here, that meant the bomb had worked, but she couldn't figure out how they'd connected it to Hannah or how they tracked her from Dublin to Edinburgh. She hadn't even used her real name on the tickets.

Oh, Christ. How long had they been looking for her? Had Dr. Portman gotten a conscience all of a sudden? Surely, he wouldn't risk his career out of a sense of nobility.

You used the name you gave that girl outside the gallery event, though, didn't you? Idiot!

Still think this isn't your fault?

She may be in real trouble here. "Shit," she murmured.

"What was that, Ms. Todd?" The blond detective asked in a voice she was coming to dislike immensely.

"Sorry, nothing. My mind wandered."

Nice isn't going to cut it.

Start acting crazy.

You've backed us into a corner. It's the only way.

Make it believable, or we're gone.

Forever.

Hannah's eyes flared wide with panic. *Make it believable...* "Did the girl like the little bird?"

"What?"

"Shame its head came off."

"Ma'am let's get back on track. Why were you in Dublin?"

"I fed the cat poison. I thought its final repose had an artistic flair. Did she?"

"Who is *she*? Are you speaking about a girl from Dublin?"

"The girl with the nine lives. I hope they've run out."

forty-eight

COLL

"ALRIGHT, MS. TODD—WE'LL PLAY," Detective Scott said, his tone flat and edged with something grim.

The detective sat across from the crazy woman at the scuffed plastic-and-steel table, the kind that made every room feel colder than it already was. Coll's men had been waiting to detain Todd as soon as she'd stepped off the bus, along with Edinburgh officers in plainclothes, only blocks from her mother's neighborhood.

Hannah didn't have a relationship with her mother for obvious reasons, which meant that she wasn't visiting for social reasons. Money. It had to be.

She watched the two detectives with a strange, unsettling calm, causing the hair on the back of Coll's neck to stand.

Coll and Thomas were being allowed to sit in the room overlooking the interrogation cell where Hannah Todd was being questioned.

Dr. Portman was being held in a cell nearby, having been arrested after admitting to forging Todd's release papers.

Thomas had gone with the police when they surprised the doctor at the hospital with a search warrant to look through his computer and personal phone for anything non-private and patient-related.

His phone was the jackpot. Hundreds of videos of Todd and three other patients performing various sexual acts on or with the doctor. The abuse went back years. Over a decade for Todd.

He admitted that Todd had blackmailed him for money and an early release. It was a mess and one that would, unfortunately, have a negative impact on the hospital staff and doctors, even though they most likely weren't involved and had no idea what Portman had been pulling.

A task force had already seized staff records. If anything untoward had been reported and snuffed out by anyone in administration other than Dr. Portman, it would come to light.

Dependent upon Todd's answers, she would either be transferred to another high-security hospital or prison.

"You should know, Ms. Todd, that your mother is concerned about your mental health. You never let her know that you'd been released."

Hannah's face turned a brilliant, angry red at the mention of her mother. "That cunt can rot in hell. Do you know how many times my dear old mom visited me these many years?"

"How many?" the younger detective asked.

"None. Never. Not fucking once."

"Then I understand your hesitation in contacting her once you were released, but it appeared to our officers that you were on a bus that would take you within two blocks of your childhood home. Were you going to your mother's?"

"Not that it's any of your business, but yes."

"Why now?"

"The bitch owes me money," she hissed before slamming her palm against the tabletop.

The detectives hoped to learn her motives for traveling to Dublin and what, if anything, she did while there. So far, she had avoided any mention of her time there, no matter how they went at it.

After her stint at the station, she would be released into psychiatric doctors' care for evaluation of her mental fortitude.

If her odd behavior was anything to go by, Coll would bet she was destined for a straitjacket, not bars.

Thomas nudged Coll's side when an officer interrupted the room and whispered something to the detective. Scott nodded and motioned to someone waiting just outside their door.

A woman brought in a large book or binder. It looked worn or haphazardly made. One thing was certain, Hannah Todd recognized it.

"That's my personal belonging, Detective. Unless I'm under arrest for something, I would appreciate my things not being rifled through."

"As I've explained, ma'am, your release was made possible outside of the law, and I'm afraid that your hospital, all the staff, and you will have to be questioned. Legally, you are still a ward of the local authority under the Mental Health Act, and your belongings can and will be confiscated until it's deemed safe."

The two detectives made a point of flipping through the pages of the ratty book, and Coll noticed that Hannah became more and more agitated, murmuring and whispering to herself.

"It seems this woman, Mirren, is of particular interest to you. Can you tell me why that is?"

Coll felt his heart lurch. Thomas cursed under his breath and sat forward. Every word from that crazy woman's mouth had become more ominous.

"Ms. Todd, Hannah," Detective Scott's partner began, "be honest with us now. Why do you have a scrapbook of Mirren

Campbell? Why did you go to Dublin? What have you been doing these past weeks?"

"It's over, ma'am. Tell us what we want to know, and you can leave."

"Leave where? Can I go to my mother's?"

"I'm afraid not today, Ms. Todd, but you do need to cooperate. What were you doing in Dublin? Were you following Mirren Campbell?"

"No, I wasn't following that dumb bitch. I hate her. She ruined my career. My life!"

Coll could see spittle flying from her angry lips. "Keep talking," Coll said quietly.

Todd's mannerisms were becoming even more erratic. She glanced over first one shoulder and then the other. She looked up, to the left, to the right, at her feet. A continuous stream of whispering, gestures, and winces throughout.

The woman was clearly battling demons of her own, and the sooner she was in the hands of doctors who would actually treat her—properly, humanely—the better. Part of him couldn't help but feel a flicker of sympathy.

But it didn't last.

Her destructive behavior had started before Dr. Portman. Long before that, she'd already crossed lines most people never even approached. Whatever had been done to her had only sharpened something that was already there.

And then there was his niece.

The moment that thought surfaced, any lingering compassion burned off. Whatever pity he might've managed was gone, replaced by something colder, harder to shake.

"If it's Mirren you're angry with, then why did you go to Dublin when she lives here in Edinburgh?" Detective Stubbs' partner asked.

"You're all wrong. Let me handle this damnit," she hissed, and it was clear she wasn't speaking to anyone in the room.

"Ms. Todd? Dublin. Why?"

Thomas spoke in a low voice so they could still hear what was going on below. "Did Margaret ever mention anything about a bird or a cat? Hannah asked what the girl thought. It didn't seem like rambling."

Coll thought about that for a moment. "Mags never mentioned anything like that to me, but Eze's guard, Nasir, has been following her for a while. He might know."

Coll dialed Nasir directly, since they'd made the calls to the family that Hannah Todd had been picked up, and he didn't need to follow Margaret anymore.

He answered on the first ring. "Mr. Barr."

"Nasir. MacGregor and I are witnessing Hannah Todd's interrogation. She mentioned dead animals and what the girl thought about them. Mean anything to you?"

"Yes. I was with Miss Morrow when she found a dead cat on the stairwell leading to her workshop. She mentioned thinking the animals were getting in some way because she'd found a headless dead bird and a kitten before that.

"She tossed the bird in an outdoor bin, she said, because it was tiny and bloodless at the point she found it. She buried the kitten in a park on the way to work. I took care of the cat.

"The woman did these things?"

"It appears that she did, which means Hannah Todd had been in Dublin for a while." Coll felt bile surge up his throat. The woman had been in Dublin for Margaret. "Anything else happen that might seem strange?"

"A car swerved onto the walking path. I saw the car swerve and only managed to pull Margaret just far enough that she wasn't run over. It clipped her and sent her tumbling.

"Witnesses believed the man purposely swerved toward

her. The police believe he was under the influence. He ditched the car and has not been caught."

He and Thomas looked at each other in horror. That was no accident. That woman tried to have her killed.

"Please hold for Mr. Otaji," Nasir said.

"Barr. MacGregor." Eze's deep voice filled the room. "I have been listening to your conversation and wish to add that before Nasir was sent to Ireland and before I had her move in with me due to her horrid living conditions, Margaret fell down a flight of outdoor stairs. She called me, and I took her to the hospital.

"She didn't mention that it was anything but an accident, but she was very quiet and reserved. At the time, I felt that she wasn't telling me something."

Thomas stood abruptly, staring at the scene below him with an intensity that put Coll on alert immediately.

"Why do you ask if Mirren's sister is still alive?" Detective Scott asked. Clearly, Coll had missed something that Todd had said.

Hannah Todd giggled. "You can't fool me, Detective. I saw her family here." Her gaze jerked toward the ceiling, and she said, "That's not true. Shut up."

"Stay on the line, Eze," Coll whispered down the line. "Have Nasir call Margaret."

"Ms. Todd, answer the question. Why do you think Margaret Morrow is dead?" Detective Scott deepened his voice in demand, standing and slamming a fist on the table, making the paper cups and water bottles tremble.

"She isn't answering. Neither is Jonathan O'Faolain," Eze spoke grimly in Coll's ear. He barely heard the words from the roaring in his ears.

Hannah smirked, enjoying the attention of the two detectives. "I assume she found my present. Bombs aren't so easy to set, I'll have you know." She grinned and clapped her hands in glee. "Tell me! Did Mirren cry over the pieces of her sister?"

forty-nine

PATRICK O'FAOLAIN

"WHERE THE FUCK IS JON, DANIEL?" Patrick demanded of his nephew, who just so happened to be his son's best friend. If anyone knew where his errant boy was, it was Daniel.

"Calm down, Pat," his brother Bran urged. "Patrick wouldn't have blown off an important meeting without a good reason. You know that."

"I understand that, Bran, but he would have let me know." Patrick was annoyed at first, but as thirty minutes turned into an hour, his irritation turned to apprehension. They had all decided to meet at Dagr's firm to hammer out the final details of buying a piece of property attached to the distillery.

Their dad had already scouted the property before he passed, and Patrick and Bran wanted to make sure they secured the acquisition before someone else swooped in and bought it out from under them.

"It couldn't have been more than a quarter of an hour before the meeting when we spoke. Jon said he was making last-minute adjustments to the helipad designs. Bébhinn brought up that she didn't want them so close to where the Three Wolves Distillery tours began and wanted them further away, yet not too far from the event center.

"I went to his office, and his notes and changes were all there," Daniel explained with a frustrated sigh.

Daniel didn't like not knowing where his cousin was any more than Patrick. Dagr had another client waiting but asked to be informed when they found Jonathan. Bébhinn said she would start calling all their friends before she left the boardroom.

As the three men were leaving the boardroom, Patrick's phone rang. "MacGregor," Patrick answered.

"Get to the hospital. It's Margaret. We're on our way. I need your family there. Now."

fifty

JONATHAN

JONATHAN WAS furious that Mags wasn't listening to him. The chance of an intruder still lurking in her office was high.

He was already running toward the underground parking garage when he realized she was going to investigate. His heart was pounding wildly, and telling himself to calm down wasn't working.

"Mags, stop. I'm on my way. Wait outside for me," he pleaded.

"I'm looking inside now, and not one thing is out of place."

"I'm still coming."

As he slid into his car, he heard Mags gasp. There was some sort of...explosion, a structural failure. Fear like he'd never felt before had him speeding across town.

Her phone had gone silent, and when he tried to call it again, he got a recorded message. Without hesitation, he dialed emergency services. The operator was giving him the runaround when he said to send fire engines or an ambulance, something, anything to the gallery. When he had to admit that he wasn't sure what had happened, another fifty questions started.

Jonathan hung up and dialed Coll Barr. He and MacGregor had friends on the Dublin force and could make things happen faster than his family could.

As soon as he heard the phone connect, he didn't waste any time. "Call the police that you know in Dublin, Coll. Something's happened to Mags. I'm not there yet, but I was on the phone with her, and I thought I heard an explosion. She isn't answering." He could hear the quaver in his voice. There was no need to pretend a stoicism he couldn't manage.

"Thomas is calling them now. The bitch admitted to planting a bomb before she skipped town. Be careful when you get there. Keep your head and call me the very second you have eyes on my niece."

"I'm pulling up now. Oh, Christ. Oh, Christ." Jonathan could hear Coll yelling his name, but it felt like a ghost had placed soundproof muffs over his ears.

People milled around the debris littering the cobbled street behind the gallery. The lower-level entrance and attic were missing portions of the walls, but for the most part, the two-hundred-year-old structure was still standing.

The attic was filled with black smoke billowing from the roof, and there was no sign of Mags, which meant she was still inside.

He left his car in the middle of the footpath and ran for the stairs, or what was left of them. Several bystanders shouted at him to stop. Never. Not until Mags was secure in his arms. At the entrance, Jonathan tore off his shirt, buttons flying. He used the arms to secure the material around his lower face, helping ward off some of the smoke choking the air.

"Mags!" he shouted as he tripped and scrabbled up what

stairs were intact while bypassing loose brick and wooden beams.

The smoke was dense, black, and choking. The fire appeared to be contained in the attic. The tarry smoke would have been sure death if the outer wall hadn't sustained enough damage to let some of it out.

He used the material from his dress shirt to wipe sweat and smoke from his forehead and eyes. He said a silent prayer when he heard sirens coming. *Thank Christ.*

"Mags! Damn it, answer me," he yelled, the effort had him bending over and coughing in gut-twisting hacks.

Almost to the top of the stairs, where the worst of the damage outside the room seemed to be, he stumbled over more debris, making him fall forward. His knees landed with a painful thud on the edge of the hardwood while his hands flew out to stop his forward momentum.

Except his palms didn't come down on more wood and debris. Instead, he felt something warm and soft. With a cry, he ran his hands over what had to be Mags' body that was sprawled at an odd angle over what must be the top few stairs.

"Mags. Mags. Mags," he chanted. "I'm here, baby, please be okay." Through the thick smoke, which only seemed to be getting worse, his fingers finally found her neck. She had a pulse, steady and thumping.

Tears stung his eyes. Her unmoving silence had portended something altogether different than life. He quickly ran his hands over her body, figuring out by touch the best way to lift her. He heard shouts outside. Soon, he would have help from the firemen and paramedics.

He lifted her body, cradling her tight against his chest and praying that she had no internal injuries that he was making worse by moving her.

He grunted as something large hit his side. In the same moment, he felt Mags' shoulder against his chest shift.

He huffed out a wheezing chuff of surprise. "You and your damn bag, Mags." As gingerly as he could with little to no sight, he found the bag's strap and pulled it free of her arm and onto his.

With one arm securing her to his chest, he used the other to feel the walls as he retraced his steps, thankful that he'd had the presence of mind to knock most of the debris to the side during his ascent.

Several tense minutes later, he stumbled out of the doorway and kept walking even as paramedics came at him.

"We've got her, sir," one woman urged as he found fresher air for Mags. "Place her on the gurney."

For a moment, he felt like his arms wouldn't, couldn't release her, but she needed to be checked out. A figure emerged at his shoulder. Eze.

"Let them have her, Jon. We will follow the ambulance to the hospital."

He finally let her go, looking at her soot-smudged and bruised face. He ripped the shirt from around his head, and before the medics could wheel her to the ambulance, he bent and kissed her. "I'll be right behind you, Mags. I love you."

He stood there for a moment, feeling lost as men and women in uniform rushed toward the building, firehoses stretched between them.

Eze's palm landed on his shoulder. "Come on, my brother. Nasir will drive your car."

Thankful for the direction, Jonathan nodded and followed Mags' good friend, his as well now, he supposed.

On the trip following the ambulance, Jonathan's brain finally started working past finding Mags alive but unconscious.

"How did you know to be there? I didn't even have a chance to call my family. I was on the phone with Coll—" he stopped speaking, pieces of the puzzle clicking together. "Coll Barr. I was on the phone with him. My thinking's jacked right now."

"Barr called Nasir earlier while they were questioning," Eze's lip curled in distaste, "that woman. She mentioned things that didn't make sense. Nasir was able to illuminate their meaning. While on the phone, the woman insinuated that she knew Margaret was dead.

"She mentioned a bomb and thought that was why she was picked up. Since we were on the phone when she admitted that, Nasir and I immediately set out. Neither you nor Margaret was answering, and then you called Barr."

Eze shrugged, but it was clear that he was as shaken as Jonathan. "Her heartbeat was strong." Eze nodded, but they lapsed into silence until the hospital came into view.

Jonathan was out of the car door and running to the ambulance as they were unloading Mags from the back. She looked so pale and fragile.

He didn't know anyone with more life in them than Margaret Morrow except right now she looked...peaceful, not at all the berserker he knew she could be.

Where was the girl who'd put a laxative in his and Daniel's hot chocolate when they hadn't let her and Bébhinn go camping with them? Where was the woman who interrupted his dates and then ate their food when they left in a huff? Where was the woman who could look at him and grin, and his whole world became brighter?

She was still and quiet. She was not his Mags, and it was killing him to stand back and do nothing.

As they wheeled her away, Jonathan shook out the filthy shirt that he'd still been gripping and put it on, not realizing until they walked into the waiting room that he was still shirtless.

Nasir interrupted his bleak thoughts. "Excuse me, Mr. O'Faolain," he said as he handed him his phone. "I found this in your car."

"Oh, right. Good." He didn't bother scrolling through his missed calls and texts, dialing Charles Morrow instead.

"Jonathan. Thank God. Aileen, it's Jon. I'm putting you on speaker. We're in Jo's family's plane. We're all here."

"We're at the hospital and they've taken Mags back, but they wouldn't let me go with her."

"How is she? How bad is it?" Aileen, Mags' mother, asked, tears in her voice.

"She's banged up and bruised, but—" he hesitated.

"But what?" Charles asked impatiently.

"She was unconscious when I found her on the stairwell, and she still is. I don't know anything, but I swear the moment I do, I'll call."

"Is your family there yet?" Thomas MacGregor must have been close to the phone because the scowl in his gravelly voice sounded like he was standing in the waiting room.

"No. I haven't called...wait, what the," he stuttered as every family member in Dublin, including Dagr's father, Ulf, and Ciar's father, Ciaran, were stampeding past the hospital staff.

"They are now."

"Good. Call me the second you know anything." MacGregor ended the call.

Before he could put his phone away, his father wrapped his powerful arms around his son, and Jonathan let him, pressing his eyes against his dad's shoulder. His father held the back of his head, just as he had when Jonathan was a child.

"Thanks for coming, Dad."

"Always, boy. You scared me when you didn't answer," he chided, "but I understand. If it were your mother…" He didn't finish. He didn't need to.

"Patrick, please," his mother tried to pry between them. His dad gave him one last squeeze before stepping back. His uncle Bran gave Jonathan a nod and put his arm around his brother.

"Thanks for coming, Mom." And of course, he wasn't only hugging his mother, but his aunts, Raven and Rowan. They patted, kissed, and cried over his chest.

He sent a desperate look his dad's way, but of course, he only shrugged.

Endure.

"Are you hurt, Jon?" His mother pulled back and asked, running her hands over his head, which she could barely reach, and over his arms.

"Throat's a little sore from the smoke, but I'm fine."

"Patrick," Raven barked. "What are you doing just standing there? Call a doctor. Jon should be thoroughly checked out."

Thankfully, his mother knew him well. "We can do that after, Rave, once Mags wakes up and Jon can see for himself that she's going to be okay."

Rowan touched his cheek, garnering his attention. "But you will get checked out. Soon," she said softly.

"I promise, Aunt Row. Don't worry," he added, hating the tears pricking her eyes. But before he could get too emotional over his aunt's distress, she turned to his dad, Bran, and Ulf. "You three will make sure he does."

Daniel used the distraction to close the distance between them and hugged him close. "I wish I could have been there to help, Jon."

"I could have used it," he huffed and shook his head, remembering the nightmare of the stairs and finding Mags.

"Mags is too much of a fighter to be knocked down for long," Daniel encouraged.

"I know," Jonathan said, swallowing a lump in his throat.

"I called everyone. They should be here any minute. Blair was giving a lecture to first years." Jonathan could only nod. He knew their friends would rally, and he was glad for it. When Mags woke up, she would be happy to see everyone.

And she would wake up. Anytime now.

Jonathan's attention was snagged when a nurse bustled in, an overflowing clipboard clutched in her hand.

"Family of Margaret Morrow?" she queried the room.

Jonathan stepped forward. "Her family should be here within the hour. I'm her fiancé. Is she awake?"

"No, but she is beginning to twitch her fingers, which is a good sign. We're done with the tests for now and putting her in a room. If you follow me, Mr.—"

"O'Faolain.

"Mr. O'Faolain," she repeated. "Fine, then. I'll take you to see her."

"Thank you," he said, nodding. "Oh," he said, searching for the two men he needed to speak to, "Eze. Nasir. Would you mind staying? Mags will want to see you both when she wakes up."

They both gave a slight bow. "Of course."

"I'll text you when Charles and Aileen get here," his dad said as Jonathan was being led from the waiting room.

There was already a nurse in the room fiddling with Mags' IV port and blocking his view. He rushed to the other side of the bed, and there she was. Her wild brown hair spread out like waves over the white hospital sheets, so fragile.

Someone had attempted to wipe the soot from her cheeks, but it had only smeared the grime, and yet she was still so stunningly beautiful that it hurt to look at her.

"She's been moving more since we got to the room," the nurse said while she finished rebandaging Mags' arm.

"She would probably like to hear your voice," the nurse who brought him here suggested.

He curled his fingers around Mags' free hand and slowly leaned forward to kiss her knuckles and then her lips.

"I love you, Mags. Wake up now, though. You're scaring me, damn it. The Mags I know always has something to say. Your mom and dad are almost here. Well, Josephine, MacGregor, Cat, and Barr as well, but you probably knew that. Both of our families turn out when there's something to celebrate, mourn, or when someone's been hurt. You've been hurt, in case you forgot, while you've been napping."

He kissed her lips again. "Come on, baby, talk to me. If you don't wake up soon, I'll redesign our townhouse by myself. I'll make it a total bro pad, no embroidery anywhere."

One nurse left, leaving him with the one who'd come to get him. She asked, "How long have you two been engaged?"

"It feels like our whole lives. It's only ever been her for me." The nurse sighed and said something about romance, but his attention was solely on his girl.

Her eyes fluttered.

"Oh, God, Mags. Come on, baby. Open those eyes for me." He leaned in close and whispered in her ear. "If you don't open your eyes, I swear I'll let Daniel sleep by you tonight, and you know how he farts when he's nervous."

"Don't you dare," Mags choked out.

"She spoke," he practically yelled. "She said words!"

"Yes, Mr. O'Faolain. I heard her." the nurse said as she shone a light in Mags' eyes since they were wide open. "Welcome back, Miss Morrow. You have a lot of people who will be excited to see you."

Jonathan's knees were shaking; his relief was so intense. "Christ, Mags. You scared me."

Mags met his eyes and reached up to cup his face. "You scared me too. Daniel's farts. Really?"

fifty-one

HANNAH

YOU TOOK *away our only advantage.*
You knew being crazy was the only way.
Pretending ignorance.
No memory of past deeds. Whatsoever!
And certainly, no fucking bragging.
You idiot.
You, absolute filthy, rotting fool.
You've screwed us all.

Hannah took every word, every slight against her character and intelligence, and swallowed it down. She had miscalculated. Played her cards too early.

She was lying in a small hospital cell strapped to a narrow bed as shivers wracked her weak body. The doctor had informed her that she would experience a range of fentanyl withdrawal symptoms like muscle pain, vomiting, panic, nausea, and, her favorite, sweating.

She tried to tell them that she'd never taken drugs, but of

course, she'd heard the voices snickering in amusement at her predicament.

According to one of the voices, she'd started using the drug the moment she'd gotten out of the hospital.

The doctor said she would be through the worst of it in a few days, and then she'd be able to stand trial for attempted murder of Margaret Morrow.

Attempted.

Always and forever a failure, Hannah.

Nothing but an addict and a filthy whore for hire.

Look, I can't say it's been fun with you all these years, but I think, we think, it's time to go.

"No," she whimpered. "I'll fix this. I escaped once. I can do it again."

Too little, too late.

Goodbye, Hannah.

Goodbye, girl.

Bye, bitch.

Goodbye and good riddance.

We won't meet again.

You're on your own now.

No one to disappoint but yourself now.

"Please, please, please, please, please," Hannah begged, tears streaming down her face while her hands fought the restraints.

Oh God, the silence. The absolute stillness inside her head. They were just being mean. They would come back. Any minute.

"Are you there?" she asked, hearing her voice crack and waver.

A nurse appeared over her, a blank expression on her face. "Things will get better from here on out, Ms. Todd. The high dose of meds you're being injected with now should already be helping to stabilize you. You might be more tired at first, but trust that the doctors have your best interests in mind. Getting free of the fentanyl in your system will also go a long way to steadying you."

The nurse scurried around the little room like the rat she was, not caring in the slightest that Hannah was truly dying right in front of her.

She couldn't live without her family of voices. She wouldn't.

It was all silent now.

A killing silence.

fifty-two

MAGS

IT FELT SO good to be home, not at Eze's flat, because Jonathan happened to be a bossy boyfriend and moved her things to his townhouse before she'd taken one step out of the hospital. Currently, Mags was reclining on the boys' living room couch. The same couch that Jonathan, Daniel, and Ciar had rubbed their manly funk all over for years, and which she and her best friends agreed needed to be thrown out the door during renovations.

Jonathan surprised her that morning by inviting their best friends over for a visit. The laughter was healing after the bomb thing. Mirren had been devastated that Mags had been targeted because of her, which was ridiculous. Her sister had no more control over what happened than that poor, disturbed Hannah Todd.

Already certifiable, the woman had then been abused by her doctor for years. The sick man had exploited his power abominably. Because of that, he'd given Hannah more freedom than she should have had, like a private bathroom. The staff admitted it was possible she could have easily gotten rid of the antipsychotics without the staff being aware.

Mags' family found out that Hannah was in the hospital for unrelated health issues, but her new doctor was giving her medications by injection, which wouldn't allow her to hide or vomit the pills later.

Thomas and Coll reported that Hannah was inconsolable about being left alone by her family.

Her family was the voices, and the medication had silenced them.

Mags shuddered at the hell that woman must have been living in and would probably always live in. Even when she pictured the destruction of her business...not destruction of the actual business, but of her materials; hoops, needles, thread, and the few completed pieces that hadn't been delivered yet.

But those were only things. She'd been so lucky. The detective who determined the cause of the explosion said that her foot had scooted the bomb sideways just enough that the solid, old, medieval attic door took the brunt of the explosion. In fact, it was the door that had knocked her senseless and tossed her body out of harm's way from the fire.

She and Mirren were so thankful that the Smiths had installed a clean-agent gas fire-suppressing system. None of the gallery's art was damaged.

Mag's friend Jina and her artist girlfriend, Anna, stopped by to make sure she was okay. Mags had almost cried when Anna told her that none of her art had been damaged and the gallery would be open for business again as soon as they removed the old back walkway.

That was incredible news all on its own, but the other amazing thing to come from the fire was pure magic. Mags had had a huge write-up in the local paper, and the story of the escaped mental patient trying to kill a "beloved" local artist had made Mags something of a local celebrity.

Jonathan was right when he encouraged her to immediately rebuy all her stock and set up shop without further delay, while she was still a hot topic with plenty of people clamoring to own one of her pieces.

She'd reminded Jonathan that she didn't have the capital at the moment to "buy everything," to which he gave her a chiding look and said, "Good thing your fiancé has plenty then."

"Fake fiancé," she reminded.

"It isn't fake to me. I called you my fiancé in public, and you didn't deny it. The Irish take bundling seriously, babe. Anyway, I gave the insurance list you provided the gallery to my father's assistant. She's been purchasing everything on the list, plus anything else Mom, Raven, and Rowan could think of.

"Remodeling is going well. The entire upstairs floor in your old townhouse will be used for overflow storage, along with a drafting table and a workstation, with the sun providing natural lighting for drawing new designs.

"The living room will handle a second workstation and comfortable seating for clients and guests, and one of the bedrooms is being turned into a changing room with another set up with your sample drawings as you make them and color choices—though I know you like to have final say about that."

That had been yesterday, and Mags' head still felt like it might explode, and not from the severe concussion and fractured rib she'd taken from the explosion.

When she'd spluttered and stuttered and tried to express some semblance of outrage at him being too high-handed when it came to her business, he simply said, "I needed something to take my mind off almost losing you, Mags. I've listened to every word you've ever said about your needlework. I think I'm getting it right."

And just like that, her prickliness fizzled, replaced by an awe-inspiring level of delight in how much he loved her.

If Jonathan had been hurt, she would run roughshod over temperance as well, so here they were now, her back resting against Jonathan's chest as their friends hung out, all of them, like it used to be before marriages and children and work.

"Jon's been impossible since that influencer named him Sexiest Hero Alive. I mean, Christ, who runs around shirtless during an emergency?" Daniel asked, rolling his eyes and elbowing Dagr, who choked on his laughter.

"Fuck off, Dan," Jonathan growled. "I wasn't thinking about my appearance, I can assure you."

"Did the O'Faolain heir hold the burning building up with his pecs of steel?" Gray mimed reading a newspaper.

"Oh," Bébhinn started, giggles overtaking her before snorting, "Sorry, sorry, but my favorite was the article where they used the picture of Ulf, Bran, Patrick, Dagr, Daniel, and Jonathan. '*Frozen* for Adults. Yum.' I literally died."

Dagr shook his head and absently rubbed his hand over his wife's pregnant belly, chuckling. "Dad wanted to sue the journalist, but your moms voted against him."

"The Byrne sisters for the win," Mags laughed.

Blair smirked at Jonathan and signed another tabloid goody. "'I wonder if he used his V-lines to direct the firefighter's water.'"

"Christ, you redheaded little imp. No one said that," Jonathan choked, his cheeks finally pinkening.

"They did," Bébhinn said.

"Oh, they did," Gray followed.

"It's true, babe. You're a sex symbol now. Deal with it." Mags grinned and tapped her elbow to his side. She giggled when he nipped the lobe of her ear. "I'm a famous artist now, and though it can be overwhelming, I'm coping," she laughed.

"Did any of the articles about Mags mention that we're engaged?" Jonathan asked the group.

All their friends gasped and looked at each other, wondering if they were the last ones to know, but everyone was equally in the dark.

"He's teasing. He told the nurse that so that he would be able to see me after the accident."

"And you went along with it," Jonathan reminded smugly.

"You're as good as married. Historical practices and all that," Ciar shrugged, like there was nothing to be done.

"Oh, shut it, everyone. We are not engaged." She shook her head at their teasing, but then she noticed the room fell quiet and everyone's eyes went wide at whatever was happening at her back.

She tried to twist around, but her tender ribs really disapproved of the move, and she gasped in pain.

"Damn it, Mags. Don't hurt yourself," Jonathan chided.

He gingerly slipped out from where she'd been leaning against him and kneeled on the hardwood next to the couch.

"What—" she gasped as Jonathan held up a ring, and not just any ring, but a gold band set with stunning round-cut diamonds around the entire circle.

"Jon," she breathed, stunned.

"I know you don't like to wear rings while you're working with your embroidery because they catch on the strands sometimes, but I had the jeweler make it so the prongs holding each diamond are smooth.

"They call this style an eternity ring, and," he hesitated, his face burning, "I thought since I've always loved you, it fit. Us, I mean. Fit us." He grimaced at his rambling but persevered. "Will you marry me, Margaret Morrow?"

She started to push herself up, but he was quicker, his hand coming to rest gently against her chest, guiding her back down before she could strain her ribs.

"Easy," he murmured. "Yes," she breathed at the same time.

And then he was sliding the band onto her ring finger, his touch steady despite everything, before leaning in to kiss her—soft, certain, and full of promise.

Around them, their friends erupted—shouting, laughing, hooting loud enough to shake the room—but Mags barely heard any of it, completely lost in him.

"You make me so damn happy, Mags. I could have lost you when I'd only just got you." He kissed her again. "It's definitely forever now," he grinned, twisting her ring.

Mags touched her fingertips along his jaw. "Definitely forever."

"Should I phone the Daily and let them know that their 'Sexiest Hero' is officially off the market?" Bébhinn asked, clapping her hands in glee.

fifty-three

BLAIR

LIFE WAS about family and friends, full of smiles and laughter, best friends and hard work. Life could be cold and blustery or blazing hot, soft breezes in the afternoon or misty mornings, suffocating parties or a solitary night.

Life was colorful with blue skies, orange, yellow, and purple sunsets, verdant hills and valleys, or brilliant leafy trees, their bark like braille under her fingertips, silently speaking their secrets.

But life was also quiet. At least for her.

Blair was born with no auditory nerves, so she wasn't a candidate for cochlear implants. She didn't mind.

Most days.

Some were excruciating, but thankfully, they were few and far between.

Blair was too fortunate to wallow in self-pity. She had loving parents, a shithead of a younger brother who also happened to be pretty amazing, and six best friends that included her cousin, Mags Morrow (soon-to-be O'Faolain),

Gray MacGregor Murphy, Bébhinn O'Faolain Griffiths, Ciar Murphy, Dagr Griffiths, Daniel O'Faolain, and Jonathan O'Faolain.

The interconnected relationships would un-saint a saint to unravel. Best to leave the branchy family and friends' tree for another day of musing.

Blair had been at a crossroads for months. Sure, she was independent and went her own way, when and where she pleased. Her life was plants...seriously, her *life*.

But her friends were all paired off now, or mostly, getting married, having children, and running their own businesses. She wasn't falling behind or dissatisfied so much as unsettled, irritable, and lonely.

Which was ridiculous. Completely outrageous. Blair was brilliant, a prodigy botanist, and highly coveted.

A university in the United States wanted her in their master's program in plant pathology. Oklahoma State University wasn't the most prestigious university, but one of its professors, Dr. Linda Bartel, wanted her, and Blair recognized a kindred spirit in the woman.

Linda had even flown to Dublin to interview Blair, woo her to OSU so to speak, and she'd been wooed. Still, Blair hadn't wanted to leave her family and friends. She might be brilliant with all things green and leafy, but unlike them, Blair needed more than sunlight and water to thrive. She needed to be surrounded by the familiar.

In a perfect world, Blair would work with Ulf Griffiths, Bébhinn's father-in-law. He oversaw a reserve passion project in Wales. She'd already spent weeks there for one of her classes, and even though she'd fallen in love with Wales' flora and it met school requirements, Blair couldn't accept Ulf's offer. She needed to leave the country.

She didn't want to.

But...it was the only way.

If she didn't leave everything and everyone behind, she would never be free.

He didn't want her to leave, had been furious when she'd admitted how impressed she was with the Oklahoma program.

Blair hated herself for even confiding in him about the opportunity, but there was something inside of her that refused to hide anything from him. He wanted what was best for her. He cared for her. Deeply. When she succeeded, he crowed about her success. When she failed, he held her and let her cry. When she upset him...well, those were dark times with even darker bruises to mark them.

Despite knowing he would be unhappy, she accepted the OSU position. He'd refused to see or speak to her for a week.

There were days she reveled in his absence and others where depression threatened to drown her.

Blair first touched her fingertips to the fading bruise on her cheek before sliding them to her ears, wondering if the hearing could ever feel as alone and isolated as she sometimes could.

She only needed to close her eyes for the dark silence to find her.

also by anne gregor

Irish Wolves Legacy

Irish Goodbye

Irish Breath

Irish Fury

The Scottish Lions

Josephine

Catriona

Mirren

The Irish Wolves Trilogy

Raven

River

Rowan

about the author

Anne Gregor has a Master of Arts in History with a Civil War emphasis. For her thesis, she focused on Irish immigrants working the transcontinental railroad across America, specifically those who settled in Oklahoma amongst Native Americans. A love for research turned into a love for fictional writing, and soon, every old document Anne studied became the premise for a novel. Though Oklahoma remains near and dear to her heart as she lives on Grand Lake O' the Cherokees, she enjoys traveling the world with her characters. **Anne is the author of three contemporary romance series, The Irish Wolves, The Scottish Lions, and Irish Wolves Legacy.**

A small press bound by the belief that every voice matters.

Sign up for our newsletter to learn about new releases and more.

Buy directly from us to save on ebooks, book bundles, and special editions.

Follow us on social media:

facebook.com/oliverheberbooks

instagram.com/oliverheberbooks

tiktok.com/@oliverheberbooks

bsky.app/profile/oliverheberbooks.bsky.social

youtube.com/@OliverHeberBooksPublisher

oliverheberbooks.substack.com

amazon.com/oliverheberbooks